WINDOW of Opportunity

The Stained-Glass Legacy 🪟 Book One

Heather Greer

Scrivenings
PRESS
Quench your thirst for story.
www.ScriveningsPress.com

©2023 Heather Greer

Published by Scrivenings Press LLC
15 Lucky Lane
Morrilton, Arkansas 72110
https://ScriveningsPress.com

Printed in the United States of America

Paperback ISBN 978-1-64917-262-4

eBook ISBN 978-1-64917-263-1

Cover by Linda Fulkerson
www.bookmarketinggraphics.com

Dedication Scripture taken from the NEW AMERICAN STANDARD BIBLE(r), Copyright (c) 1960,1962,1963,1968,1971,1972,1973,1975,1977 by The Lockman Foundation. Used by permission. www.lockman.org.

All other scriptures are taken from the KING JAMES VERSION (KJV): KING JAMES VERSION, public domain.

All characters are fictional, and any resemblance to real people, either factual or historical, is purely coincidental.

To those who live their faith, even when it means doing the difficult things.

"For in it the righteousness of God is revealed from faith to faith; as it is written, 'But the righteous man shall live by faith.'"
Romans 1:17 (NASB)

Chapter One

1926 - Harrisburg, Illinois

"Isn't it just the berries?"

The feminine voice drew Brendan Dunne's attention. Straining to see without moving away from the barber's scissors, Brendan realized the woman had gained the attention of every other male in the shop. A few stared curiously. Others glared. He smiled at the sentiment contained in their eyes. How dare a woman invade this man's world of haircuts and razors and shaving cream?

Even back in Chicago, a young woman took a gamble having her hair bobbed. Those around her would either love it or hate it, and neither side kept their opinions to themselves. A far cry from some of the more rural towns he'd seen, Harrisburg was still a long way from metropolitan Chicago, and the backlash from such a bold fashion move could be disastrous.

The tall, brunette preened in front of the mirror. Her newly shorn locks were as straight as a pin, and her bangs were equally so. The only hint of curl was in the very front where her hair curved slightly forward to frame her face. He didn't see the attraction, but if her smile was any indication, the woman loved her new look.

She used the mirror to look at the impossibly petite woman who'd accompanied her into the barbershop. "Evangeline, you simply have to bob your hair. With all your waves, it would be darling on you."

Evangeline raised a slender hand to the honeyed tresses secured in a low bun at the nape of her neck. Her voice was quiet when she spoke. "I think I'll keep my hair the way it is for now. Maybe another time."

Brendan smiled. She wouldn't cut her hair. It was written all over her face.

"Where is your sense of adventure?" The brunette chided Evangeline as she pulled the bills out of her purse to pay the barber. "Haven't you seen the latest issue of *Harper's Bazar*? It won't be long until all women give up their corsets and long hair for good. Everything will be short from hair to hemlines, and women everywhere will be better for it."

Men cleared their throats, some in shock and some in disgust. Brendan sucked in a breath. The women he'd known in Chicago had adopted the same brazen attitude, but at least they had the sense to voice it in the clubs, speakeasies, and at parties where such bold attitudes were less shocking in mixed company. This girl might have the spirit of a girl from big-town Chicago, but she definitely lacked the finer points of finesse and discretion, which was saying a lot considering those were two words he'd never considered to describe those girls in the first place.

As the barber spun his chair away from the mirror, Brendan took a closer look at Evangeline. Poor girl. She obviously didn't share her friend's boisterous nature. An embarrassed pink tinged her skin from her neck to the roots of her hair.

He doubted she was a simple farmer's daughter. Her dress wasn't homespun or overly worn like many of the rural farm girls who came to town with their families. Her short stature left only the briefest glimpse of leg even with her dress hem stopping at mid-calf. Her black oxfords were well-polished and even the laces lacked signs of wear. While the length and loose fit of her dress were in keeping with the times, Evangeline didn't share her friend's need to showcase the trendiest styles of the twenties either.

Evangeline peered uncomfortably in his direction. Brendan hadn't realized he'd been staring and hated the idea that he'd added to her discomfort. He smiled in acknowledgment before pulling the watch from his pocket to fiddle with it absentmindedly. Out of the corner of his eye, he watched as Evangeline joined her friend and walked out the door.

A collective sigh of relief filled the barber shop. Awkward silence was replaced with talk of cars, the economy, and baseball. Brendan smiled. The men could be men again. He settled back against the chair and listened to the chatter without joining in.

A final spin of the chair, and the protective drape was whisked off his shoulders.

"There you be."

Brendan took out his wallet and thumbed through, finding the correct bills. "Looks great, Mr. Miller. Thank you."

Brendan plucked his black fedora from the coat rack and placed it on his newly slicked back hair before looping his umbrella over his wrist. As he pushed open the door, he caught a glimpse of the girls coming out of the Woolworths across the street, arm in arm. Evangeline carried a small paper sack in her free hand. What a pair those two made. Of course, he didn't know them well. Didn't know them at all, really. He was only familiar with their types, and what he'd experienced of those didn't seem to blend naturally in his opinion.

Brendan buttoned his ulster coat as he stepped from the warmth of the barber shop into the fall air. The staccato honk of a horn disturbed the peace of the afternoon. A blue Chevrolet pulled up beside the girls.

Evangeline held back while her friend tugged her arm free and flitted over to the men trying and succeeding in gaining her attention. She leaned down enough to see the car's occupants. Didn't she realize she was treating them to a peek at her womanly assets? Of course, she did. Her flirtations were obvious from across the street. It would be foolish to think she was oblivious to the show she teased them with.

She glanced over her shoulder and must have spoken because Evangeline shook her head. Her friend threw her hands up in the air. Evangeline shook her head again, and a firm "no" carried across the intersection.

"Evangeline, don't be such a blue nose. It's only a ride."

The frustrated whine, like nails on a chalkboard. Still, Evangeline stood her ground and shook her head.

"Fine. Walk home then, but don't complain to me when you're caught in the rain." She pulled the door open. "Scoot over boys."

Evangeline stared after the car pulling away. Her shoulders sagged. A gust of wind stole the sack from her hand, depositing it in the street not far from where Brendan stood. She moved to chase it, but he held her in place with a raised hand and retrieved the lightweight bag. Curiosity nearly got the better of him. What could she have purchased that would be so light? A gentleman would never ask or look. He folded over the top of the sack and trotted across the street to where Evangeline waited for him.

She tilted her head slightly to see him from under the brim of the purple cloche hat perched on her head and smiled. "Thank you. That wind came out of nowhere."

Brendan nodded his head. "Happy to help. Miss Evangeline, is it?"

She frowned.

He rushed to explain. "I couldn't help but hear your friend call you by name in the barber shop."

She glanced at the barber shop across the street before looking back to him. The confusion fell from her face, and she smiled again. The sweetness and innocence of it nearly stole his breath before she spoke.

"I'm afraid you have me at a disadvantage, sir. I don't know who I'm indebted to."

"Brendan Dunne, at your service. But only if we agree that you owe me nothing. Any man worth knowing would have done the same."

She gazed down the road a moment before looking back at him. "No. I don't think they would have."

Ah, the men in the Chevrolet who whisked away her friend. "You're right. I doubt those dandies would have taken the time to help. But, then again, I did say any man worth knowing. I'm not convinced they fit either requirement."

Her laugh was soft, bringing warmth despite the chill in the air. "Maybe you're right."

"Of course, I'm right. Your friend ..."

"Dot, Dorothy."

"Miss Dorothy may find that out soon enough, though I hope for her sake she doesn't. As for you, Miss Evangeline, please allow me to escort you home, since you were so rudely left to fend for yourself."

"I'm not sure that's such a good idea. We've only just met." Her slender fingers absently rubbed the pendant hanging around her neck. "Mother would have had a fit if I got into a man's car, but I'm not sure I would fare any better with a practical stranger walking me home. Besides, it's only a few minutes' walk."

"Then I won't walk with you. I'll walk behind you, just to make sure you arrive safely. There's no harm in that, is there?"

Her voice was hesitant. "I suppose that would be all right. Besides, I can't prevent you from walking down the street now, can I?"

"Very well. After you."

Brendan awkwardly trailed several steps behind Evangeline. Walking next to her would have afforded him the opportunity to get to know her better. Of course, when she had words with her mother about it, she probably wouldn't find gratitude among the list of feelings she had for him. It was better this way.

5

When the first fat drops of ice-cold rain hit his cheek, Brendan rethought his stance. It wouldn't do to care for propriety if it meant Evangeline could take a cold. He lengthened his stride to catch up with her and opened his umbrella above them.

"Miss Dorothy was right about the rain. I hope your mother understands, but I cannot in good conscience allow you to walk in the rain when I've got a perfectly useful umbrella."

"Under the circumstances, I'm sure Mother will understand."

"Evangeline Grace Moore get down here right now, young lady."

Mother's screeched order bounced off the walls causing Evangeline to pause halfway up the flight of stairs. Had the town's busybodies already passed down a report of Brendan walking her home? Surely they couldn't disseminate information that quickly. She'd only been home for thirty minutes.

It would do no good to pretend she'd not caught Mother's order. Besides, it would be disrespectful. No matter what she felt about her parent's strict decrees and constant disappointment in her choices, God had shown her long ago that honor and respect of her parents was required. The fact that she was nineteen, soon to be twenty, didn't change anything. She lived under their roof, and she would show them respect whether they realized it or not.

The echo of each step as she made her way down the stairs sounded like the beating of a drum leading to an unfair trial and execution. She'd taken that path many times. While the execution might only be figurative, it occurred in regular intervals after every perceived grievance.

Evangeline took a deep breath and stepped around the corner into the parlor where her mother waited, her foot tapping impatiently on the polished wood floors.

"Yes, Mother?"

"Would you like to tell me what you were doing getting in a car filled with boys today—

and after visiting a barber shop, no less?"

Evangeline sighed. "You may want to tell your informant to have her eyes checked, Mother."

"You will not be so disrespectful. It is highly unbecoming in a young lady."

"Nevertheless, whoever told you such a tale was wrong. I refused the ride, though doing so left me walking home in the rain. Whoever tattled must not have witnessed the whole scene."

Her mother's chin went higher in the air if that was possible. "And the barber shop? Turn around and let me see your hair. I can't believe you would visit a place like that much less adopt a hairstyle that suits only those of a certain, low-class temperament and interest."

Before Evangeline could comply, her mother gripped her arm, spinning her around. Evangeline winced. Waiting until her mother's free hand touched the bun she'd arranged that morning, Evangeline answered, "I went in with Dot. She was the one who got her hair bobbed, not me. Besides, it was a barber shop, Mother. That's hardly like frequenting a speakeasy."

Her mother inhaled sharply. "What do you know of such things? I sensed Dorothy Taylor was no good for you. She's a horrid influence, and I was wrong in letting you befriend her. Your father is a judge, and as such, we have certain standards that must be maintained. Dorothy is simply not the sort to help your image in the community."

Evangeline took advantage of her mother's position behind her to roll her eyes. Carefully schooling her features to a neutral position, she faced her mother. "I'm not concerned with what people in the community think. I've done nothing wrong, and Dorothy has been my friend since elementary school. I agree she doesn't always make the wisest choices, but as you can see from my restraint today, I do not follow along like a mindless sheep. If something is wrong or questionable, I don't do it."

Pursed lips and silent regard were Evangeline's reward for choosing not to get in the car. What would have happened if she'd actually taken a ride? She repressed a shudder at the thought. It didn't matter. Mother would find something to complain about.

"May I be excused to my room now?"

Mother's lips flattened. "I suppose. I need to get supper started anyway."

Evangeline left her standing in the parlor and made her way to the semi-sanctuary of her room. At least she'd only had to face her mother over the car ride. It was hard to berate her for that one when she'd passed up the opportunity. Sharing an umbrella with Brendan Dunne for the last few blocks on her walk home would be another matter, rain or not.

Brendan. He'd been so polite. It was this fact, not the way his tall, slim form made her feel protected as she walked beside him, that brought a tiny smile to her lips. Her reaction had nothing to do with his dark hair. No. Those waves she'd spied in the barber shop that couldn't be fully tamed didn't cause her grin. Neither did his sky-blue eyes. Though they were framed more perfectly than the Georgia O'Keefe paintings she'd seen in the Chicago museum her father had taken her to. No, those things didn't matter at all. And they were not what left her daydreaming about seeing him again.

Chapter Two

E vangeline jumped at the sudden sound of what she assumed was her father's fist smacking against the dining room table. Her foot hovered over the next step as she paused in her descent. It would work more in her favor to find out what had riled her father before walking blindly into a bad situation. It wasn't eavesdropping. It was self-preservation.

"As if we don't have enough problems from the Birger and Shelton gangs and the Klan. Now we have to import trouble from Chicago."

His angry voice traveled to Evangeline on the stairs without any problems. Her mother's voice was more controlled. Evangeline shut her eyes to concentrate on the quiet words but still struggled to hear her response.

"Now, there's no need for you to get riled up. Madeline Thompson told me Mr. Birger is perfectly respectable. Why, he even helped one of her neighbors who was down on his luck. Does that sound like a man bent on causing trouble to you?"

Her father growled. "Madeline Thompson is a ninny. Her know-it-all husband is nothing more than a grocer gathering gossip from all the other ninnies in town." His tone softened. To Evangeline's ears, it sounded placating and not at all sincere.

"Trust me, darling. Our neighbors, no matter how well-meaning, are not worth listening to on matters of gangs or bootlegging. As a judge for the county, I believe I am a trifle more qualified to discourse on such matters. I assure you, Mr. Birger is indeed a less-than-savory individual, and he's not the only one."

Mother's defeated sigh floated up the stairs despite the weight it carried. "Yes, dear. I apologize. I didn't mean to question your authority on the matter. Now, what's this you were saying about trouble from other areas?"

Father's voice dropped, and Evangeline gingerly tip-toed a few steps closer, careful to avoid creaky spots that would alert her parents to her presence.

"I shouldn't bother you with such things. Forgive me, Mabel. You don't need your pretty head filled with the worries I carry home from work. Besides, they aren't subjects meant to serve as fodder for your bridge club."

"I would never divulge such information as carelessly as that."

At least the wall separating Evangeline and her parents prevented them from seeing her doubtful frown that would earn their ire. Despite knowing her mother was in the next room with her hand fluttering to her chest in dramatic offense at her father's suggestion, Evangeline had been home during several bridge club meetings. While she never joined the ladies at the table, she'd listened to her mother commit that exact offense on numerous occasions. However, her father's next words confirmed the success of her mother's pretended offense.

"Don't be offended, dear." His voice sweet, if not downright patronizing. "I didn't mean anything by it. I know you wouldn't mean to gossip about such matters. I believe at times, it simply slips out into conversation. But I must remember you are not as cotton-headed as some of the other wives in this town. You're educated, and due to my position in the government, you already know more of what's going on than most women."

"There. You see. You can share with me. What kind of trouble has arrived at the doorstep of our town? And what can be done about it?"

"It's nothing to be alarmed at, I'm sure. We've had a couple new arrivals to town who hail from the Chicago area. The Dunne brothers."

Her mother's gasp covered her own. Dunne. It couldn't be. Her stomach grew queasy as she replayed their conversation in her mind. Brendan Dunne. She was sure he'd said his name was Brendan Dunne.

Paper rustled as Evangeline assumed her father laid the newspaper aside. "It's a name well-known in certain less-savory circles in Chicago."

"You don't mean they're involved with gangs? Or are they bootleggers? That's all we need. More bootleggers."

"Gangs. Bootleggers. There's no difference. I suppose you have some smalltime bootleggers who work on their own, but the ones you have to worry about are those with the numbers to make threats and the means to carry them out."

"You're afraid a new gang is moving into Harrisburg?"

"No. Not a new gang. I believe a merger of sorts may be in the making. Apparently, the family patriarch sent his boys down here because the oldest one has landed himself in too much trouble back home. The youngest has been charged with keeping him out of mischief. But rumor has it they've already visited Shady Rest a time or two. Whether or not their family follows, these two may be falling in with the Birger gang."

Evangeline covered her groan by clearing her throat. Time for getting information was over. Really, she shouldn't have waited that long, but curiosity had gotten the better of her.

She continued down the stairs as if she'd not been standing like a statue for the past five minutes.

Turning into the dining room she pasted on what she hoped was a believable smile. "Good morning, Mother. Father."

She took her seat at the table and reached for the teapot to fill her cup. As she spooned sugar into the steeping tea, her thoughts swirled around her newfound knowledge regarding Brendan. He was sweet. An old-fashioned gentlemen in an age of pompous dandies. Part of a mob family. Could it be true? As her mother said, even Mr. Birger presented himself as an upstanding citizen.

Evangeline was pulled from her thoughts by the sharp tone in her mother's voice. "Pardon me. I think I missed the question."

Her father chortled. "I'd say so. What is so interesting that has you wool gathering through breakfast and unable to answer your mother?"

Side-stepping her father's inquiry, Evangeline blinked at her mother. "Yes, Mother?"

"I was telling your father about Dorothy's escapades yesterday, and I asked if you have plans to see her again today. I really think you should distance yourself from the girl. She isn't the type of person you need to associate with."

Evangeline forced a deep breath and a sip of tea before replying. "I personally don't think that's a very Christian attitude to take. Dot and I have been friends since childhood. Yes, she's making bad choices. Yes, she knows better, but so do I. We can be friends without me making those same mistakes. One day, I hope she listens to reason and grows up. Until then, I don't think abandonment will solve anything."

She steeled herself against the coming disagreement. Her mother's open mouth snapped shut before she could retort as her father placed his hand over hers on the table. While continuing his silent reassuring, he turned to Evangeline. She refused to look away from his probing gaze. After several seconds, a slight curve turned the corners of his lips up.

"I believe you are right, Evangeline. Dorothy could learn a lot from you. You're a level-headed young lady. I trust you will not allow her to lead you down a destructive path."

His emphasis on the final sentence left Evangeline feeling his warning. It was not to be mistaken as a statement of belief that her moral compass would remain true. A slight narrowing of his eyes confirmed her suspicions. Evangeline raised her chin only enough to signal her acceptance of his challenge.

She smiled. "Of course not, Father."

He stood and crossed to her mother, placing a kiss on the top of her head. "Very well. I will see my ladies tonight at dinner."

The front door closed as her father left, and Evangeline drank her tea in the remaining silence. She could feel her mother's eyes on her but refused to give in to the urge to look up. After her father sided with her, it would only encourage another barrage of reprimands regarding her choice of friends, and that was the last thing she wanted. There were more important things to think about—like Brendan Dunne.

Evangeline's shoulders relaxed as her mother finally made her way from the dining room. She wasn't naïve enough to think bootlegging was an enterprise enjoyed by only the dirt poor or the filthy rich. Even though Harrisburg lacked the ostentatiousness of the big cities that Dot was drawn to, there were plenty of men and women enjoying the rebellion against prohibition laws. It wasn't unusual to see a man who frequented the speakeasy on Friday night sitting in the front pew on Sunday. And bootlegging was a lucrative business, especially if you were the one in control. Gang activity was the next natural progression.

Evangeline's stomach knotted as she considered the possibility that the handsome man who'd helped her home in the rain was involved in less-than-legal activities. Her father said the younger brother was sent to watch out for an older brother who'd gotten in trouble with the law.

But which brother was Brendan?

Chapter Three

Evangeline threw out her hands to keep her balance as Dot's shoulder connected with hers. "What in the world is wrong with you?"

Dot rolled her eyes. "Don't cast a kitten. If you hadn't been lost in your own daydreams, that little nudge wouldn't have bothered you. It's definitely nothing to lose your temper over." Dot motioned across the street with a tilt of her head. "Besides, that's enough to set everything right again."

Evangeline swallowed the urge to respond as she peered toward whatever had caught Dot's attention. Though modestly sized, the rock exterior, stained-glass windows, and heavy wooden doors of the church made it seem immense compared to the one her family attended across town. But Dot wasn't interested in sanctuary architecture. Movement at the doors explained her friend's snared attention.

She sucked in a breath and glanced away from the two men exiting the building.

Dot turned to her with a mischievous grin. "What did I tell you? Those two will turn heads all over town. Maybe we should go introduce ourselves."

Evangeline grabbed Dot's arm to pull her along. "We will do

no such thing. I can't believe you'd even suggest it. That's brazen, even for you."

Dot laughed as she freed her arm. "Brazen? Evangeline Grace, I can't believe you'd say that to me. You're supposed to be my best friend. Is that what you think of me?"

Evangeline pursed her lips. She had no desire to hurt Dot, but lately, her friend's behavior had grown more rebellious and reckless than ever before. She sighed. "Maybe brazen isn't the right word. But you must admit, you've been giving your attention to young men more freely than you used to."

Dot laughed again. "You're a sheltered girl, Evangeline. You need to learn to leave your pious opinions in the pews on Sunday morning. They don't have a place in the day to day. Getting the attention of those young men is the reason God gave us certain assets in the first place. There's no harm in a little flirtation. It keeps life interesting."

Evangeline refrained from arguing. At one time, Dot was as dedicated to things of faith as Evangeline. Lately, she actively put as much distance as she could between herself and God. It amazed Evangeline that their childhood friendship had survived the changes. She had no doubt part of that was due to choosing her battles carefully and covering their friendship in prayer on a daily basis. Evangeline had learned a long time ago this was one of the battles she could never win. No need wasting her breath trying.

She opted for a truce of sorts. "To each their own, I guess. It doesn't matter right now, anyway. If we don't get going, we won't make it to the Orpheum before the show starts."

Dot shook her head as she looped her arm through Evangeline's and continued down the sidewalk away from the men. "We couldn't have that, now, could we? Fine. Onward to the Orpheum."

Brendan followed his brother's gaze to the pair across the street. It was Evangeline and her friend. He was as sure of their identity as he was that the women had spotted them as well. In fact, if he were a betting man, he'd be willing to place a wager that he and his brother were the topic of conversation. Quick glances from Evangeline and more forward, lingering ones from her friend all but proved him right.

James clapped a hand along his shoulder. His smile was too full of the devil to have just exited a church. "This town may not be as dull as I thought after all. What do you say we mosey across the street and introduce ourselves?"

Brendan suppressed a groan. "No."

While he was fairly certain James would have no interest in Miss Evangeline, he couldn't deny her friend's more flamboyant nature would be like honey to a fly. James's antics with the women in Chicago hadn't elicited their father's edict to get him out of town, but it hadn't helped his cause. The last thing they needed now that they'd relocated to Harrisburg was a replay of their Chicago troubles.

Relief swept through him as the girls, arm in arm, walked away. At least he wouldn't have to argue with James in the middle of the street. Whatever else they might be, the Dunne family was better than that. Their father would be horrified if they made a public spectacle of themselves.

James swore under his breath before he glared back at Brendan. "Looks like we missed our chance for now. It's your fault. Buy me a pack of smokes before the show, and I might be tempted to forget the whole thing."

Irritation crept through Brendan as James's brows lifted in challenge. He forced a good-natured smile. Contrary to the Irish blood flowing through his veins, fighting wasn't the answer, especially when it was over something as ridiculous as this. "Whatever you say, James. Let's go to Woolworths to get your cigarettes. But you're not making me late for the show. Understand?"

"Yeah, yeah. Big talk from my little brother. But seeing as how I don't want to miss any of the show either, I'll agree. But only this time."

On the walk across the street and down the couple blocks to the store, Brendan's thoughts were taken up by a certain woman with wavy honey-blonde hair. As much as he'd like to see her again, maybe get to know her a little better, James and Miss Dorothy shouldn't be anywhere near each other. James was used to trouble. The girl struck him as one who thought she wanted the life of fun and freedom touted in all the latest magazines, but she didn't have an inkling as to what it was really like. He hoped James would not be the one to teach her that lesson.

Chapter Four

The cool of the darkened theater did nothing to prevent the heat of Evangeline's temper. She glared at Dot, who was once again turned nearly all the way around in her seat, making eyes at the men behind them.

"Would you please turn around?" Her voice was low but insistent.

Dot rolled her eyes and sighed. "Didn't you see who came in right behind us?"

Evangeline licked her tightened lips. She wasn't blind. She'd seen Brendan Dunne and his companion claim empty seats three rows directly behind them. But she'd also seen the men surrounding the Dunnes. Most of their reputations were well known in the area, and it wasn't because they were pristine. Were Brendan and his friend part of that group, or had they simply chosen their seats poorly? It didn't matter. She was here for the show.

Without turning from the screen, Evangeline spoke loud enough for Dot to hear without drawing the attention of the other patrons. "I am here to watch the picture. Can you please stop trying to ruin it for me?"

Evangeline clamped her mouth shut as Dot's hand shoved her shoulder.

"You're no fun. A new Buster Keaton is shown every other time a new picture comes to town. How often do two incredibly handsome men end up sitting behind you? Do you really want to miss this opportunity?"

"Yes. I do. Now please be still so I can watch the movie."

Dot must have sensed her ire for she pushed no further. But while she left Evangeline in relative silence to enjoy the antics of the Confederate railroad engineer in his attempt to rescue his fiancée from Union spies, Dot still cast several less intrusive, yet still obvious, glances over her shoulder in the men's direction.

As soon as the movie ended, Evangeline grabbed Dot by the wrist and dragged her through the crowd to the women's toilet. Once they were away from prying eyes and listening ears, Evangeline dropped her wrist and spun to face her.

"What do you think you're doing? Could you, for once, act like a mature adult rather than a girl who has just discovered boys exist? I came here today to watch a movie. I thought that was your reason for coming too. Then, you spot some dandy, and the money I paid to watch the show is wasted because you can't stop making eyes at him."

Dot's jaw tightened. "Pardon me, Mrs. Grundy! I didn't know being twenty meant I had to forgo fun in favor of being uptight and unapproachable."

"Uptight? Unapproachable? Just because I don't flirt with everyone who doesn't wear a dress doesn't mean I'm unapproachable."

"Do you think so?" Dot placed her hands on her hips as her voice issued her challenge. "When was the last time you even spoke to a man other than your father or the clods at church who've known you forever?"

Evangeline lifted her chin. "Not that I have anything to prove to you, but just yesterday I spoke with one of the men you've been gawking at."

Dot snorted. Evangeline couldn't help answering with an eye roll. When Evangeline refused to speak further, Dot straightened as the disbelief in her eyes changed into equal parts question and something akin to pride. If Dot was proud over something so pointless, how had their friendship managed to remain intact?

Dot dipped her head. "I'm speechless. I didn't think you had it in you. Maybe I'll make a 1920s woman of you yet."

"Keep trying. On second thought, no, don't. I'm perfectly happy with my life. I don't need you scheming to transform me."

Dot regarded her for a moment before allowing a small smile. "Evie Grace, you're something else. Let's get out of here. I'll even buy you a chocolate shake at Holloway's Café on the way home since I ruined the movie for you."

Forgiveness was a given. And Dot's use of her childhood nickname was a sure sign she was ready to move past their disagreement as well. The words "I'm sorry" rarely left Dot's lips. In fact, Evangeline couldn't ever remember hearing them. But she'd enjoyed more apology milkshakes through the years than she cared to count. Thank goodness she was naturally slim, and the rich treat didn't sit on her hips like it would for some.

Evangeline sighed. "Fine, but I'm getting extra whipped cream and a cherry on it."

"Excuse me, Miss Evangeline," Brendan said as he stepped up to Evangeline and Dot's table at the diner. "My brother and I couldn't help noticing our paths crossing this afternoon. We wondered if we might join you?"

Evangeline didn't know him well, but she would swear that his smile was forced. It most certainly failed to reach his blue eyes, which shone with apology. She flicked a glance at his brother. He had identical blue eyes, right down to the thick dark lashes framing them. But rather than remorse, his were full of interest and trained on Dot alone.

21

She opened her mouth to speak, but Dot answered for her as she slid farther into the booth. "Of course, you can join us. We'd love the company. Wouldn't we, Evie?"

It was all the invitation the brother needed. He'd dropped into the booth next to Dot before Evangeline had time to make room for Brendan to sit next to her. She smiled up at him as politely as she could manage.

The corners of Brendan's eye crinkled as he frowned. "Are you sure you don't mind, Miss Evangeline?"

A negative answer would get them to leave. Dot silently pleaded with her from across the table. She swallowed a sigh before turning back to Brendan. Was the sudden unsettled feeling in her middle due to dread over the possibility of her parents finding out or excitement at the opportunity to get to know Brendan? Maybe a little of both.

Evangeline scooted farther down the bench seat. "I'm sure. You're welcome to join us if you like."

A slight narrowing of his eyes as he slid in next to her told Evangeline all she needed to know. Her feeble smile didn't fool Brendan—he perceived her hesitation. He probably thought she was immune to his charm and good looks. Nothing could be further from the truth. She simply wanted to avoid trouble at home. Associating with these men might very well gift wrap trouble and leave it on her doorstep. But which one would be the instigator?

Brendan was more polite and well-behaved, but good manners could be a front to hide his true self. After seeing them together, even in this limited capacity, Brendan was likely the more responsible younger brother her father had spoken of at breakfast. Evangeline hoped she was right, but she wasn't sure why it mattered. If the rumors were true, Brendan was part of a crime family no matter how gentlemanly he appeared.

Brendan's brother waved the waitress over to the table. If the way she flitted over immediately at his request didn't give enough indication of infatuation with the undeniably handsome man, her bright-as-the-sun smile certainly did. He gave her one of his own, though Evangeline could tell from across the table his grin was a means to an end.

"I hope you don't mind, but we've decided to eat with our friends at this table. I'd like a burger and fries with a coffee, black. And my brother will have ..."

All eyes fell on Brendan whose smile was less feigned as he focused on the waitress. "I'll have the same, please."

As the waitress made her way back to the order window, Brendan's brother turned his attention to Evangeline. "It seems you have me at a disadvantage, Evie. My brother seems to know you and your friend, but I haven't had the pleasure."

Evangeline cleared her throat. "It's Evangeline, if you don't mind. Dot, Dorothy, is the only one who gets away with calling me Evie."

His smile was too perfect, and his voice too smooth. "Of course. I didn't mean to offend."

"Miss Evangeline and I have had occasion to meet, but I have yet to officially meet Miss Dorothy." Brendan extended his hand across the table. "Let me introduce myself, as I should have right from the start. I'm Brendan Dunne, and this is my brother, James. We're pleased to make your acquaintance."

Dot took his hand briefly. "None of this Miss nonsense. Just call me Dorothy. Miss is too stuffy for my taste."

When she included James with a look in his direction, he grinned. "I like you, Dorothy. Or can I skip all formality and call you Dot?"

Evangeline bit her lip to keep from reacting to the coy smile Dot flashed at James.

"Dot suits me just fine." Before their flirtatious looks became too awkward for the rest of the table, Dot turned back to Evangeline. "I have to admit, when you said you'd met Mr. Dunne, half of me didn't believe you."

Evangeline smiled tightly. How could she answer without seeming petty and juvenile? Just as uneasiness encroached on the silence, Brendan Dunne's smooth, deep voice filled the space with its subtle Irish lilt.

"Please, Brendan is fine."

Dot nodded toward him before returning her attention to Evangeline. "How exactly did you and Brendan meet?"

"He offered me his umbrella when you left me to make my way home while you rode around town in a certain blue Chevrolet."

James quirked an eyebrow in Dot's direction. "A blue Chevrolet. Is that right? And who was driving this automobile that tempted you away from your friend? Should I be disappointed that you'd give your attention to others so easily? Maybe I'm not as special having received an invitation to join you as I originally felt."

Evangeline hid her desire to gasp at the brazenness of James, practically a stranger to both of them, by giving her attention to the milkshake in front of her. Dot's giggle did not ease Evangeline's displeasure. From the corner of her eye, she could see Brendan's jawline tense. Apparently, he wasn't pleased with his brother's antics either. Maybe she would have an ally to dissuade their interest in each other.

Evangeline seethed as Dot's giggling continued.

"You don't have to worry about them. They are only some local boys. Barely grown, and not even that if you want to get picky."

Evangeline glanced between James and Dot. His charming smile was laced with insincerity. Her long eyelashes provided a fetching, flirtation as her batting eyes extended an invitation to continue his flattery. Good grief. This was not good at all.

"Here you boys go. I made sure the kitchen fixed you up real quick." The waitress set their meals in front of them with a smile that rivaled Dot's in the area of blatant flirtation.

Brendan turned to James, who had eyes only for Dot. He sighed before turning a polite smile up at the girl. "Thank you. It looks delicious."

Evangeline couldn't help feeling a little bit sorry for the girl. Her flirtatious smile morphed into something akin to a grimace. She'd gone out of her way to impress and received nothing in return. The result might have been different if he weren't trying so hard to woo Dot. Much to Evangeline's chagrin, he was succeeding.

Brendan tucked into his food, while Evangeline concentrated on her milkshake. The other two at the table obviously did not need or want their input. Conversation flowed ceaselessly, accented by James's smooth words and Dot's giggles. It wasn't until Evangeline had finished her milkshake that Dot decided to include her.

Dot's excited squeal brought the rest of the restaurant patrons' activities to a halt.

Evangeline's cheeks heated at the unwanted attention. She glared at her friend. "What did you say?"

Dot had a cat-that-ate-the-canary smile as she clasped her hands together in front of her. "You should invite Brendan and James to your birthday party. It would be so much fun!"

Evangeline felt her face flush. "No. I mean, I'm not having a party. It's only supper with Father and Mother. Not a real party."

"And me. That makes it a party, especially if James and Brendan come. It isn't every day you turn twenty. You need a party."

Evangeline forced the tenseness out of her jaw before answering. "Dot, you know what Father and Mother are like. They wouldn't be pleased with that. It's all I can do to get them to allow me to extend an invitation to you."

Dot swatted the empty air. "Oh, pish posh. Don't let Evangeline fool you. Her parents simply adore me."

Evangeline could not contain her laugh. "My parents strain their sensibilities putting up with you, and you know it. You've gotten yourself into one too many scrapes to be a proper companion to a judge's daughter."

James turned his attention to her. "A judge's daughter?" One brow raised as he stared at his brother. "We have stumbled on new friends of the highest caliber, wouldn't you say, Brendan?"

Unease filled Evangeline at the look James gave Brendan, but she couldn't quite decipher the meaning behind it. She glanced at Brendan. His own expression was equally inscrutable. She had the distinct impression that no matter what James had said, Brendan was not impressed by her father's position. In fact, if she wasn't mistaken, he was more than a little uncomfortable at the thought.

His expression and voice were flat. "Yes, so it would seem."

Dot and James were too wrapped up in their own ideas to notice the discomfort their conversation created in those across the table from them. Dot laid a hand on James's arm.

"She's right, you know. Oh, not about her parents disliking me. They know I'm the kind of friend Evangeline needs." Dot waved the concern away. "But about the party. Judge Moore can be the biggest bluenose. It's rather tiresome. A party would've been a bright spot in a dreary week."

James patted the hand still resting on his forearm. "Quite right. We should remedy that."

Dot sucked in a breath as her mouth formed an *O* as big as her wide eyes. Her voice rose a full octave in her excitement. "You mean, we should throw her a party ourselves?"

James smiled at her. "Now you're on the trolley. The four of us could pile into my Packard Six and head over to Shady Rest tomorrow afternoon for some of that barbeque everyone talks about. And though the afternoon may not be the busiest time to visit, we might even be able to enjoy a dance or two to celebrate."

"We should. That would be perfect. What do you say, Evie? Before we go to the stuffy old supper with your parents, we can join James and Brendan for a real celebration! I've been dying to visit Shady Rest."

Dying might be more appropriate than Dot imagined. As much as Charlie Birger might pass as a good neighbor in Harrisburg, his dealings outside of the town were known to be less respectable. And trouble had been brewing between him and the Sheltons for a while now, if her father's rants at supper could be believed. Besides, even if the afternoon out didn't put the four of them in harm's way, it would still land Evangeline in trouble with her parents. Evangeline toyed with the locket around her neck. And she had no doubt her father would quickly find out.

Brendan frowned. "While I am certain Miss Evangeline's birthday is worthy of celebrating, I don't think Shady Rest is our best option."

Evangeline exhaled the breath she didn't realize she'd been holding. "I'm inclined to agree with Mr. Dunne."

"I didn't mean to extend permission to use my name only to Miss Dorothy. Please, it's Brendan."

Evangeline dipped her head. "I'm inclined to agree with Brendan."

How could simply saying his name cause that flutter to race through her middle? She was a grown woman, turning twenty, no less. She'd chided Dot more than once for such childish nonsense, but the tables were turning. And not in her favor. His voice, with its slight Irish accent, made everything he said sound like the sweetest poetry and arrested her attention more than she cared to admit.

"We simply must celebrate your birthday."

Dot's insistent voice bordered on a whine, pulling Evangeline from her musings. Dot and James watched her with equally expectant looks. Their eagerness had little to do with her birthday. Of that, she was sure.

She flashed a regretful smile to Brendan. "Can you excuse me, please?"

Waiting until he stood, Evangeline scooted across the vinyl seat, careful of her skirt. "I'll be back in a moment."

Seeking time to think, she made her way to the women's toilet in the back of the café. The dingy mirror hanging over the sink reflected her frustration. The last thing Evangeline wanted was to spend the day with two complete strangers, no matter how attractive they were. It wasn't lost on her either that celebrating her birthday was the last thing on Dot's mind. Not that she would admit to such a thing.

"If they expect me to agree," she spoke to her reflection, "they're going to be disappointed."

Raising her chin, Evangeline left the privacy of the little room ready to put her foot down on her friend's plans. In her absence, Brendan had assumed the inside seat of the booth. His gaze gave her a silent apology.

"Thank you." She remembered her manners though her words were accompanied by a confused frown.

Giving her attention to Dot, Evangeline braced herself for a fight as she chose to deal with the situation head-on. "I don't mean to be rude to our new friends, but I thought it might be nice for the two of us to spend the afternoon together tomorrow before supper with my parents." She included James and Brendan with a quick glance. "It's only that Dot and I have been friends for so long. I think spending the day with only her and me sounds perfect. I hope you understand."

"Don't worry your pretty little head about it." James took a drink of his coffee. "We understand. Don't we, Brendan?"

Before he could answer, Dot's hand covered hers on the table. "It's fine. Really. We talked about it while you were gone and decided it wasn't the best plan. Tomorrow, you and I can picnic by the river. It'll be a beautiful day. What do you say?"

If she were honest, the entire conversation was a little too easy to redirect. In all the years she'd known Dot, Evangeline had never seen her acquiesce so readily to plans that ran counter to her own. That she would willingly abandon plans that included attractive men, visiting Shady Rest, and the possibility of dancing made it even more suspicious. Dot's lips were tipped in a sweet smile Evangeline was convinced held nothing but feigned innocence. However, pointing that out, especially with present company, would only cause Dot to huff.

"That sounds wonderful." Evangeline smiled back before glancing at the men. "I do hope you understand."

"Evangeline," Brendan spoke when she made eye contact. "You should know—"

"You should know that we aren't men who easily take offense." James interrupted. "Spend the day with your friend and family, as it should be. Now, I'm afraid you'll have to excuse us. There is somewhere we have to be."

Pulling his wallet from his coat pocket, James placed two bills on the table before standing. Brendan cleared his throat.

"Oh goodness, my apologies." Evangeline shot out of the booth allowing Brendan to vacate the inner seat.

"Good day, ladies." James barely waited for Brendan to stand before moving toward the door.

Brendan turned to Evangeline. "About tomorrow ..."

"Brendan," James interrupted from the door. "We have to go. Now."

"I hope you understand." Evangeline repeated.

"Of course, I do. It's only—"

"Brendan. Now."

Evangeline smiled. "I think you had better go. Your brother does not appear to be the most patient of men."

"You have no idea." Brendan tipped his head and moved toward the door.

Chapter Five

"Dorothy Elizabeth Banks, how could you do this?" Anger surged through Evangeline as soon as she spied what could only be James's Packard Six parked near the picnic spot Evangeline and Dot frequented. She'd known Dot was up to something at the café the previous day, but Evangeline let Dot's talk of Brendan's possible interest override her common sense.

Dot laughed beside her, as carefree as any other time. Not even a hint of guilt for her duplicity.

"Do come on." Dot prodded as she exited the driver's side of the Chevrolet. "Brendan's stuck on you. I can tell these things. And you fancy him as well."

A raised palm stopped Evangeline's denial. Dot's red lips twisted in a wry smile. "You can't fool me. You like him. Now, get to know him better. He's a real sheik, not like the other men in this town. You can thank me later."

Dot's hips swayed strategically as she sauntered toward where the men stood waiting. Evangeline sucked in a deep breath. At least this far away from town, there was a chance Mother and Father might not hear of Dot's latest escapades. It remained to be seen how many more of her antics they would tolerate without expecting Evangeline to cut all ties with her friend.

"Happy Birthday, Miss Evangeline." James's boisterous voice assaulted her as she approached. "Your picnic awaits."

A sweeping gesture drew her attention to the edge of the river. A heavy, white blanket rested on the sea of green grass not far from where it faded into the grays and browns of the riverbank. Anchoring one side of the blanket, a woven picnic basket waited to be relieved of the edible treasures it held.

"Come, ladies." James extended his arm to Dot who allowed him to tuck hers in close. He led the way to the blanket.

Brendan offered Evangeline his arm. "Miss Evangeline, if I may have the honor."

The smile that came with his offer showed he was less than thrilled with the arrangement. So much for Dot's intuition. The man obviously didn't want to be here, though Evangeline had no idea what she'd done to put him off.

"You don't have to." Evangeline hoped her smile covered her disappointment. "I know it's the expected and polite course of action. But I promise I won't hold it against you if you want to forgo social expectations in this case."

A frown creased the area between Brendan's brows. With a shake of his head, he dismissed her suggestion. "Absolutely out of the question. Even if it weren't expected of a gentleman, I would still ask, just to have the pleasure of your company."

Heat filled Evangeline's cheeks as she wove her arm through his. From James, the compliment would have sounded insincere. She had a feeling it was that way with most things James said. But from Brendan, the words meant more. His tone assured her of their truth.

"I had James and Brendan pick up all your favorites." Dot sounded pleased with herself as she unwrapped chicken salad sandwiches and placed one on each plate.

Dill pickle spears, probably from those Dot's grandmother canned each year, joined their sandwiches before Dot retrieved a sealed waxed paper bag from the basket. Evangeline's mouth watered. While relatively new, she had a feeling the crisp, fried potato chips sprinkled with salt inside would one day be very popular.

Dot smiled. "Don't stand there like a statue. Sit down. Enjoy your birthday lunch."

As much as Evangeline wanted to stand her ground and make a statement, the draw of chicken salad and chips was too great.

Yesterday a milkshake, and today a bag of chips. Was forgiveness purchased this cheaply? The first crunch of chip assured her it was. And at that moment, Evangeline didn't really care.

"Miss Evangeline, I hope our presence doesn't disappoint you." James's tone spoke more than his words.

If Evangeline shared Dot's temperament, she would take James to task for his attitude. He no more cared about her reaction to their being in attendance than he would if someone were to swat a fly. But she wouldn't tell him that. Instead, she took a sip of her sweet lemonade before offering a polite smile.

"Not at all." She glanced at Dot. "I'm used to surprises. Dot is a master at arranging them whenever it strikes her fancy."

Dot's chuckle was forced. Good. She understood Evangeline's words were less than complimentary no matter how nicely they were spoken. One of these days, Evangeline would need to put her foot down on her friend's antics. The thought was enough to turn the chicken salad to rock inside her stomach.

Though it started with all the grace of a newborn foal taking its first steps, conversation about the inconsequential flowed as the group finished their meal. Dot wasted no time in gathering empty plates and returning them to the basket.

"After that meal," Dot began, "I think I might like a stroll along the river. It's such a pleasant day. I'd hate to waste it. Would anyone like to join me?"

Evangeline's heart sank. The way Dot's gaze only included James was all the proof she needed. Her friend didn't care a whit about their celebration. Evangeline had hoped her birthday was the real reason Dot planned the party. That it was simply convenient to ask James and Brendan to join them. But the truth was plain. Dot planned the picnic to meet James. Her birthday was simply the excuse to get Evangeline to join her and keep Brendan from being as wanted as an outbreak of smallpox.

"No. I don't think I'm in the mood for a walk today." It was the truth. Dot didn't need to know she was the reason.

"I'll escort you, Miss Dot," James offered a bit too quickly before shifting his attention to Brendan. "Why don't you stay and keep Miss Evangeline company? I'd hate to see her sitting here all by herself while we wander down the river's edge."

How gallant. Evangeline silently seethed as James helped Dot up, and they strolled toward the river. Evangeline focused her heart on prayer. *Lord, help me control my attitude. I don't want this to fester between Dot and me. And I don't want to let her selfishness ruin my birthday. I can't let her steal the joy from my day.*

A flirtatious giggle floated from where Dot and James walked away. If she was to keep a good attitude, God needed to intervene and be quick about it. At that moment, she wanted nothing more than to take Dot's car and leave her to find her own way home.

Unmistakable emotions played across Evangeline's face. Disappointment, frustration, and hints of betrayal took turns peering from the depths of her brown eyes. Brendan fought his own frustration. He expected this kind of behavior from James. His brother didn't know Evangeline and wouldn't care to use her. But Miss Dorothy was supposed to be her friend. What kind of friend behaved in such a selfish manner?

Brendan cleared his throat. "I'm sorry."

"Sorry?" Evangeline turned to face him. "Why?"

"I should have warned you last night. I tried. I should have tried harder."

"Warned me?"

Brendan nodded. "While you were away from the table, Miss Dorothy and James plotted this whole affair. She claimed you'd come and be too polite to say anything about it. I would not have mentioned their scheming, except that your own expression betrayed your understanding of the situation."

"You don't know Dot well." Evangeline straightened her shoulders though disappointment clung to her eyes. "And you have no reason to apologize. If I cared to think on it long, I would have realized her plan before we pulled into the parking area and spotted your brother's automobile."

"That may be. However, I am still sorry she's used you in this manner. Especially on your birthday."

"Believe me, when it comes to friendship with Dot, one learns to expect the unexpected and understands there is little that takes place without Dot wanting it to happen."

Brendan frowned. "Beg your pardon, Miss Evangeline."

"Please, Evangeline is fine. If we're to be companions for the afternoon, I think we can forgo the formalities."

"Evangeline." He tested the name without the proper 'Miss' attached and found it as refreshing as the lemonade he'd enjoyed with lunch. "As I was saying, and do forgive me if this is too forward, but if your friendship is that one-sided, why do you continue pursuing it?"

Two slender fingers rested against Evangeline's pale pink lips as she considered his question. Brendan didn't think he'd offended her. Of course, he wasn't well enough acquainted with her mannerisms to know for certain. As the silence continued, his initial confidence waned.

"I shouldn't have pried."

"Oh, no." Evangeline's smile put him at ease. "It's only my first answer sounds so silly."

"I'm sure that's not true."

One shoulder lifted in silent challenge of his assertion. "I was going to say, Dot and I are friends because Dot and I have always been friends. We met in our first year at school, and we have been together ever since."

"There is something to be said for loyalty." It was the only truthful answer he could give. Nurturing a friendship only because it had always been that way did seem a trifle silly, especially when one in the relationship thought only of herself.

"It wasn't always this way." Evangeline gazed toward the shoreline Dot and James had long since vacated for a more secluded area of the riverbank. "Dot and I were not so different as children. Oh, she was always more outgoing and adventurous. But that was good for me. I tended to be a bit of a bore."

"I can't believe that."

Evangeline nodded. "It's true. I guess I still am. I much prefer spending time with one or two friends to activities like dancing and parties. And reading outside under the oak tree in my back yard is as near to heaven as I can get on this earth."

"That doesn't mean you're a bore. Many people prefer spending their days in quiet and relative calm. I tend to prefer conversation to parties myself."

"As children, Dot encouraged me to play with the other children and have fun. But she was different then. As we left childhood behind, I became more serious about my faith. While I was learning to have a relationship with God and live the way He wants me to, Dot challenged every rule. She decided God doesn't care what she does, if He even exists. Life is here to make her happy. And she has made it her goal to chase everything she thinks might give that to her."

"Which brings me back to my initial question. If you and Dot do not share interests or beliefs anymore, why do you still foster friendship?"

"Hope is a tiny word with a great deal of power, Mr. Dunne."

"Aren't we skipping formalities?" He wagged a finger at her with a grin. "Call me Brendan."

"I have hope, Brendan. Hope that one day, Dot will see the futility of chasing all the wrong things. I pray every day for her to remember the faith she had as a child. To remember God's love and return to Him. It's my hope that in remaining friends with Dot, she sees God in the way I live, and when she's ready, that example will help her find her way."

Brendan regarded her silently. Barely more than strangers, yet she shared freely about subjects obviously close to her heart. He'd been given a treasure.

Evangeline's pale cheeks pinked. Brushing an invisible speck from her dress, her gaze darted from blanket to grass to the riverbank without once landing on him.

"I'm sorry to prattle on so." She continued to look out over the water. "Dot always tells me I sound like a dumb Dora when I speak of such things. While I don't like her phrasing, I fear she's right."

There was nothing unintelligent or uninteresting about Evangeline. A spark of anger lit in his chest at the realization she thought so. How could a friend make her feel that way?

"Applesauce." The rebuttal slipped from his lips without thought. "My silence was in no way an indication of boredom on my part. Quite the contrary."

Her expression filled with yearning as if she were lost at sea and he'd thrown her a lifeline. Was there no one in her life to make her feel worthy? As strong as her faith appeared, did she truly feel like she paled in comparison to Dot's vivacious personality?

Brendan squelched the urge to reach out, touch her hand. "It was your passion that moved me to silence, not boredom. Your faith and your love for Dot motivate you to keep giving with nothing in return but the hope that one day, your friend's heart may change. I find that challenging."

"What do you mean?" Her soft voice barely rose above a whisper.

"Like you, I am a person of faith. My brother keeps up the pretense by attending mass, as does most of my family. For me, faith is more than living without giving thought to my actions and then seeking absolution after the fact. Faith is about becoming the person God made us to be. That's a novel idea for most of my family, especially considering ..."

He inwardly cringed. A judge's daughter didn't associate with a gangster's son. One slip of the tongue about his life in Chicago, and the fact that he found Evangeline an engaging companion for an afternoon picnic wouldn't matter.

"Considering?"

Wariness narrowed her eyes. Had rumors already reached her? No. Dot's scheming or not, Evangeline wouldn't have enjoyed a picnic with them if the truth were known. He was being paranoid.

Brendan shook his head. "It doesn't matter. Listening to your passion for Dot to live a life of faith convicts me of my shortcomings with James. While you are tenacious in your loyalty to Dot and seeing her come to faith, I admit I've struggled with the desire to be free from my responsibility to keep James out of trouble."

"Please don't put me on a pedestal. There are times Dot sorely tries my patience too. There have been many instances where I had to reconsider my commitment to our friendship."

"But you've stayed."

"Yes." Evangeline nodded. "However, I've also had to come to terms with the idea that God can save Dot with or without me. Ultimately, her faith is not my responsibility. Accepting that as fact has enabled me to give our friendship to God and trust Him if He asks me to distance myself from my friend."

Would he feel as confident in faith if God asked him to step away from James? Or would it simply be a relief born of escaping responsibility? Evangeline possessed an assurance of her motives that Brendan lacked. Of course, familial obligations added to the reasons for his choices. But he couldn't get into those with Evangeline. He could, however, pray about his attitude toward his brother. Then, maybe, he could display the same passion for James that Evangeline showed for Dot.

"Look at that, Dot, baby," James's voice drew his attention.

"What did I tell you?" Dot sank into James as she slid her arm around his waist. "They haven't moved an inch."

"You need to relax, baby brother." James chided before letting his gaze travel up and down the woman in his arms. "You never know what fun might be around the curve of the riverbank."

"We had a perfectly nice time." Evangeline's voice was icy as she stared at the pair before them.

"Doubtful." Dot retorted.

James planted a loud kiss on Dot's forehead. "I hate to end the party, but if we don't leave soon, you'll never make it to supper with the judge." He turned to Evangeline. "Happy birthday." His gaze transferred to Brendan. "Let's blouse. I need to pick up a deck of Luckies."

"Ugh." Brendan stood and gathered the picnic paraphernalia. "You really should quit with the cigarettes. They stink."

James laughed as he strode toward the car.

"Bye, doll," he called over his shoulder. "We'll see each other soon."

As the men drove away, Evangeline glared at Dot.

"I don't want to hear it." Dot's raised brows issued the warning not to challenge her. "Get in the car. James is right, we're going to be late."

Chapter Six

With one hand on the steering wheel, James clapped Brendan on the shoulder. "Smile, brother. It's a beautiful day."

Brendan rolled his eyes. "You hate picnics."

"True." James's laugh was harsh. "But I love a choice bit of calico. And that Dot? She's as choice as they come. Hotsy-totsy and a bearcat to boot."

"Do you have to be so coarse?" Brendan used some of the vernacular popular with those of his generation, but never the ones describing women. They were degrading, not taking into account the person so much as their physical attributes and how willing they were to engage in less-than-moral activities.

"What's your beef? I guarantee Dot didn't mind. Lapped up the compliments like a kitten with a bowl of milk. Don't you appreciate a beautiful-looking woman?"

Brendan stared straight ahead. "Of course, I do. But unlike you, I tend to look a little deeper than a woman's appearance and what she will or won't do when we take a stroll down the river."

James flicked a glance at him before giving his attention to the road in front of them. After a moment of silence, his face lit up.

"Hoo-hoo!" His guffaw filled the car. "While I got the

bearcat, you got stuck with the canceled stamp. It's true. Isn't it? Your girl is just a shy little wallflower too proper to let loose and enjoy herself."

Anger erupted in Brendan's chest. He sucked in a cooling breath. If he answered before regaining some semblance of calm, the fire of his fury would spew from his mouth and cover James.

If it be possible, as much as lieth in you, live peaceably with all men. Brendan silently allowed the verse from Romans to play in an endless loop. All men. Including James. Especially James. They were brothers, after all. And no matter how strained relationships became when Brendan didn't want to take part in the family business, they were still family. And family was second only to God.

The mantra had been drilled into him from the day he was born. While Brendan understood his father, brother, uncles, and cousins only put God above family in word, it meant something to him. That's why he couldn't condone their heinous actions to keep control in the neighborhood or their fanatical protection of each other after the fact. It was also why his father sent him with James when protecting him from the consequences of rash actions became impossible at home in Chicago.

Their father might not understand Brendan's resistance to their family's ways, but he understood that Brendan's refusal to participate in bootlegging, bribe collecting, and worse meant the family could trust him to try to keep James out of trouble until tensions eased. Too bad they didn't realize how unquenchable James's appetite for trouble was.

"Don't go all stoic on me." James's voice was teasing. It always was when he tried to pacify Brendan after angering him. "I didn't know. How could two women, two friends, be so entirely different? Don't worry. We'll find you someone. She'll be the cat's meow. You won't even remember Evangeline."

At least he'd dropped the 'Miss' from Evangeline's name. James excelled at the pretense of being proper when it suited the situation. Most of the time the insincerity grated on Brendan's nerves, especially so with Evangeline.

"I don't want to forget Evangeline." He refused to look at James. Whether incredulous or teasing, seeing James's expression would irritate him more. "Just because she isn't like Miss Dorothy doesn't mean she isn't worth my friendship."

"Hmm."

Brendan chanced a quick glance at James. His brows *V*'d in thought. *Oh, no. What did I say?*

"Maaybe." The word was drawn out like a slow drag from the cigarettes he enjoyed. "You just don't kiss and tell. I couldn't help noticing, Dot is Miss Dorothy. Evangeline, however, is simply Evangeline. If you've dispensed with the formalities, perhaps more took place than the chaste image of you two sitting prim and proper on the picnic blanket would suggest."

"Don't do that." Brendan growled the warning through clenched teeth. "Do not attribute your immoral proclivities to me. And do not disparage Evangeline's reputation. She behaved as a perfect lady."

James's jaw tightened. His eyes peered out the windshield toward the road, but Brendan could see the moment they went flat.

"Oh, I touched a nerve." His voice carried as little emotion as his eyes. "How about we strike a deal? You keep your opinions to yourself regarding my time with Dot, and I won't hassle you about your relationship with Evangeline. Deal?"

"I don't have a relationship with Evangeline."

"Call it a preemptive measure." James regarded him. "One look at your face confirms it. You want to get to know Evangeline as much as I want to have some fun with Dot."

"You are supposed to be staying out of trouble. It's why we're here instead of Chicago."

"That's not what our father meant. Besides, Dot isn't going to be trouble. She's simply a good time."

Knowing James thought nothing of Dot yet was willing to

play with her affections soured Brendan's stomach. The girl might be a terrible flirt and too enamored with a culture she obviously didn't understand, but that didn't make using her right. Brendan considered his options. Going against James would only make their time in Harrisburg unbearable.

If he worked it right, he might even be able to warn Dorothy away from James through Evangeline. James was correct about one thing, though—Brendan did want to get to know Evangeline better. And where Dorothy went, Evangeline was sure to follow.

"Deal." He wouldn't even have to plot and plan to see her. With James and Dorothy involved, arranging to meet would be taken care of without any help from him. And while Evangeline wasn't the scheming type, Brendan wouldn't be surprised to learn the girls were discussing the day as much as he and James had.

"Oh, quit looking at me like that, would you." Dot whined with a sigh.

"You've not taken your eyes off the road since we got in the car. You can't begin to know how I'm looking at you." Evangeline was quickly losing all semblance of patience. This time Dot had gone too far.

Dot shoved a wayward strand of hair from her cheek. "I don't have to see you to know. I can feel you glaring at me, and it's not nice. You're worse than my mother was with that look of disappointment."

"What do you expect?" Evangeline struggled to keep her voice at a normal level. "Do you think I'm blind? You were completely disheveled when you came back from your walk. You may think me naïve, but I know there wasn't a lot of walking going on."

Dot giggled. "We're adults."

"You barely know the man!"

"I know all I need to know." The blunt statement left no room to argue. "James isn't some Reuben like all the other

44

backwoods hicks around here. He's from Chicago, Evangeline." Her voice was breathless, like she'd found the Holy Grail of relationship standards.

Evangeline sighed. "That doesn't mean anything."

"It means everything. I'm stuck here in this no-account town. But James? He's experienced all the things I dream about. The things I've only read about in magazines. He's going to take me away from here."

"Did he tell you that?"

Dot's chin raised.

"Well?"

"He didn't have to. I can tell."

"Oh, Dot."

"Don't you do that. Don't treat me like I'm a wayward child who doesn't understand. James really likes me. And the more we're together, the more he'll realize I'm just like those women from Chicago. When he and Brendan go back home, James will beg me to go with him."

A tendril of fear spiraled through Evangeline. "I know you want to move on to what you believe is a more exciting life, but you don't know James or his family. You don't know what kind of lives they lead."

"Didn't seem to stop you from chatting with Brendan all afternoon."

"That's different. Brendan isn't like the rest of his family" She didn't have proof of that, but she needed to make her point. Adjusting the skirt around her legs, she rummaged through her thoughts for an explanation. "Do you know about their family?"

Dot shrugged. "James mentioned being sent here while some kind of trouble worked itself out."

"They're a mob family." Despite being the only two in the automobile, her voice dropped to a whisper.

"Oooh," Dot cooed. "I could be a gangster's moll. Wouldn't that be the cat's meow? Think of all the parties. I'd be a real somebody."

Evangeline groaned. "You're already somebody, Dot. Somebody who's not involved with the police or worried about watching your back or anything like that. You don't really want that life. Do you?"

"What if I do? What's it to you?"

If she had to ask, was there any hope? Or was it only a guilty conscience reacting? As Dot pulled up to the house, Evangeline placed a hand on Dot's arm and waited for her to make eye contact.

"We're friends. It matters. You're heading down a road that doesn't lead anywhere good. God's plans for you are so much bigger."

An unladylike snort cut Evangeline off. "Don't start up with that again. *God loves me. God has a purpose for me.*"

The mocking tone shouldn't hurt, but it did. Evangeline should have expected it. Dot had grown less and less patient with matters of faith. But still, Evangeline had to try.

"Dot ..."

"I'm serious, Evangeline. That's enough. Of course, you believe in a loving God and purpose and all that. Look at all God gave you. You're the judge's daughter. The best of everything is simply handed to you. But what would you do if you had to give it all up? If you had to scrimp and save and lose like the rest of us?"

Evangeline blinked back tears.

"You'd realize it's nothing more than hokum and start doing what you really wanted."

"Please, don't."

Dot was just getting warmed up. "Don't what? Don't tell you the truth? It's time you open your pretty little eyes. The world isn't all prim and proper, waiting to give you your own personal fairy tale. And if you ever, just once, lost something you care about, you'd see it too."

"My beliefs aren't based on fairy tales."

"You could have fooled me. Seems your big house with your

perfect parents and your ridiculous birthday supper are just another chapter of your once upon a time."

Evangeline bit her lip. *Please God, help me. I didn't know she was so bitter.*

"I don't want to fight with you, Dot. Let's forget all this and go enjoy supper. What do you say?" If they could just move past this, everything would be fine.

"I say," Dot glared at her, "you're going to be late, and I'm not hungry. I think I'll pass on supper."

"You don't mean that."

Dot stared out the windshield. Tense silence pulsed between them. Evangeline worried her pendant between her fingers. Surely Dot wouldn't do this. Not today of all days. Not because of a man. But Dot said nothing, keeping her focus outside the automobile.

Pressure building in her chest, Evangeline stepped from the car and strode into the house without a backward glance. It was time for her birthday celebration.

Chapter Seven

"Would you like to take a walk, Mother?" Evangeline leaned away from the table, allowing the housekeeper to whisk her empty plate away from the table.

Usually, the family met their own needs in the evenings, but Mother had asked Mildred to stay. The excuse was that keeping Mildred would allow the family more time together. Evangeline smiled, sure it had more to do with the fact that her mother abhorred household tasks. Dot would probably see that as another mark against her family. Her easy smile tried to fade, but Evangeline pasted it in place for her mother's benefit.

Mother dabbed the cloth napkin against the corners of her mouth before placing it on the plate Mildred added to her stack. "I don't think so. Not tonight. But if you do, please be sure to wear a cardigan. Fall has arrived, making the evenings a bit cool."

"Please, Mother. Won't you go with me?" After the disaster with Dot, being by herself was not appealing. "We can make it a short walk."

Her father cleared his throat at the head of the table. "Am I not a suitable walking companion for my only child?"

Evangeline straightened and tried to look repentant. "I'm

sorry, Father. I didn't realize a walk would appeal to you. Would you care to join me?"

"I think after such a hearty meal, a stroll would be a welcome choice."

"Let me go get my cardigan, and we'll be off." Evangeline wasn't quite sure what to think of her father's offer to accompany her. It wasn't that they had a bad or tumultuous relationship. Her interests simply rarely aligned with his, leaving them little to do together or talk about.

It amazed Evangeline how different silence could be between people. Dot's stubborn refusal to speak after her outburst earlier weighed heavy on Evangeline. The same quiet as she strolled with her father toward the main street of town was peaceful. Both content to leave the other to their thoughts.

Waving as they passed neighbors sitting on their porches, Evangeline's thoughts wandered to her disagreement with Dot. Chicago tempted Dot with a siren song promising excitement, fun, and freedom from all the things she believed held her back. Evangeline desired simple pleasures. If only Dot could see that without a relationship with God, she would find nothing to fill the cravings inside her. Evangeline wasn't fooled. Part of Dot would always enjoy new and exciting things, but God could show her how to find those without going down the dangerous paths she was toying with.

"How about a milkshake for my favorite girl?"

Speaking of cravings. Evangeline nodded at her father. "That sounds like the perfect birthday treat."

"You're not too full after dessert, are you? I wouldn't want you to have an upset stomach on your birthday."

Evangeline leaned into the arm looped around her own. "Not at all. There is always room for a milkshake."

"Enjoy them." The admonition was accompanied by a chuckle. "Not all of us were lucky enough to have them when we were growing up. Ice cream was rare enough."

Father could be stern and domineering at times, but on days

like this, Evangeline cherished the blessing of her family. His strong arm holding hers close was a comfort after the turmoil of the afternoon. Thinking about the day's events brought to mind another gentleman's arm that held hers that day. How could the same action spark thoughts of support and security one time and another time cause her heart to race and her cheeks to heat. Why, even just reminiscing on it left her flush.

"Hello. Let me hold that for you."

Brendan's voice jerked her from her thoughts. When had they arrived at the café? And why was Brendan there holding the door for her and her father? Afraid stormy clouds of disapproval would push aside the pleasantness of her evening with her father, Evangeline couldn't acknowledge knowing Brendan.

"It's good to ..."

Her eyes widened with panic. Hoping to warn him off, Evangeline offered a slight shake of her head. Maybe he would catch the meaning, and her father wouldn't notice.

"See others out enjoying the fine evening." Brendan managed to salvage the situation before saying something to make her father suspicious.

"Thank you, Mr. ...?" Her father let the question hang.

Brendan smiled. "Dunne. Brendan Dunne, sir."

Evangeline moved inside. To her horror, Brendan and her father remained outside the open doorway. Her father knew exactly who Brendan was. Would he confront him here in so public a place? That would be too embarrassing.

Her father held out his hand, waiting until Brendan accepted it with a hearty shake. "Judge Herb Moore. You're new in town, aren't you, Mr. Dunne?"

"Yes, sir." He nodded. "But please, Judge Moore, call me Brendan. My father is Mr. Dunne."

"Well, Brendan. I'd like to welcome you to our fine little town. Harrisburg prides itself on a neighborly spirit and old-fashioned family values."

Having already claimed a seat in a nearby booth, Evangeline

watched in fascination and horror as her father took two steps in her direction and paused. He turned to Brendan, who narrowly missed running into him with the sudden stop. While Brendan tried to hide it, Evangeline could see the questions in his eyes.

"Brendan, how would you like to join my daughter and me this evening? Give us a chance to get to know one another a bit better."

Evangeline's mouth dropped open. This could be a disaster. Her mind screamed "No," but she was the only one to hear it. Brendan's gaze darted to hers. Any possibility of a look to warn him away was squashed as her father also glanced her direction. Instead, her mouth snapped shut as she pasted on the polite smile she'd been trained since childhood to offer in social settings.

"I couldn't impose."

Relief.

"Nonsense." Her father motioned toward the table. "Evangeline and I would love nothing more than getting to know a newcomer to our fair town. As I stated before, Harrisburg is a friendly place. Neighborly. Could one be any more neighborly than sharing a table and conversation?"

Brendan removed his hat as he stepped fully into the room. "Put that way, how could I refuse? Thank you, Judge Moore. I believe I will join you."

Sliding across the bench seat, Evangeline made room for her father to sit beside her. Brendan claimed the space across from them. Of all nights for Brendan to happen upon them, why tonight? Knowing the crime connections in Chicago, why would Father choose hospitality instead of keeping his beloved daughter as far from him as possible?

"Brendan Dunne, let me formally introduce you to my daughter, Evangeline."

"Miss Evangeline, I hope I'm not intruding on a special father-daughter outing."

It wasn't lost on Evangeline how he avoided lying by leading her father to believe they'd only just met. Her smile relaxed a bit.

"Not at all. We were enjoying a stroll after supper when my father suggested we get a milkshake."

"It's Evangeline's birthday today." Her father's hand patted hers. "I thought a special treat was in order. Evangeline loves milkshakes."

"Your birthday? Well, then I am intruding on a special occasion. Please, allow me to take care of your milkshake this evening."

The urge to giggle welled up in Evangeline at Brendan's raised eyebrows and mock surprise, but she refused it. Instead, she allowed her humor to brighten her smile erasing the last vestiges of her previous unease.

"I'm sure that's not necessary. Is it, Father?"

He raised his hands in a halting gesture. "Not at all. I've invited you to join us. Tonight will be my treat."

Before Brendan could argue further, the waitress stopped at the end of their booth. Evangeline breathed a quiet sigh of relief that it was the usual evening server, Pearl, and not the waitress who had served the four of them only the day before. It wouldn't do to have their previous meeting brought to light, especially when her father was present to chastise them both at the same time. And though her father held onto his public image with a tight fist, Evangeline was positive he'd have no qualms about making a public spectacle in this case. He would be livid and let everyone know it.

Her father smiled at the waitress. "Good evening, Pearl. I'd like a cup of coffee, please. And Evangeline will have a milkshake."

"What flavor, honey?" Pearl asked, jotting down the order in her notepad.

"Chocolate, please. With extra whipped cream and a cherry?"

She smiled and scribbled on the pad. "We can do that for you." She glanced at Brendan. "And you, sir."

"Feel free to order whatever you like," her father reassured Brendan before he could answer.

Brendan nodded toward her father. "Thank you." He turned

his attention to Pearl. "I believe tonight, I'll have a grilled cheese sandwich and a cup of coffee."

One more scribble before the waitress turned to deliver their order to the kitchen.

"While we wait," Evangeline's father turned his attention on Brendan. "Why don't you tell us about yourself? Where are you from? What prompted your move to Harrisburg?"

Before Brendan could answer, Pearl returned.

"Here you go." She set the milkshake in front of Evangeline before placing one of the cups of coffee in front of Judge Moore.

Turning to Brendan, her smile grew warmer. She placed his coffee on the table. A blush filled her cheeks when her hesitance to fully relinquish the cup caused Brendan's fingers to brush hers as he reached for the drink. From the corner of his eye, Brendan could see one of Evangeline's brows raise high as Pearl rested her hand on his forearm.

"And don't you worry." Her voice was drenched in sticky, sweet honey. "I'll have your sandwich out in a flash."

Brendan gave only the required polite smile and a small nod. "Thank you."

Had he imagined Evangeline's amusement at the exchange? Turning to face her, her features were schooled into an expression as bland as boiled potatoes without the butter. Judge Moore cleared his throat. A judge with a question that had yet to be answered. That was never a good thing in Brendan's opinion.

"My apologies, sir." Brendan took a sip of coffee. "My brother, James, and I hail from Chicago. We're here at our father's request."

With an almost imperceptible narrowing of his eyes, and lips that pursed after each taste of his coffee, Judge Moore contemplated Brendan. The man noticed more than one typically would. Brendan was sure of it. Next to her father, Evangeline absently worried the pendant around her neck.

"And what business prompted a man in Chicago to send his sons away from the hustle and bustle of the city into our fair town, Mr. Dunne?"

"Please," Brendan fell back on pointless chit-chat while he scoured the recesses of his mind for a suitable answer. "I must insist you and Miss Evangeline call me Brendan. I realize Chicago might stand on such a formality. But, as you've pointed out, I'm in the neighborly town of Harrisburg now. It seems more neighborly to abandon strict levels of formality."

"Brendan, it is, then."

"If you are to be Brendan, then please, call me Evangeline." Her sweet smile telegraphed only innocence and sincerity.

Though the slight lift of his chin indicated Judge Moore might not be completely in favor of her edict, he didn't forbid it either. At least Brendan could continue without concern for giving away their previous meeting with accidental familiarity. It was one less thing to worry about in a conversation rife with opportunity to say the wrong thing.

"But you've asked me a question." Brendan turned the mug in his hands. "Father is a businessman. He's always looking for new areas for expansion."

It wasn't a lie.

"And what business is your family in?"

Evangeline eyed him warily. Then, she already suspected the true nature of the family business. That meant her father did as well. Omitting the less savory aspects of his family's life was necessary for their protection whether he agreed with them or not.

"My family owns and manages several rental properties, both residential and commercial." All true. And hopefully, enough to satisfy the curiosity of Judge Moore.

Shrewd eyes pinned Brendan to his seat. He straightened his shoulders. The family's methods were not his own. Time had taught him the folly in taking on the guilt of those who bowed to his father's ways. Especially when even guilt gave them wide berth.

Judge Moore cleared his throat. "I've heard rumors of tenants, both families and businesses, finding themselves stretched beyond their means to buy safety from the very people who offer their protection. Have any of your people found themselves in those situations?"

The judge had about as much finesse digging for information as the coal miners on the outskirts of town as they blasted holes in the earth until it gave up its riches. While her father waited with thinly veiled condemnation, Evangeline gave up all pretense of enjoying her birthday treat. Pushing the mostly empty glass away, she tucked her bottom lip between her teeth.

Brendan took a bite from his sandwich giving himself time to chew over his options before answering. "It's nasty business when people take advantage of others in that way. Disgusting, really. But, yes, I know many who've found themselves in those situations. I try to give aid, but the small ways I'm able to are as helpful as offering a homeless man a pair of gloves to stave off the cold of a blizzard. It only manages to slow down the impending loss and barely does that."

"I'm sure," Evangeline's soft voice broke into the conversation, "those in need appreciate whatever help you've offered."

Her father patted her hand. "Very true, Evangeline." His tone held far less agreement than his words would suggest. "It is despicable to watch a few in our society get fat, not off the misfortune of others, but through duplicitous means that prey on innocent lives."

The challenge was clearly extended.

"I couldn't agree more, sir."

"Someone needs to purge these men from our society." A placating smile twisted Judge Moore's lips. "Not that Chicago is the only area dealing with people of this sort. Ruffians—well let's call them what they are. Criminals. These criminals have a foothold in southern Illinois as well. Though Harrisburg, for the moment, seems unscathed by their attempts."

Careful. Weighing his words was vitally important if Brendan intended to stay on Judge Moore's good side. This man was not a Reuben, despite talk around town confirming the Moore family was Harrisburg born and raised. And though it was large for the southern part of the state, Harrisburg still wasn't another Chicago, no matter how up and coming it fancied itself. Country hick clung to it like a tick on a dog. But not on the man sitting across from him.

"Harrisburg does seem a rather peaceful town. And as you pointed out earlier, it's full of that neighborly charm so often missing in larger cities. I pray your town continues to grow and thrive and doesn't attract the less desired element."

Evangeline perked up. "Are you a praying man, then, Brendan?"

"Yes." He nodded. "And, though I applaud our police forces and our judicial system trying to stem the tide of criminal activity, I believe, in the end, it is God who will mete out justice for the innocent victims."

Coffee pot in hand, Pearl stopped at the end of their table. "Y'all want a refill?"

Judge Moore raised a hand. "Not for me. Thank you, Pearl." He motioned toward Evangeline. "I believe Evangeline and I are finished. If you'd be so kind as to bring me the bill."

Glancing at Brendan, Pearl raised the coffee pot in his direction. He shook his head. "None for me either. Thank you. I'm just going to finish off the last of my sandwich, and your table will be free."

As she went to retrieve the check, Brendan nodded to Evangeline and then Judge Moore. "It has been a pleasure dining and speaking with you tonight. I want to thank you, again, for your generosity in inviting me to join you and for my meal. Harrisburg hospitality in action."

Standing, Judge Moore extended his hand to help Evangeline

slide gracefully across the seat to join him. "Thank you for dining with us and indulging me in a few questions to get to know you better. I'm sure you will be a valuable addition to our town, however long you intend to stay."

"It was a pleasure." Evangeline's easy smile proved her words.

Brendan didn't doubt her sincerity. Her father was another matter completely. He watched them through the window as they exited and couldn't shake the feeling that he'd been weighed and measured. But had he been found wanting?

Chapter Eight

Seeking out Evangeline was a risk when he was unsure on his standing with her father. Still, Brendan couldn't get her rich brown eyes out of his mind. The way her hair shimmered in the sunlight during their picnic didn't help either. It made him think of silk and brought with it the urge to run his fingers through it to prove its softness. And her smile. That smile could steal the breath from any man, especially when accompanied by her easy laugh.

Too many women he'd had occasion to meet were like Miss Dorothy. Brash. Bold. And so insistent on being unique they melded into one indistinguishable mass of crude rebellion. If only the trends would give way to women like Evangeline. Sweet. Beautiful. Pure. Classic.

"Hmm."

The soft sound of a woman's voice pulled Brendan from his thoughts. One of the Moore's neighbors was strolling his direction. He must seem like a lunatic, standing on the sidewalk gawking at the house with a bouquet of daisies.

Before she had opportunity to chide him for standing in the middle of the path, Brendan moved onto the walkway leading to the Moore's wrap-around porch. Turning to acknowledge the woman's presence, he doffed his hat and nodded.

"Good morning, ma'am."

Lips a tight, straight line, she barely flicked a glance in his direction. "Good morning." The words came out as staccato as the click of her heels on the concrete as she hurried past him.

He turned back to the house. Shoulders back, he fortified himself with a deep breath before making his way up to the front door. A quick assessment of his attire ensured nothing was amiss. His fist hovered only a moment over the door before announcing his arrival with a knock.

The woman who opened the door had to be Evangeline's mother. Though gray strands stole some of its shine, her hair was the same honey blonde as her daughter's. Eyes of an identical deep, chocolate brown shade, though framed with the subtle lines of life, peered at him with open curiosity.

"May I help you?"

Her voice, trained in the requirements of polite society, was friendly but held no warmth. Of course, he was a stranger standing outside her door. Did she have reason for warmth?

"Hello, ma'am." Brendan used his free hand to remove his hat. "My name is Brendan Dunne, and, with your approval, I hoped I might visit a spell with Miss Evangeline today."

"Dunne. The man my husband said dined with him and our daughter last night?"

"The very one." Brendan smiled. "I enjoyed the time immensely. Your husband is a man who cares for his family and his town. That was evident in our conversation. And Miss Evangeline was such a joy to speak with. I would be grateful for the opportunity to get to know her a little more."

Pleasure warred with doubt in Mrs. Moore's eyes. "It's customary for you to seek my husband's permission with such a request. However, since you are standing here, and he is not due back home until supper, we won't make you leave and come back another time."

She eyed the bouquet in his hand. "I doubt those flowers would look as fresh if you delayed even a day. If you will wait here, I'll inform Evangeline of your intentions and see if she is inclined to join you."

"I appreciate that, Mrs. Moore."

The words were barely out of his mouth before the door shut in his face. At least she'd warned him first. Once the idea settled, any doubt he'd known fled in the face of excitement. Did that mean Evangeline didn't see many gentleman callers? Why did the image of her passing time with another man twist his stomach? He and Evangeline weren't even courting.

Something had Mother worked up, if the sound of feet galloping up the stairs was any indication. Evangeline had heard the knock on the door, but since she was in the middle of her morning Bible study, she'd let her mother answer.

Curious, she set her Bible on the bedside table. Before she could move from where she reclined against the headboard of her bed, her mother burst through the door. Evangeline would not have to wait to find out what excited her mother so early this morning.

"What are you doing in bed?"

The horror expressed in her mother's tone tempted Evangeline to cower like a naughty toddler. But that was ridiculous. Nothing about Evangeline's behavior was wrong or even unexpected.

Evangeline frowned. "I'm doing my morning Bible study, as I have every morning for at least the last five years."

"You have time for that later."

Her mother's hands flapped about, reminding Evangeline of a disgruntled chicken. When she started toward Evangeline's vanity before turning to the closet only to fly back to the vanity and then turn to stare at her, Evangeline had to stifle a giggle. The way she bounced from place to place without reason, the chicken wasn't simply disgruntled. It'd had its head chopped clean off.

"What are you standing there for?"

"What am I supposed to be doing?"

"Making yourself presentable. You can't entertain him while looking like you just tumbled out of bed."

Evangeline ran her hands down the front of her skirt. Not freshly pressed, but definitely not slept-in wrinkled either. And it was perfectly clean. She'd only been reading in bed, not wallowing in it. Wait. Her hands stilled.

"Who am I entertaining, Mother? I was unaware I had a guest."

"I told you when I came in."

"You most certainly did not. And for the record, you've still not told me. Not really."

"Oh, dear me." She held out a brush to Evangeline and waited for her to take it. "Run that through your hair and then we'll add a bit of color to your cheeks."

Evangeline complied with Mother's demands. But she needed answers. "Mother, who?"

Without waiting for Evangeline to follow her first command, her mother grasped her by the wrist and practically dragged her to the vanity. "Now, let's see. Just a bit. We don't want you looking garish." She began applying a light touch of rouge to Evangeline's cheeks. "We wouldn't want Mr. Dunne thinking you're the sort of young woman who is less than acceptable."

"No." Wait. Mr. Dunne? "Brendan Dunne is here? To see me?"

When her mother kept inspecting her, Evangeline took both her mother's hands in her own and looked her in the eye. "Mother. Please. Is Brendan Dunne waiting downstairs to see me?"

"Well, no."

Evangeline shook her head. What had gotten into her mother?

"I left him on the veranda." Her mother's expression was sheepish.

Oh, bother. Evangeline dropped her mother's hands and quickly ran the brush through her hair, smoothing it, before pulling it back into a quick but expertly fashioned knot at the base of her neck. She double checked the rouge her mother had applied. Finding it subtle enough, she gave herself a complete once-over. Presentable, even with her simple cotton dress. It would have been wonderful if her mother had told her straight away what was happening. She could have traded her comfortable at-home dress for one more suited to company.

There was nothing to be done about it now. Brendan had already waited much longer than he needed to for her to appear. After slipping on her T-strap shoes, she made her way to the door, forcing herself to slow on the stairs. She couldn't appear rushed or disheveled when she joined Brendan on the porch. Not even if her mother's announcement had caused her heart to gallop.

Chapter Nine

"Mr. Dunne, how nice to see you." The expected greeting slipped from Evangeline's lips as she opened the door. He'd freed her to call him Brendan, but with Mother hovering near by that would never do.

He offered her a simple bouquet of daisies, heating her cheeks in a way that would add more color than the rouge Mother had applied only moments earlier. "These are for you, Miss Moore. I hoped they might earn me a short visit."

"They're lovely." She accepted them from his hand and ran a finger over a few of the delicate petals. "Thank you. But I assure you, there is no need to resort to bribes, no matter how beautiful, to enjoy a chat with me on the front porch swing."

He gestured to the swing. "After you, then."

"Oh, no." She shook her head. "I'm not letting your gift go to waste. Let me put these in water first. You sit. I'll hurry back, I promise."

"Then I'll wait for your return."

Evangeline stepped back through the still open doorway and closed the door. She startled as it shut, revealing her mother's hiding spot behind it. Though Evangeline hadn't doubted for a moment her mother would lurk nearby and make sure her conversation with Brendan was polite yet formal, she hadn't expected her quite so close.

"Mother." Her voice was a whisper but her tone a shout. "What are you doing?"

"I couldn't help overhearing, and I thought I could be of use." She reached for the flowers. "Here let me take those. You don't want to keep the young man waiting."

Evangeline forced herself to contain an eye roll as she relinquished the flowers. Of course, her mother couldn't help overhearing. The only way to hear better would've been to join them on the porch. At least societal expectations prevented that choice. And really, Evangeline couldn't blame her.

How often did one's only daughter entertain an unexpected gentleman caller? For other mothers maybe it happened more frequently, but for Mother? This was a first. Her excitement was palpable.

Evangeline smiled. "Thank you. And I trust you'll not be joining us on the swing?"

"Of course not." Her eyes spoke of her offense. "I would never do something like that."

"I was teasing, Mother." Evangeline laid a hand on her arm. "I know you would never stoop to behavior such as that."

A curt nod sent Evangeline back out the door. After their exchange, her mother's false attempts to save her time more than likely took more time than if Evangeline had simply found a vase for the flowers herself. And though she spoke truthfully when Mother said she would not join them on the swing, Evangeline didn't doubt she wouldn't stray far from it.

Brendan lounged on the white porch swing like he didn't have a care in the world. One arm draped along the back railing while he sat at an angle in one corner. Evangeline smiled as she joined him, mirroring his position on the other end of the swing. The only difference was she kept both hands folded together in her lap.

Brendan cleared his throat. "You look lovely today, Miss Moore."

"Please, it's Evangeline." She kept her voice low. "I only addressed you formally because I knew Mother was close. I didn't realize how close until I closed the door and revealed her hiding spot behind it. She nearly caused my heart to stop right then and there."

"Mothers have a way of doing that." Brendan chuckled before turning serious. "I have to admit. You made me a little apprehensive too. I wondered what I could have done last night that caused us to regress from Brendan and Evangeline to Mr. Dunne and Miss Moore."

"I'm sure it wouldn't have troubled you too much."

An intensity Evangeline didn't expect lit in his eyes. "On that point, you couldn't be more wrong."

Evangeline fidgeted with the pretense of smoothing the material draped over her legs. The words, though serious in tone, sounded flirtatious. What did Evangeline know about the ways of men? Here she was twenty years old, and Brendan Dunne was the first to brave her doorstep. Maybe she was misreading the situation completely.

Movement behind the curtained window to the right of the door drew Evangeline's attention. She smiled, and Brendan turned as well. Drapes parted to either side of the glass revealing the beautiful daisies Brendan brought her. They'd had such a subtle, sweet fragrance. Her mind must be playing tricks on her, because she could smell it even now.

"Thank you, again, for the flowers." She nodded in their direction. "It was kind of you."

Brendan returned his attention to her. "I wasn't sure which type to purchase. The florist told me I couldn't go wrong with daisies."

"They are very cheerful."

"I'm glad you like them."

Their small talk stalled as Evangeline searched for something to discuss. Of course, it would be helpful if she understood why Brendan had called on her in the first place. The flowers indicated interest. Then again, she'd seen visitors bring flowers to a hostess on many occasions. It could be nothing more than a polite gesture.

"Why are you here, Brendan?" She slapped a hand over her mouth. Oh bother. How could she be thoughtful in one instant and lose the filter between her mind and her mouth in the next?

She allowed a brief look at his face finding surprise etched into every feature. "I believe I owe you an apology." Her gaze fell to her hands, twisting in her lap. "I'm not accustomed to visitors, not gentleman callers anyway. And now, I've broken a cardinal rule of entertaining. You're uncomfortable."

Calm radiated from Brendan's hand as he placed it over hers, stilling her anxious movement. "There is nothing to be sorry for. At least not on your side of things. It seems, however, I owe you an apology."

She frowned. "Whatever for?"

His fingers moved from hers to a strand of hair rebelling against the haphazard knot she'd forced it into. Flutters filled her at the light touch of his hand over her cheek as he brushed the wayward lock behind her ear. Her eyes slid shut as if tucking the moment safely away in her mind to revisit in the future.

A slight shifting of the swing brought her back to the moment. Brendan had closed some of the distance between them, though not far enough for either of them to be accused of impropriety. The intensity was back in his eyes.

"Why?" Her question was a whisper. "Apologize, I mean. Why apologize?" They had to return to familiar ground or Evangeline would never find her balance.

"Because ..." he said with a smile that hinted at roguish, "if you have to ask me why I'm here, I've not been as open with my interest as I thought."

"I-interest? In me?" The words squeaked out in her wonder.

His laugh should have embarrassed her, but Evangeline

was still wrestling with the idea that Brendan Dunne, the most attractive man she'd ever met, had just told her he was interested in her. Besides, his laugh was as rich as warm maple syrup on a stack of fresh pancakes. Evangeline would humiliate herself a thousand times to hear it again. Though she secretly hoped continued embarrassment wouldn't be necessary.

Evangeline fidgeted with the pendant around her neck drawing Brendan's attention. He sobered, his brows dipping in a *V* as a frown replaced his smile. Evangeline dropped her hands back into her lap and scarcely dared to breathe. She had no idea what she'd done to warrant such a drastic change. Part of her wasn't sure she wanted to know.

Unable to sit still under his scrutiny, Evangeline rose and, as gracefully as possible, made her way to the banister. Tension in her shoulders eased as she glanced around at the houses of neighbors she'd known since birth and the flower gardens where, as a small child, she'd pilfered blooms for bouquets to give her mother. These were familiar and understood.

Her breath hitched as the creak of the swing announced Brendan's presence behind her. Though she could sense him near enough to touch her, he didn't reach out.

"I didn't intend to make you uncomfortable."

Still, she didn't turn. It was easier to think without looking into those eyes that told her everything and nothing. "You didn't."

"Then why were you playing with your necklace?"

This time, she did turn to face him. "Playing with my necklace? What do you mean?"

"I know we've not known each other long, nor do we know each other well. But I have observed you grasping your necklace multiple times. In every instance, you were thinking or unsure of something."

Was he right? Evangeline couldn't argue against the charge. Her parents had given her the necklace on her sixteenth birthday.

Not a day passed without her clasping it around her neck as she readied for the day.

"I didn't notice the habit."

She lifted her hand. Seeing a self-satisfied grin turn his lips, Evangeline realized she was about to live up to his charge. Not wanting to admit how correct he was, Evangeline redirected herself away from him and to the banister where she gripped the smooth wood in place of her necklace.

A chuckle sounded behind her. "You've still not answered my question."

"What was it, again?" Why was his presence rattling her usual calm? No. She was sure that wasn't Brendan's question.

"Strictly speaking, I asked why you were playing with your locket, if I wasn't making you uncomfortable." Another low chuckle. "But I think we can skip it. The real question is why does my interest in you make you uncomfortable? Have I done something to warrant your nerves? Or, perhaps, the feeling isn't mutual, and you're at a loss as to how to tell me?"

Disappointment tinged his voice with the last suggestion. *If he only understood.* He'd arrested her attention the moment she spotted him at the barber shop. She'd been sorely tempted to get the bob Dot pestered her about simply for the opportunity to enjoy looking at him a little while longer.

Evangeline swallowed the knot of nerves residing in her throat. "No." The lump refused to vacate the premises cutting off further explanation.

"No, I haven't offended you in some way? Or no, my interest is not returned?" The question sounded strangled.

"I've never entertained a gentleman before."

Brendan fought to control the laugh threatening to burst from his lips. Without a doubt, Evangeline would take offense at such a rude reaction. But she had to be playing coy. Didn't she? It went against all his first impressions of her, but it was the only explanation.

"A woman as beautiful as you never having a suitor? I find that hard to believe." Did he sound surprised or accusatory? Her answer would tell.

"I'm not sure what to say. Either men from Chicago have vastly different ideals of beauty than the men from Harrisburg, or the idea of courting the judge's daughter is enough to scare potential men from my doorstep." Slender shoulders raised with a heavy sigh. "Maybe it's a bit of both."

"I can't deny most men from Chicago do have standards more in line with my brother's tastes. But I do not share his proclivity." He moved to the railing beside Evangeline and covered her hand with his own as he gazed at her. "And you, Evangeline Moore, are beautiful by any standard. I'm inclined to agree with you. Your father's standing in the community may hamper your prospects."

The rose filling her cheeks took away any lingering doubt she might not return his feelings. She moistened her lips. Perfectly shaped lips. An adorable cupid's bow over a full bottom lip. Neither one sporting the over-dramatic red so many gravitated to. They looked as soft as rose petals and just as inviting.

The desire to test the comparison welled up. Although the behavior was completely out of bounds, knowing so did nothing to squelch the urge. Temptation blazed in him when she turned her attention from the street to fully face him.

"Do you really think so?"

One kiss is all it would take to erase the vulnerability present in her question. A single, chaste kiss to take away her doubt. But could Brendan taste her lips against his without everything in him begging for another and another until chaste had no place in the act? His imagination had already experienced her kiss and was preparing to receive another. If his thoughts were so traitorous, would his actions be any less so?

He could not, would not, put Evangeline in such a situation. Especially not on her front porch in the light of day where anyone

71

could walk past. Shaming her in that way would be inexcusable. Besides, his faith demanded he treat Evangeline with love and respect, as a cherished treasure.

Taking his thoughts captive, Brendan nodded but moved no closer. "Your beauty is undeniable. I want to get to know you, Evangeline, and knowing your father is the judge won't deter me."

"What do we have here?" Dot's voice oozed contempt as she walked up the sidewalk.

The change in Evangeline was immediate. Her hopeful, expectant expression fled. The sparkle died in her eyes, and her beguiling smile flattened.

"I came to apologize for ruining your birthday." Dot sauntered up the steps. "But looks like I wasted my guilt."

"I never said you ruined my birthday,"

The tremor in Evangeline's voice tore at Brendan.

Dot waved her hand through the air with a harsh laugh. "That's right. How could I ruin your big day? You don't need me. You have everything you could ever want in your fairy tale life. I'm just the baggage from your childhood kept around to irritate your parents."

"That's not true, and you know it." The words burst from Evangeline in a rush.

Brendan didn't understand what happened to create a rift in their friendship, but Evangeline grew more agitated by the second.

"Dot," he interrupted without apology, "whatever happened between you, this isn't the way to work things out."

"Would you look at that?" Dot sneered. "It seems the little princess has found herself a prince. Isn't that simply the berries?"

"I think—"

Dot jutted a finger in his direction. "You don't get a say in this."

"No." Evangeline's chin rose as her shoulders straightened. "But I do. I'm not sure what your problem is right now. I'm not even sure you know. But I won't stand here listening to you insult me on my own porch. Until you're ready to deal with whatever this is in a more adult way, I suggest you leave."

Dot shrugged. "If that's how you want it. Anything you say, princess."

It only took Dot retreating around the block and out of sight before Evangeline's defensive stance crumbled. Shaky breaths and a quivering lip announced her struggle to keep her emotions in check. Brendan lightly grasped her arm and led her to the swing, taking a seat beside her after she'd settled into it.

Fury pounded against Brendan's chest as if trying to escape its confines. Why did Evangeline allow Dot to treat her in this manner? While it was true Brendan didn't fare any better in dealing with James, they were brothers. If he had a clam for every time he wished they weren't, Brendan would be a rich man. Then again, it was easy to know what you would do in a situation that could never happen.

Evangeline had no such biologically enforced boundary with Dot. The time and energy she'd poured into their friendship through the years had to weigh heavy against the thought of walking away. Especially knowing Evangeline was the constant in Dot's life, an example of God's love and the faith Dot didn't share. Brendan didn't envy her the choice.

"She wasn't always like this." Evangeline reasoned quietly.

"So you've said."

"I think she's disappointed in the way her life is going. I'm an easy target."

Brendan frowned. "I'm not sure what you mean."

"It's easier to say my life is *the berries* because of benefits I've had that she's missed out on." Evangeline shrugged. "As crass as it may be to speak of it, my family has more financially than Dot's. We always have. Not that Dot's family is destitute or anything. Father is a prominent figure in town. Dot's father is known and respected as a miner, but it's not the same."

"She's jealous."

Evangeline shook her head. "No. It's more like she sees the

trouble she has in life and the so-called ease in my life and has decided it's due to those circumstances. It's her way of ducking responsibility for the consequences of her actions."

For a moment, only the occasional chirp of birds broke the silence. Brendan still wasn't sure he understood the issue, but he had no idea how to put his confusion into a coherent question.

"Dot wants excitement." Evangeline sighed. "She's read all these magazines highlighting the latest trends and fashion. It's her goal to model herself after the women on the pages. Life in Harrisburg is dull in comparison. Always the rebel. She's running headlong into a lifestyle promising glitz and glamor, but one I'm afraid will deliver heartache instead. Whether she is blind to it or simply chooses to ignore it, is yet to be seen."

Brendan scratched his head. "I'm failing to see how her push for those endeavors leaves her at odds with you. Your life isn't filled with that kind of self-centered opulence."

"No. I stand against it. Mine is the voice of reason that plants the seed of doubt about her choices. At least, that's what she believes. I can't help but think it's the Holy Spirit nudging her back in God's direction that is really the focus of her ire."

"What are you going to do about the situation?"

Evangeline dropped her head back and stared at the whitewashed ceiling above her before turning to Brendan. Resignation took up residence in her eyes.

"I'm not sure there is anything I can do."

Chapter Ten

"I shouldn't have said it. Now, let's blouse. I'll get you a milkshake over at the café."

Dot's patronizing tone set Evangeline on edge. She'd accepted a thousand apology treats through the years, but sadly, none of them came with an actual apology. Generic phrases like the ones she offered were the closest Evangeline came to hearing, "I'm sorry," much less, "Will you forgive me?" Old age would render her ears incapable of hearing the words long before they would actually be uttered.

"No." Evangeline reached her limit. She plopped down on the sitting room sofa. "I don't want a milkshake. I don't want a bag of chips. Or even a cola."

"Aww, come on, Evie." Dot steepled her hands and batted her eyes from the doorway. "You don't mean it. I know I was positively rotten to you the other day. I *was* jealous, I guess."

Evangeline crossed her arms over her chest. "And what about all the other times? You've bought me more food in the last couple months than I should accept in an entire year."

Dot tried for a nonchalant shrug, but the chagrined expression on her face gave her away. "You're right. I don't know what's gotten into me. But yesterday, I was jealous. I'd gotten the icy mitt from James, and I came here to find you and Brendan all cozy together on your porch."

"We were not cozy. He was a perfect gentleman."

Another shrug. "Be that as it may, he was here with you. James hasn't spared a word for me since your birthday picnic."

"Don't pretend that little get-together was in my honor." What had gotten into her today? She never defended herself this fervently. Still, understanding never helped in previous situations. "You planned the shindig so you and James could have time together. The food was barely swallowed before you two took off alone."

Was that a hint of natural color on Dot's cheeks? Could she possibly feel embarrassed at her behavior of late?

"It was horrible of me. And all for a chance to snag the attention of a Chicago sheik."

"Don't do that." Something loosened inside Evangeline's chest. Compassion replaced her anger. Dot's desire for love and acceptance were thick in the air. "You're more than a sheba to any sheik. You don't have to be that person to be special. Just be the woman God created you to be."

Dot's jaw tightened before she relaxed into a smile that was a little too bright. "God created me to have fun. Maybe it won't be with James, but that's fine. He's just one little fish in the great big sea. One day I'll find the perfect fish for me."

"Poetry aside," Evangeline said rolling her eyes. "God created you for more than … fishing."

"There's nothing wrong with fishing, especially when you have the right bait." Dot laughed and shimmied her shoulders. "And God gave me the perfect bait."

Evangeline groaned. They'd exceeded Dot's tolerance for all things serious. Silently, Evangeline petitioned God that her words would sink into Dot's heart. No amount of reasoning would free Dot from her belief that real life resided only in Chicago and other metropolitan areas. The conviction that her worth was determined by men's desire for her had been planted and taken root long ago. Then again.

"I'm not convinced that was His plan."

"Maybe. Maybe not. But one thing is certain."

"What's that?"

Dot winked at her. "In the course of this conversation, I think you've forgiven me."

"Forgiven?" Evangeline arched an eyebrow. "Yes. But that doesn't mean you can keep acting out when your world is less than ideal. One of these days, forgiveness won't include another opportunity for you to treat me this way. I'll shake your dust from my shoes and move on."

Dot's red lacquered lips opened and closed while her face scrunched in confusion. It was as if she'd never had boundaries placed on her friendship, and she didn't quite know what to do with the change. Evangeline refused to relent. Standing up for herself was long overdue in their friendship.

"Look at that." Dot finally cooed. "You get your heart stolen by a good-looking man for the first time and suddenly you're lousy with confidence."

Gritting her teeth, Evangeline fixed Dot in place with a narrow-eyed look.

"Fine. Fine. Everything's jake. I wasn't trying to insult you." Dot's laugh was friendly as she held her hands in front of her in surrender. "I'm impressed. I didn't know you could be this assertive. Always forgive and forget, seventy-times-seven, and all."

"I'll always forgive. I told you that. Nothing's changed."

Another laugh. "Yes, it has. Oh, not about you being willing to forgive. But you've got to admit, never in all our years of friendship have you stood up to me."

"That's not true." Evangeline huffed. "I can come up with a list of several of your hare-brained ideas that I emphatically passed on participating in."

Dot rested her shoulder against the door frame. "Sure. You've stood up for your morals and your beliefs. But never, not even once, have you stood up for yourself."

"I shouldn't have had to. You're my friend."

Her argument was dismissed with a shrug. "Be that as it may, you've had opportunity and never taken it until today."

There wasn't an argument to refute the claim, at least not one Evangeline could employ with one-hundred percent truthfulness. And perhaps the assumption she'd always held, the one that said if Evangeline wanted Dot to see her faith, she'd hold her tongue even when treated wrongly, was faulty. Was her change of heart due to Brendan's influence?

"Maybe I've opened my eyes to the fact that I'm worth standing up for."

"It's about time. Even if it does mean you're standing against me."

Dot shoved away from the doorway and crossed to the mantle adorned with family photos. Picking one up from the row, her thumb rubbed over the glass, her smile wistful. It was a photo of Dot and her, dressed in their Sunday best. Both miniature versions of themselves held tightly to flower-adorned Easter baskets. Their faces were filled with excitement, and their friendship was evident. How many times had Evangeline reminisced over that same picture, especially after a row with Dot?

"You know I'm never truly standing against you though. Don't you?" Evangeline joined her at the mantle, laying a hand on her shoulder.

Dot glanced at her over her shoulder before returning the photograph to its place. "I know. Even if your new attitude feels a little like it. There's too much water under our bridge to seriously entertain the notion. Besides, no matter how frustrating and goody-two shoes you can be, I know you say what you do because you love me."

"I do love you." Evangeline clasped Dot's hand and nudged her with her shoulder. "Friends until the end."

"Friends until the end." Dot repeated their childhood mantra before turning to Evangeline with a mischievous glint in her eyes. "Now, give me all the details about you and Brendan Dunne."

"There isn't anything to tell."

"I don't believe that at all."

"Well, maybe," Evangeline started as a girlish giggle escaped. "I think he might actually like me."

Dot rolled her eyes and laughed. "Now you're on the trolley. And it's about time. I saw it that first day in the barber shop. So, what are you going to do about it?"

Great question, but Evangeline had no clue how to answer.

Chapter Eleven

"A nd where do you think you're going, young lady?" Father's voice filtered from the dining room as Evangeline was about to slip out the front door.

"Dot and I made molasses cookies yesterday." Evangeline poked her head into the room where her father sat at the head of the table with the day's newspaper. "We're going to visit Miss Myrtle and the Barnett family today. We thought they would enjoy the treats, especially since Mr. Barnett hasn't been able to work at the mine since his accident. His little ones probably aren't getting many sweets."

"You and Dot?" His eyes narrowed. "There's no young gentlemen joining you in this quest of mercy?"

Evangeline frowned. "No. None that I know of. Is there someone, in particular, you're concerned about?"

"Your mother mentioned young Mr. Dunne came calling a few days ago. I meant to speak with you about it when she told me, but the opportunity never arose."

She'd expected her good fortune on that front to run out before now. "Brendan Dunne did come calling. Mother gave approval, and he acted the perfect gentleman. Why, he even brought me a bouquet of flowers."

"Ultimately, it isn't her permission you need. Although she did explain that my good report of our time at the diner encouraged her to allow it."

"You do approve of him. Don't you, Father?" Could he see in her face how much she wanted him to say *yes*? "You appeared satisfied after your talk with him. And he did express faith. That is a reassuring characteristic, is it not?"

"I'm not one given to rumors," he began as he folded the newspaper and laid it aside.

Evangeline could argue that point. More had been spoken around their very dining room table than she cared to admit. However, now was not the time to broach that subject. Instead, she waited for him to continue.

"But my sources tell me his family's business may venture into less than acceptable activities."

"He is not his family." Evangeline set her basket of cookies on the table and took the seat next to her father. "I believe he even made mention that he did not condone his family's business practices."

"True." Her father stared into the dark, steaming liquid in his cup. "His brother hasn't expressed the same hesitancies."

"Well, then, it's a good thing Brendan has shown interest in me and not his brother."

He took a slow sip before answering. "It's my job as your father to protect you."

"Brendan poses no threat to me."

"Trouble doesn't often discriminate. I'm afraid James's ties to their family's ways might bring trouble to Brendan and inadvertently to you if I allow him to court you."

Evangeline wouldn't make promises regarding things she had no control over. Besides, her vows of safety would mean little to Father. She laid her hand over his and allowed him to search her face, hoping her peace would give him the assurance he needed.

"Father, I've not known Brendan very long, but I believe he is honorable. I also believe he would do anything to keep me out of harm's way." Dare she tell him about Dot's temper? Their friendship had weathered worse. "Just the other day, while we enjoyed our visit on the front porch swing, Dot said some very hurtful things."

Her father grunted. "What did that girl say now? Did this have anything to do with your birthday? You never did clear up what took place between you two."

"That's not the point, Father." She needed to get him back to the subject at hand. "Brendan understood how her words hurt me, and he stayed with me until I'd calmed. He didn't dismiss her behavior or tell me I was being a ninny."

"Of course, you weren't being a ninny." Father's fist emphasized his words against the tabletop. "That girl, Dorothy, she's got a tongue sharper than the knife that carves our Thanksgiving turkey. Brendan seems like a bright enough boy. He's wise enough to know the fault lies there and not with my sweet daughter."

"And it shows he cares about my well-being."

"True." Her father nodded. "I can't fault him for seeing to your emotional state. Too many young men only want the fun a young lady can offer."

The knowing look he gave her caused heat to fill her cheeks. Never had her father spoken of such things, at least not when he thought she was within hearing. She could only hope his urge to do so now would pass with the conversation.

"But Brendan even joined us at the café. Someone concerned only with chasing good times would not have done that, would they?"

"I suppose you have a point. I can't see the likes of any of the young men who chase after Dorothy doing so, at least not without overt signs of placating to get what they want. Brendan was refreshingly sincere."

"So ... I may continue to entertain Brendan? If he wishes to see me again."

His hand covered her own with a pat. "Don't doubt for a

moment that young man will be back. I've a feeling he knows a good thing when he sees it. And you, dear daughter, are the best. You have my blessing with one caution."

"Yes, Father?"

"Remember to guard your heart. Even the most well-meaning of young men can find themselves tempted beyond distraction by a young woman as pretty and sweet-natured as you. And while I find your innocence in such matters a refreshing change from most of today's young ladies, it could lead you into situations that are best avoided."

Evangeline toyed with her locket as heat once again flooded her cheeks. Victory came at a cost, but she would endure daily reminders about propriety and virtue if it meant her father's approval of Brendan.

"I understand, Father. I'll be careful."

She rose and gathered her basket of cookies before planting a kiss on her father's cheek. Dorothy would be impatiently waiting. Evangeline was now more than twenty minutes late, and she still had to take the trolley to Dot's house. Hopefully, the news of her father allowing Brendan's visits would placate her. Anything revolving around entertaining men would no doubt be met with Dot's wholehearted approval.

If only she had assurance that Dot's drama hadn't scared Brendan off. Would he decide Evangeline wasn't worth the hassle? She prayed it wouldn't be so.

Chapter Twelve

Adjusting the basket of treats on her arm, Evangeline turned up the gravel drive. Normally, the uneven path would wreak havoc on her ability to navigate the drive with the low heel of her shoes, but time and weather had worn a lot of the rock away leaving more dirt and even patchy grass to grow up in its place.

Before she reached the sun-bleached porch of the house, the door swung open.

"It's about time," Dot chided without so much as a how-do-you-do. "Where on earth have you been? The trolley has never been this late."

"It wasn't the trolley." Evangeline looped her arm through Dot's. "Father wanted to speak with me about Brendan's visit the other morning."

Dot whistled. "And how did that go?"

"Let's stroll over to the Barnett family's house first. Then, we can catch the trolley back to Miss Myrtle's place to leave her cookies. I'll tell you on the way."

Though the road leading to their first stop wasn't lined with sidewalks like those closer to town, the ground was fairly flat, providing an easy walk. Evangeline was able to share the morning's events without struggling for breath as they kept a gentle pace.

Dot skipped ahead of Evangeline and turned toward her, grasping her hands, nearly upsetting the basket on her arm in the process. Not even the glare Evangeline threw her way could curb Dot's enthusiasm.

"I just knew your father would see reason! Oh, Evangeline. I'm so happy for you."

Darting her gaze to the yards around them, Evangeline sighed realizing no one witnessed Dot's gushing congratulations. Their trek could continue with Evangeline's pride intact. Extracting her hands from Dot's grasp, Evangeline waved her free hand in dismissal and moved around her friend.

"I don't know what you're so happy about. It's not as if Brendan secured my father's blessing to ask me to marry him. Father only said he may court me, if he even wishes to."

"Of course, Brendan wishes to, you Dumb Dora. He's absolutely smitten with you. Not want to see you? Complete hokum. That's what that is."

Though pleasure zinged through her at Dot's assertion, Evangeline wouldn't give in to the giddiness welling up. She cleared her throat and fussed with the cloth covering the treats in the basket. "I do hope you're correct."

Dot rolled her eyes. "We'll see soon enough. Now, let's get these cookies delivered."

The Barnett house was just ahead. The three middle children played kick the can in the front yard. The cry of the youngest rang out from inside the house, and the oldest daughter, Elizabeth, was hanging worn dresses and shirts on the line in the side yard.

"Hello." Evangeline waved as she drew the attention of the yard's inhabitants.

The little ones paused their game only momentarily as visits from Evangeline and Dot were not unusual. For all her quirks, Dot had a soft spot for this family, and Evangeline was more than happy to encourage it.

Elizabeth stuck a wooden clothespin over the shirt sleeve she strung across the line. Swiping a hand across her apron, she moved to meet them before they reached the house.

"We best not go inside today. Pa's been a bit cantankerous what with bein' off work so long. And baby John was up all night with the colic. Mama's at her wit's end."

Hopefully, Evangeline's smile put Elizabeth at ease. "Don't you worry. We don't have to go inside."

"We brought you a plate of cookies to sweeten your day." Dot whipped the cloth off the basket and produced a plate of cookies from inside. "It's not much. But my pa also sent fifty cents so you can get a gallon of milk for you and the little ones."

It wasn't true. Evangeline knew the money came from Dot and not her father. In her experience, Dot's father thought little enough about the needs of others. But Dot wouldn't want the attention, and it was less apt to happen if her parent had sent the precious gift.

"Please, tell your pa I said thank you." Elizabeth took the offering as reverently as if she'd been given gold. "Mama will be so surprised. And the young'uns will think they've died and gone to heaven. Cookies *and* a glass of milk? I don't know the last time they've had such a treat."

The gratitude over something Evangeline took for granted was humbling. Seeing the desperate circumstances the Barnett's faced, she determined to bring more next visit. No. That wouldn't do. It might embarrass the family. But she could use her own limited funds to secure a weekly milk delivery. She had little she needed to spend her money on. And if something did come up, her mother and father would see to it.

Plan in place, Evangeline smiled. "Well, we had better let you get the cookies in the house and get back to your chores before the sun gets too hot."

"Evangeline's right." Dot nodded. "We've got another stop to make, and you've got your hands full."

"Thank you. Next time you'll have to stay and chat a

while." With the plate of cookies balanced on one hand, Elizabeth leaned in to give them both a quick side hug. She waved and turned to the house, calling the youngsters in behind her.

Chatting about everything and nothing at all as they strolled back to the trolley stop, Evangeline missed this side of Dot. When they were children in Sunday School, it was this Dot who cemented their friendship.

Thinking about the needs of others and how they could fill those needs was as natural to Dot as her rich, brown hair. The relaxed, contented smile she wore now was present nearly every day back then. Only after her mother tired of life married to a miner and left without a word as Dot was entering her teenage years did her attitude change. Evangeline surmised Dot's rebellion against God and her way of life stemmed from the hurt her mother caused.

Father God, reach through Dot's pain to show her Your love. Let her come to know You. Use me, Lord, in any way You see fit. The plea sprung from Evangeline's heart as it did each day, sometimes multiple times a day. Evangeline always gleaned encouragement from these little moments, letting them revitalize her prayers for her friend.

"What brings you ladies out on such a fine day as this?" James's voice met the pair as they arrived at the trolley stop. Lounged against the side of his automobile, he raised his hand in greeting.

A groan grappled with excitement as Evangeline's gaze connected with Brendan's. Rather than being annoyed with Dot for being Dot, Evangeline focused on the pleasure of the masculine smile directed at her. And after securing her father's blessing, no matter how tentatively given, she could relax and fully enjoy Brendan's company.

"We're on a mission of mercy." Dot practically skipped over

to the car. "We've just been to the Barnett's home to deliver some fresh-baked cookies. They've had a difficult time lately."

"Suzy homemaker and an angel of mercy." James's voice held a hint of insincerity that grated as he smirked at his brother. "Looks like we've found the real riches in Harrisburg, no matter what Mr. O'Gara might believe."

This time, Evangeline allowed an eye roll. A brazen attempt at flattery. And a clumsy one to boot. Would any woman find comparison to the black rock mined in the area a compliment, no matter how rich it made mine owners, such as Mr. O'Gara?

Dot giggled and swatted his arm. "My how you go on."

Evangeline's lips twisted in a humorless smile. Maybe flirtatious exchanges between the sexes were simply not in her nature to enjoy. James won Dot over. Was her reaction true or as contrived as James's compliment? Whatever the case, Evangeline wanted no part of the nonsense.

"At least, you didn't compare us to the gob piles that wreath our town in red with their constant burning." As a naïve young girl, she'd imagined the reddish horizon a thing of beauty, maybe even something for poets to wax on about. But one didn't grow up in a coal town without realizing the sight's allure only lasted as long as one's ignorance. Unlike a sunset, these colors hemming in the town were reminders of the dangerous business of coal mining. What other industry's refuse spontaneously burned night and day as it lay on top of the soil?

Dot's mouth swung open in a decidedly un-Dot like way. Nothing ever scandalized her. Of course, Evangeline never loosed her sassy side in public either.

"I would never compare a woman to a refuse pile." The offense in his tone was as insincere as his compliment. "Women should be held in highest regards."

"And you feel a hunk of dirty, black rock that lines men's pockets with riches is the best way to accomplish this?"

"Evangeline!" Dot tugged on her arm. "What has gotten into you?" She shifted her attention to James. "I must apologize for

Evangeline. I'm sure she didn't mean to discount your compliment."

A smirk twisted his lips. "Applesauce. She meant exactly that."

His eyes took Evangeline in from head to toe and back again. It was enough to provoke a squirm in Evangeline and a spark of jealousy in Dot. That was the last thing Evangeline needed in their friendship.

"I thought you were a bit of a canceled stamp." James's gaze hadn't shifted from her. "Interesting to see maybe a bearcat lies underneath that buttoned-up exterior."

"Assumptions are rarely our friends." Evangeline flattened him with a glare. "Take for instance, your ability to be anywhere we are at any given time. One might assume you're a spoiled rich man-child who doesn't have to do an honest day's work like the rest of us."

"You could." He took the bait. "But I believe you're already aware the business our father sent us here to conduct is more a feeling out of the area to ascertain its suitability. And our father is, indeed, footing the bill, so to speak."

Evangeline raised a brow. "I didn't say *I* assumed that to be true. I said *one* might jump to that conclusion. Once again, you've proven your propensity to pass judgment without fact-finding first."

Brendan cleared his throat, breaking the growing tension. "All of this aside, where are you ladies headed now?"

Relief flooded Evangeline's chest. She'd never spoken to anyone with such frankness, and Brendan's olive branch provided a welcome retreat. "Miss Myrtle has been shut in with a bit of a cold recently. We're on our way to deliver a care package to her and have a short visit."

"Very short." Dot smiled. "We wouldn't want to tire the old dear out, with her ailing and all. In truth, we'll more than likely drop off the cookies we made for her, inquire if she needs anything, and then take our leave."

This was news to Evangeline, but she didn't dare contradict

the statement. She didn't have to look at Dot to know the exchange with James had soured her mood. Determined to see it lifted, Evangeline decided to go along with the new plan. Anyway, what Dot said made sense. Miss Myrtle would need plenty of rest. She didn't bounce back from illness as she once did.

"Why don't you forgo the trolley?" James kept his focus on Dot. "Brendan and I will give you a ride, and then we can all go get lunch together."

Dot laid a hand on his arm. "How generous of you, James. Thank you. That would be wonderful."

James opened the passenger door and waved Dot inside. "Your carriage, my lady."

Apparently, Evangeline's thoughts on the offer didn't matter. Then again, she didn't know what she would have chosen. Time with James taxed her. Those same minutes spent with Brendan flew from reality into memory too swiftly.

"Evangeline."

The soft way Brendan spoke her name pulled her from her musings. With the rear passenger door open, he waited for her to take her place. She slid down into the seat with as much grace as she could muster and tucked the hem of her dress under her legs. With it safely pushed out of the way, Brendan closed her door before circling to the other side to climb into the seat behind James.

Once on their way with Dot and James animatedly talking in the front seat, Brendan leaned toward her. Though his nearness set loose a warm feeling inside, propriety demanded he not scoot close enough for her to physically feel his warmth.

"I've never seen a woman go toe-to-toe with James over his treatment of the fairer sex."

A sly smile accompanied a wink so quick Evangeline almost missed it.

Evangeline shrugged. "I shouldn't have let him goad me that way. My mouth got away from me."

"I must admit, I rather enjoyed the scene." His finger traced lazy circled on the back of her hand as it rested between them. "You're as witty as you are breathtaking."

His words and touch teased her full smile into being. Maybe she'd been hasty to dismiss the possibility of enjoying flirtation between a man and a woman. Coming from Brendan, with complete sincerity, playful banter between the sexes brought immense pleasure.

Chapter Thirteen

A shrunken woman peered between Dot and Evangeline standing on the porch. Both of the younger women glanced over their shoulders with small waves. James barely acknowledged the attention, but Brendan smiled politely and waved before the pair turned back to their hostess.

James tapped an impatient beat on the steering wheel. "I wish they'd say good-bye already. We're going to be late."

Pulling his pocket watch out, Brendan opened it. Half-past eleven. He frowned. There was still plenty of time before the dinner hour. And James couldn't be too hungry. He'd polished off a stack of pancakes and bacon at breakfast, along with a couple cups of coffee.

"Have I missed something? When did we acquire a schedule?"

"Perfect. Here they come." James relaxed into the driver's seat as the pair approached. Once they'd resumed their positions, he wasted no time in moving them on their way.

Brendan laid his head back against the seat and focused on the scenery zooming past the window. Despite nonstop chatter coming from the front, provided mainly by Dot, peace settled in his chest. The sun's rays warmed his face, while his thumb once again circled the silky-smooth skin of Evangeline's hand as he held it in the space between them. Turning from the window, he contented himself with gazing at the woman next to him.

Only when Evangeline's face puckered into a frown did uneasiness erase his sense of well-being. He glanced out his window and the windshield. How long had they been heading west? And when did the home and business lined streets give way to uninterrupted trees and fields?

"Where are we going?"

"It's getting close to dinner. We said we were going to eat together."

Anxiety snaked a slow trail through Brendan. "But where are we going?"

"Thought the ladies might enjoy some barbeque."

He wouldn't. As he so unceremoniously pointed out, there were ladies present. One the daughter of a Saline County judge. Of all the dumb choices James made in his life, this had to be one of the worst.

"Where are we going?" Evangeline's innocence hadn't allowed her to come to the same conclusion he'd reached.

"Shady Rest." Brendan's lungs barely provided enough air to force the distasteful answer from his lips.

A quick intake of breath next to him alerted Brendan to Evangeline's immediate distress. If only he could think of some way to remedy the situation. While the barbeque stand outside Charlie Birger's compound was what it advertised, the clientele frequenting the place left little to be desired. Given James's proclivities to the gangster life they'd known in Chicago since their birth, the choice shouldn't surprise him. But it did.

"Oh, Shady Rest!" Dot's hands on her cheeks framed her face. "How exciting. I can't believe I'm going to *The* Shady Rest."

"Going?" James laughed. "Baby, you're already there."

Brendan surveyed the spot as James parked. The scene was innocuous enough. Little more than a shed by the highway with picnic tables dotting the grassy area around it. Brendan wasn't fooled. The stand was a front for the real money-making activities taking place in the cabin, which loomed in the shadows farther off the road.

While the large log structure might seem homey to unknowing passersby, the only home it provided was one for less than savory activities. Rumor was if you arrived at the right time, in addition to the enticing tones of the day's popular songs, one might also hear the hostile growls of bulldogs or the angry shouts of roosters as dog fights and cock fights frequently took place beyond the cabin. This was no place for the ladies, even if one of them was practically salivating at the opportunity.

"Let's get a wiggle on, then." Dot's eyes lit with curiosity.

"No." The word was hard as granite, freezing everyone in their places. Brendan tried to soften his tone as he continued. "James and I will go grab some sandwiches. There was a field of wildflowers not too far back. It would make a nice place for a picnic."

"But I wanted—"

"Here there's nothing but picnic tables and travelers to ogle you while you eat. If we picnic elsewhere, we can have all the privacy we want." Brendan brushed his hand lightly up and drown Evangeline's arm, praying as he did that she understood he was only baiting Dot into agreement. Sure enough, Dot's gaze followed the path of his hand before she glanced at James. The hunger in her eyes had nothing to do with the tangy scent of barbeque swirling in the air around them. Of that he was sure.

"Brendan's right."

James's agreement caught him off-guard. What was his older brother up to? Did he really want to know? At least he wouldn't have to deal with a disappointed Dot on his own.

On cue, Dot's lip puffed out in a pout. Pleading eyes framed with batting lashes regarded James.

"Please, James ..."

"Another time." He swung open his door. "For now. Stay put." A quick glance in her direction prompted a suggestive smile. "I just want you for myself, baby. We can do this another time."

Her answering smile was all James needed before shutting the door. Brendan hurried to join him on the short walk across the dirt and gravel parking lot.

"You get the sandwiches. I'll be back before you're done."

Brendan followed his brother's gaze to a man lounging against a nearby tree. One of Charlie's boys. He'd bet his life on it. Nothing he could say would dissuade James. There was no point in trying. In silence, their paths diverged. Brendan stepped up to the window and placed his order. In his periphery, James and the unknown man moved out of sight around the corner of the building.

"Here ya go." The man behind the counter pushed the brown paper bag across the surface.

Brendan nodded. "Thank you."

"You go on back to the girls. I'll be just a moment more." James returned right on time.

Again, Brendan did as he was bid without question. James stepped up to the counter and held up two fingers to the man behind it as he said something too softly for Brendan to hear. As James joined the rest of them and plopped the bag onto the front seat the telltale clink of glass confirmed Brendan's suspicions. Seething, Brendan hoped the drinks inside wouldn't make an appearance at their impromptu picnic.

"Have you, um, frequented Shady Rest often since your arrival?" Evangeline's tentative question broke the silence.

Brendan turned his attention from the now empty spot in the surrounding woods where James and Dot disappeared after their lunches were eaten. Disappointment had taken up residence in Evangeline's usually sparkling brown eyes. Disgust at the situation his brother put him in restricted his throat, making it difficult to breath. A cough dislodged the tightness.

"Please, believe I have never before stepped foot on that property. And I never would have taken you to such a place."

Evangeline chewed her bottom lip. "Then, you know what goes on there?"

"Yes." One would be hard pressed to find someone from the area who didn't have knowledge of Charlie Birger's place and the illegal activities happening there. Why did admitting his own understanding of it leave him awash in shame?

Fiddling with her locket, Evangeline nodded sharply. Did she not believe him?

"Your family." She rubbed her lips together. Took a deep breath. "Some suggest they might know Mr. Birger well enough."

The question was evident, though it had not been framed as such. Equally obvious, though she tried to appear confident, was her fear. Eyes wide, Evangeline sat poker straight across from him. Acid burned his throat. He swallowed it back.

Pulling his watch from his pocket, he unclipped it and extended it to Evangeline. Her brows formed a *V* as she accepted it from him.

"Look at the back."

She flipped the gold timepiece over and ran her finger across the inscription that taunted him daily. "United." She shook her head. "What does it mean?"

Brendan ran a hand through his hair. "It's a reminder from my father. There's an Irish saying, 'A family of Irish birth will argue and fight, but let a shout come from without and see them all unite.'"

"Unity is a good thing in a family." She smiled and returned the watch.

Brendan shook his head. "It is—until it isn't."

While Evangeline probably understood more than most young women due to her father's profession, knowing the truth could push her away for good. He'd alluded to it, but often hearing things outright proved to be an entirely different matter.

97

Still, he'd determined long ago to steer clear of the deceptions so prevalent in his family tree.

"If your family is dedicated to honoring God, living lives of faith, unity is a bond that pushes each member to be more Christlike in the day to day."

"But your family?"

Searching the trees surrounding them offered no easy answers. Nothing would not soften this hard truth, though he wished to shield her from his harsh reality. "My family sits in church every week. They offer up the expected prayers and partake of holy communion. For my mother, it might have made a difference in her life at one time. Meeting Sean Dunne changed that forever. My father, my brother, all my family, save myself and one other, attend because we're supposed to. Not to draw closer to God."

Evangeline laid a hand on his arm. "Surely hearing the Word has made some difference?"

"No." His jaw tightened. How he'd prayed through the years for the message of salvation and forgiveness to wind its way into his father's heart to no avail. The prayers continued. Fruitless, if his father's actions were any proof. "My father sits in silence, but he doesn't listen to the truth. He doesn't want to."

"If not faith, then what unifies your family?"

"My father's wishes."

She stared at him in silence, the wheels turning in her mind almost visible in her expression. Understanding hovered just below the horizon, waiting for its time to dawn. But even the bare-boned facts couldn't bring it into the light. He'd been struggling to make sense of why his family chose the path they did since he gave his own life to God at fourteen. It defied logic.

"What I told your father at the café that night was true. My father owns several buildings and rents them out to businesses and individuals. What your father understood, and I believe you at least suspect, is that his legitimate business dealings are a cover for his real enterprise. Tenants have a certain level of protection under my father's care, but they pay dearly for it. Though on paper he doesn't own them, several of his renters are on his payroll. Gambling, bootlegging, prostitution. You name the vice —my father controls it in his territory."

"A gangster."

The word slipped out with her breath, quiet, but carrying a weight that settled across his shoulders. One last chance to deny it, but he determined not to take it.

"Yes."

"And is your family here to, um, expand your holdings?"

He shook his head. "No. At least, that's not the main purpose. James is the reason I'm here. He got into trouble with a rival family. In the fracas, a young woman was killed. The fiancée of the mob boss's son."

"Oh, no. The poor girl."

"It is sad." He could acknowledge that much. "She was far from innocent in the matter, but still, she didn't deserve death." He cleared his throat. "My father needed to get James away while matters cool down. I was sent to keep him out of trouble. Family taking care of family. Standing against those who oppose us, even if we cross lines to do it. That's my family."

"But." Evangeline paused. "But it isn't you."

"No. My father knows I won't engage in the family business. If there are plans for expansion, he wisely kept them from me." He answered even though it wasn't a question and held up his pocket watch. "But this. Family united. My father gave it to me before we left. It belonged to his father before him. A reminder that whether or not I accept their lifestyle for myself, they are my family. And as such, my loyalty belongs to them."

"What happens if you walk away?"

Brendan shrugged as he stuffed the watch back in his pocket. "Only my Uncle Patrick ever managed to do it. His cost? He's no longer family. My father's own brother, and no one will acknowledge his existence."

"Is that such a bad thing?"

"I don't know." He'd asked himself the same thing a million

times. Could he leave if it meant condemning his brother to eternity in hell? Not that he truly believed he was responsible for his brother's faith or lack of it. But to walk away, for his own sake, knowing his brother didn't have a personal relationship with God, somehow seemed wrong. Brendan prayed he'd never find out.

Chapter Fourteen

"You don't know what you're missing." Dot plucked a kernel of popcorn from the bag Evangeline held and popped it into her mouth.

Evangeline had her doubts. Carefully navigating around a tent stake as one of the many circus goers jostled her as they passed, she hurried to catch up to Dot, who'd continued on as Evangeline had fallen behind.

"James is a real Oliver Twist." Dot continued between buttery bites. "And the music is like nothing you've heard before. It's so much more alive when it's not filtered through radio speakers."

In the three weeks since their trip to the barbecue stand, the quartet had enjoyed several outings together. Evangeline believed the Shady Rest incident was behind them. Dot had just destroyed that belief with the announcement that she and James had visited the cabin at Shady Rest on multiple occasions. Now, she was trying to get Evangeline to join them.

"You may as well give up, Dot." Evangeline shook her head. "I have no desire to return to Shady Rest, no matter how alive the music may be. And if James really cared about you, he wouldn't take you there either."

"That's where you're wrong. James knows I enjoy it. And he's always the perfect gentleman." She touched a hand to her hair, brushing it into place. "Why, there was a woman there, I believe the men all called her the Blonde Bombshell, and she was singing and dancing. And my, was she ever dancing. I've never seen anything so provocative in my life. Men were catcalling her, and she was eating it up. Can you believe James never even looked her way? Told me there was no reason to. He had the most beautiful woman there on his arm."

Evangeline sighed. "Listen to yourself. James shouldn't have taken you to a place like that to begin with."

"And there, ladies and gentlemen," Dot waved a hand toward Evangeline, "we have a bona fide Mrs. Grundy." She laughed at her own joke. "Come on, Mrs. Grundy. We're going to miss the show if we don't get back to the boys."

Hoping they wouldn't have to revisit the conversation later, Evangeline followed Dot into the enormous white tent. Weaving through the crowds, they found James and Brendan near the front row by the tent's middle ring. James patted the wood plank next to him, and Dot happily plopped down. Scooting a bit farther down the wood, Brendan left enough space for Evangeline to sit comfortably between them.

"Ladies and gentlemen!" A voice boomed from the middle of the ring. "Boys and girls! Welcome to the greatest show on earth."

A menagerie of exotic animals, painted clowns, and performers of all sizes paraded through the middle of the tent. Ostentatious costumes that would be deemed inappropriate in other circumstances, sparkled with sequins under the lights, while other outfits jauntily bounced with each step, thanks to fluffy feathers that rivaled the proudest of peacocks.

Enraptured, Evangeline couldn't tear her eyes away from the action in the center ring. As aerialists swung high above the crowd, her heart pounded. A beautiful high-flyer, freed from the slender bar keeping her aloft, sailed through the air, though her partner was nowhere close. Evangeline sucked in a breath and held it. The man's perch arced toward the woman, but she was falling fast. Breath rushed from her lungs when his hands clasped her wrists at the last possible instant.

When the lion tamer was greeted with a mighty roar, Evangeline couldn't suppress her shudder. To be trapped in the metal cage with such natural power was overwhelming. Her fist clenched on the seat as the man stuck his head in the lion's mouth. One snap of his jaws and the joy of the circus would turn into its horror. She startled when Brendan's hand covered her own but relaxed as he threaded his fingers through hers.

"It's all fine."

His warm breath against her ear as he leaned close sent a shiver through her.

"They wouldn't let him do anything that might cause him harm. It's all part of the show."

Brendan's quiet words did little to reassure her, but his nearness did momentarily distract her from the action in the ring. The lion tamer finished his part of the show and made way for a line of elephants to take his place. The giants might be gentle enough, but Evangeline didn't doubt they could unleash an uncontainable power if they desired. She didn't want to know what kept them from doing so.

Thunderous applause filled the tent as the performers took a final bow in the ring. Evangeline joined them with abandon. Never before had she seen a show such as this one, and she wouldn't soon forget it.

"Thank you, Brendan." She allowed him to take her hand as they worked their way through the crowd. "When you suggested the circus, I wasn't sure what to expect. Today was a perfect indulgence before the coldest fall months keep us indoors."

"It really was amazing." Dot threw her empty popcorn bag into a nearby receptacle. "I don't know what we'll do to top this outing."

James stopped, causing all of them to halt their exit.

Evangeline smiled silent apologies to other circus goers grumbling as they made their way around the group.

"Brendan has one good idea, and you both start fawning over him." Mock outrage filled James's voice. "What about my idea?" He nodded toward Evangeline. "I would think you, of all people, would appreciate the outing I have planned for tomorrow."

"Don't cast a kitten, James." Dot laughed. "No one is suggesting the hayride and bonfire won't be just as fun as the circus. It's simply a different kind of fun."

Evangeline took Brendan's arm, prompting them to keep moving. "And you're correct. I love a good bonfire and hayride. Nothing says October like sitting around a fire, under the stars."

"Or cuddling close to someone to help fight off the chill?" Brendan quirked an eyebrow as he squeezed her hand.

Heat filled Evangeline's cheeks. In the weeks they'd known each other, Brendan had only held her hand as they walked or while riding in the backseat of his brother's automobile. On the rare occasion his hand grazed her lower back as they strolled together, the intimacy warmed her head to toe. What would it feel like to snuggle in close, even if merely to ward off the chill in the air?

Dot's snort was unladylike. "Evangeline couldn't begin to tell you. The bumpkins around here have shown their ignorance time and again by failing to give her the time of day."

Embarrassment drove her gaze to the ground. "I'm afraid Dot's right."

"Even as reserved as she is, there's no excuse for it." Dot's voice grew more animated. "Anyone can see she's prettier than most any woman out here. And she's one of the kindest, most patient women you're ever going to find. The men around here are ignorant Reubens, I tell you."

They wouldn't need a bonfire for warmth if Dot kept on. Evangeline's cheeks would supply more than enough heat. It was silly, really. But once Dot got going, it was hard to derail her.

"I'm inclined to agree with you, Miss Dot. And it's an

oversight I look forward to remedying, with your permission of course."

Evangeline's head snapped up. The smile Brendan gave her was flirtatious. At a loss for words, she was happy to let the conversation drop as they reached their automobile. Even as small talk circled around her, Evangeline kept to herself. Just the thought of Brendan's arms around her drove her to distraction.

"We will see you ladies tomorrow evening at five o'clock sharp." James reminded them as he pulled the car into Evangeline's driveway.

Dot leaned in to allow James to plant a kiss on her lips. Too bold for Evangeline's sensibilities, but Dot would do what she wanted to do. Not once had Evangeline's warnings been heeded. More often, they caused a fight. Lately, Evangeline kept her mouth shut about such matters. The Lord would show her when to speak again.

Dot popped out of the car with a wave. Evangeline slid her handbag onto her arm and moved to follow. Brendan's hand on her arm stopped her.

"Don't even think about it." Brendan exited the car and made his way to open her door. With a slight bow, his hand swept from her in the direction of her house. "Now, you may get out."

"Thank you."

"Please, don't ever let anyone treat you as less than the gift you are." Brendan's eyes were serious. "You may not need a man to open your car door, but always allow them the opportunity to spoil you in this one small way. In fact, expect it of them."

Keeping a respectful space between them, Brendan leaned toward her. Breath caught in her chest. Was he going to kiss her? Her heart raced at the prospect even as her mind told her it would not be appropriate. How could she politely decline?

A tiny smile as his head tilted toward the side of her face. The touch of his lips to her skin was feather-light and over so quickly she might have imagined it. Only the tingle where lips touched cheek proved she'd not dreamed it up. Well, that and the tenderness in Brendan's eyes.

"Until tomorrow."

He'd assumed the front passenger seat, and the car was driving away before Evangeline came to life once more. She caressed the cheek he'd kissed while smiling at the retreating automobile.

"Until tomorrow."

Chapter Fifteen

"I give you my word, Evangeline. I had no idea it was going to be like this." Brendan took her hands in his as he spoke, prompting her to look at him directly.

The regret in his voice cooled Evangeline's temper but did nothing for the knot twisting inside her stomach. When they arrived at the bonfire, a strange unsettledness hung over her. Nothing overtly proclaimed danger or impropriety. But where were the neighbors she'd grown up with? Those making up this crowd were less familiar to her, though there were a few whom she could match faces and names. Others she only recognized as their names were spoken and only then because her father used them around the dining room table, in less than glowing terms.

Hoping to reassure him, Evangeline pasted on a smile. "I know you would never do anything to put my reputation at risk."

She swallowed, spying over Brendan's shoulder, a man passing a flask to his friend. Her father would see to it she never went out in public again. Even now, some of the other guests were eyeing her before whispering to those sitting closest to them. Nods and even the occasional finger point increased her discomfort.

Did they know she was the judge's daughter? His position in

town left her little anonymity, but she hoped it was enough. The last thing she needed was news of her attendance to reach her parents.

A man by the fire pulled out a jug and passed it around.

No. Scratch that. The last thing she needed was a group of prohibition raiders to arrive, making it public knowledge that Evangeline Grace Moore was at an illegal event. Would the authorities make an example of her? Would her father allow it? Her head spun.

"Easy, Evangeline." Brendan grasped her arm. "Why don't we join those on the hayride? Get you away from the fire and smoke."

He didn't have to add alcohol. It was implied. Evangeline nodded. Brendan's arm, looped around hers, was as stiff as her father's starched robes. His jaw muscles were hard and twitched in the firelight.

After lifting her into the wagon, Brendan allowed her time to straighten her skirts before climbing in beside her. Soon, the driver called to the horses and the ride began. Only the quietest of conversations and the neighs of the horses broke the silence. It was the strangest hayride Evangeline had ever experienced.

Songs and laughter rang into the night every time her church held a hayride. A glance around showed her the reason for the difference. Couples paired up around her, their shadows in the moonlight closer than propriety allowed. Her face flamed. At least she hoped the darkness hid her mortification from Brendan. He would think her awfully naïve if her unfamiliarity with male, female interactions was brought to light.

Brendan cleared his throat quietly and angled his head toward hers while keeping his gaze on the other passengers. "Again, I must apologize. It seems we've gotten away from one fire only to find ourselves in another."

Tears threatened. "This isn't what I imagined the night would be. I hoped maybe you would sit close and hold my hand. Possibly even let me rest against your shoulder as we laughed with friends under the stars. I didn't expect ..."

She couldn't go on with her emotions clogging her throat. Humiliation upon humiliation. First, from the brazen actions of those around her. Then, from her own lack of control over her words. She'd not meant to alert Brendan to her silly romantic notions. The words tumbled out of their own accord.

Swiping a stray tear, Evangeline refused to allow any others that would only make a fool of her in front of these people. She pulled her lip between her teeth to still its quivering.

"My sweet, Evangeline. I am so sorry." Brendan draped his arm over her shoulder, allowing her head to fall back against his chest.

Having Brendan hold her should have induced thoughts of kisses and warm embraces. Romantic thoughts revealing just how much of her heart she'd already given him. Instead, Evangeline soaked in the comfort he provided. Under the circumstances, if he'd offered anything else, she wouldn't have been able to accept it.

"What is the matter with you?" Brendan stormed up to his brother as soon as he helped Evangeline from the hay wagon.

"Pffft."

The acrid puff of smoke James breathed in his face along with a wave of dismissal were reminiscent of their time at home in Chicago. How many speakeasies had Brendan found himself in against his will? How many times had he been forced to drag James away from the bar before he could land himself in legal trouble, or worse, a fight with a rival family? Too often to count.

Brendan's hope of James embracing a new way of life along with the move their father insisted on plummeted to the dirt beneath his feet. Flicking a glance at Dot standing behind him with a silly smile on her face, hair mussed, and bodice buttoned incorrectly, confirmed James had failed to leave any of his Chicago vices behind. When would he see the futility of these things he chased with reckless abandon? Would James ever answer God's call to a better way of living life?

Anger pushed its way through Brendan. "You're pathetic. Do you care about anyone other than yourself? No. It's always what you want, when you want it."

"An' why shouldn't it be." James's words slurred. "I take care o' myshelf. And everyone else can go—"

"Get in the car." Brendan refused to let him finish the curse. Grasping James by the arm, he glanced over his shoulder to make sure Evangeline followed with Dot. "Evangeline, put Dot in the back. You're riding up front with me. There's no way I'm letting James get us killed tonight."

He would apologize to Evangeline after he took James and Dot home. It wasn't his intention to sound high and mighty, but his anger left no room for polite requests. Evangeline's eyes conveyed her concern, but not offense, as she took her seat next to him. Good. Maybe she understood his vehemence. An apology was still in order, but he didn't doubt she would forgive him.

Other than to give him directions to Dot's home, Evangeline sat silently next to him. James, on the other hand, railed at him until Dot cooed something in his ear. He answered her with sloppy kisses Brendan tried to ignore. He was almost relieved as James cycled back to complaining to Brendan. Once Dot was dropped off, the circle was broken, leaving only his brother's slurred fuming until Brendan managed to get him home as well.

The house they shared was several blocks behind them when Brendan worked up the nerve to speak. First, he needed to deal with his brother's offensiveness. "I'm sorry you had to hear such coarse language. It's not ever appropriate, but especially not in the presence of a lady."

"It's not your fault."

She meant it. Of that Brendan was certain. He was equally convinced of her shock. Her voice lacked any emotion or inflection.

"Still, I do apologize for it. And for this whole evening. I had no idea it would be such an event." He ran a hand through his hair. "Your father trusted me with your care, and I ... You deserved better."

Evangeline stared out the window. Should he apologize again? Was there an infraction he failed to consider?

"Evangeline?"

Her shoulders lifted and fell with her sigh. She stared out at the passing scenery. Giving her time was the proper response to her silence. And after all she'd experienced that night, she deserved the proper thing. Waiting rubbed him worse than a new pair of shoes.

It was no secret he'd found Evangeline attractive from the first moment at the barber shop. She drew him more every time he got another glimpse inside her character. Each conversation, each minute spent in her presence, caused another piece of his heart to turn traitor, giving its allegiance to Evangeline. Still, they'd not known each other terribly long, and he had no way to judge what she might be thinking.

Without reprieve in sight, he pulled into her driveway. The interior lights were on, as was the porch light, providing a bit more illumination to the interior of the automobile. They didn't have much time as Brendan was positive Judge Moore waited just out of sight by one of the windows for his precious daughter. Brendan searched for the right words. But what more could he say?

Evangeline faced him. "I wish I could say I had a pleasant time tonight. But we both know saying so would make me a liar."

"I'm ..."

"Do not apologize, again." Evangeline leveled him with a look that might stop a rampaging bull. "You've already told me. You didn't know about the atmosphere at the gathering. You cannot be held responsible for your brother's actions, no matter what your father sent you here to do. James is a grown man. He is the

111

only one at fault for tonight. Well, and possibly Dot. But both are their own people. We cannot force them to make wise choices."

Absolution soared through him.

"But I feel it best if we don't see each other again."

The crash came hard and fast. Pressure to argue built inside, but he wouldn't. Evangeline had the right to distance herself from him.

The hand she placed on his did little to buoy his spirits. Hope deferred left him feeling adrift. Lifting his gaze to her face, he tried to memorize her sweet, hint of a smile. The eyes radiating warmth even as she broke his spirit.

"You do understand. Don't you?"

He nodded. Ran a hand through his hair. "Yes. I won't bother you again."

Her eyes widened. The smile faded into a frown. She swallowed. "If that's, if that's what you want."

"Isn't that what you want?" His voice sounded unsure even to his own ears.

"No. I just don't think it would be wise for us to see each other with either Dot or James present."

Air rushed from his lungs as his eyes slid shut. Another deep breath in to steady himself before looking at her. "Why didn't you say so?"

"But I did."

She frowned like he'd taken leave of his senses. Maybe he had. He went back through it in his mind. The apology which she stopped. Her insistence that blame lay firmly with James and Dot. Then came those dreadful words. She didn't want to see him again. Closing his eyes so he could see it more clearly, he concentrated on Evangeline instead of his dread. Her lips had kept moving, even as he died a bit inside. She'd continued speaking, and he completely missed it once those words were spoken.

The groan he uttered coaxed a smile from her. She'd caught him in his distraction.

"I'm so sorry." Would the night's apologies never end? "I

stopped listening after you said we shouldn't see each other again. In my defense ..."

Her brow arched.

"I was devastated at the thought of losing you. I know it's only been a short while, but I've come to care deeply for you."

The change was immediate. All teasing fled her expression allowing a shy blush to color her cheeks. Her gaze dropped from his, resting about the top button of his shirt. One corner of her bottom lip tucked between her teeth, even as she smiled, drawing his attention to her mouth, full and free from the unnatural red so many women favored. It beckoned to him.

He used his thumb to free her lip from its captor, before tracing a gentle path across it. He reached her cheek before dropping his hand back to her side. The silky softness of her skin under his worked like a magnet, increasing her pull on him with a power he didn't know she possessed.

Raising his gaze to hers, he found her eyes searching his with an innocence he couldn't claim. He'd stolen many kisses, but praise God nothing more, before he understood that wasn't God's way. Evangeline trusted him. It was right there in her eyes next to the innocence.

If he leaned in, she wouldn't deny him. But he wouldn't take. Her gift had to come freely.

"May I?" His hoarse voice was gravelly with desire.

"Yes."

If he hadn't seen her mouth move or her head dip slightly, Brendan would have missed the quiet affirmation. He slipped a hand up her slender neck to rest just below the hair twisted and pinned at the nape. One day, maybe he would be free to loose those silky strands from their prison and run his fingers through them.

For tonight, he was more than content to lean close as his hand urged her to do the same. He paused when her lips were so close to his, he could practically feel them. The warmth of her breath against his skin took his desire from spark to flame. As his lips met hers, the flame blazed hotter.

He pulled away, though everything in him argued to return to her. His touch was brief and gentle. It wouldn't be if he gave in to the urge for a second kiss. That was not the image of this night Brendan wanted for Evangeline. She'd seen too much coarseness thanks to the evening's events. He wouldn't taint this beautiful memory with a lack of control, even knowing their intimacy wouldn't extend past kisses.

The shy smile was back, this time accompanied by wonder-filled eyes. A shadow moved across one of the house windows. As much as he wished otherwise, it was time to let Evangeline go for the night. Heart light but movements heavy, Brendan stepped from the car and circled to open her door.

Before she had a chance to walk away, Brendan took her hands in his own. They were so delicate to hold such sway over him. But despite their power, their softness begged him to be her protector, her champion. It was a job he gladly accepted.

"Thank you." He tipped his head low, trying to look in eyes that again refused to raise above his collar. Slowly, she met his gaze.

"I had a lovely time."

His mouth quirked to the side. She blushed.

"Fine. It was a horrible time." She smiled. "Until it was perfect."

Perfect. He would heartily agree. "You'd better go put your father out of his misery. His little girl has spent far too long bidding farewell to her suitor. I believe he's taken to pacing the floor if the passing shadows are any indication."

She laughed. Not one to shirk his duties as a gentleman, Brendan walked her up the stairs to the door.

"Good night, Evangeline. Until next time."

"Until next time."

After she slipped inside, Brendan made his way back to the

automobile to begin the short drive home. What a night. Only God could salvage such a disaster.

And God could handle the worries of tomorrow and the repercussions the bonfire would have on his relationship with James. Tonight, Brendan determined to relish the assurance that Evangeline still welcomed him. He would allow their kiss to take up residence in his mind, providing the sweetest of dreams through the night.

Chapter Sixteen

"You're doing this with our father's blessing?" Brendan's breakfast sat uneasily in his stomach.

James's smirk irritated. "Now you're on the trolley."

Pacing, Brendan slipped his hand in his pocket. The cool metal of his pocket watch did nothing to soothe his temper. Instead, the reminder of his family's wishes being law only agitated him further.

"But he sent me along with strict instructions to keep you out of trouble." Why did his voice sound like a whiney toddler? And why did his brother's revelation come as a surprise? Brendan understood his father as well as James. Maybe better in some ways.

"You're acting like a chump." James's laugh was harsh with judgment. "You know your onions. Our father is a man who loves power. If he can expand his empire, forge alliances with Birger or Shelton, or play them both, he will snatch up the opportunity."

"That's courting the trouble he said he wanted me to help steer you clear of."

James sighed. It was an impatient sound conveying his belief that Brendan was no better than the rubes his family took advantage of at every turn. Had Brendan been naïve?

Circumstances proved it was true. But he'd hoped for something better. Futile, but he'd done it, nonetheless.

"Father only wanted distance between me and the jam I was in with the buttons after Duncan's boy ratted me out."

Of course, James wouldn't acknowledge it was his own actions that got him in trouble with the law. No. The fault in his mind rested squarely on the shoulders of the man who divulged his actions to the police.

"But ..."

"But nothing. Your only job here is to make sure I don't get caught up in the same kind of trouble in Harrisburg."

"How am I supposed to do that with you pulling the same kinds of stunts?"

James fixed him with a flinty stare. "Step up and act like a member of this family. If someone's got a beef with me, they've got a beef with you. Handle it. However you have to, for once in your life."

"No." Brendan shook his head. "You know I won't cross those lines."

"Then it's a good thing for you I'm not engaging in the same activities here I was in Chicago. I'm passing the time, having a bit of fun with a choice piece of calico while making friends with the locals, like Birger, who wield the real power around these parts. When we finally get out of this place, it will be with the friendship and cooperation of Mr. Birger himself."

"Don't speak of Dot that way."

"She's a means to an end. And don't fool yourself. That's all I am to her too. Her ticket out of here."

Brendan paused his pacing and stared at his brother. "You're taking her back to Chicago with us?"

"Maybe." James shrugged. "Maybe not. Time will tell. For now, I'll let her think what she wants and dream her big city dreams."

Brendan grimaced, shaking his head in disgust. James laughed in response.

"Stop feeling sorry for her. She's getting what she wants out of our time together—at least for now."

"And when she finds herself with the same problem Nora faced after enjoying a little too much of your fun?"

Brendan didn't see James's fist until it was too late. Pain seared through the left side of his face as bone connected to fragile bone with only a thin covering of skin giving any sort of protection. From the time they were kids, James had a short fuse, but not once had he turned his temper on Brendan. Why now? Because he mentioned the fling from the rival family that got James in trouble? It didn't seem possible. Unless ...

"You cared about her, didn't you?" Brendan probed his cheek with careful fingers. Tender. Swelling was a given. Might be sporting a shiner before morning. But nothing appeared to be broken.

"Don't *ever* let me hear Nora's name come from your mouth again." James spat the warning without a trace of guilt marring his irate features.

Shock stole Brendan's ability to respond. He'd assumed Nora was a fling like every other meaningless dalliance James had engaged in. What better way to insult their family's enemy than sharing a bed with the patriarch's only daughter—his princess? Brendan's fist-battered cheek declared otherwise.

He strode past James to the ice box and chipped off a hunk before wrapping it in a dishtowel and pressing it to the throbbing area under his eye. With the pain reliever in place, Brendan crossed to the sitting room sofa and plopped down, letting his head fall back against the cushions.

With his good eye, he scrutinized his brother. Jaw tight and shoulders thrown back, James still seethed, but something new flashed in his eyes. Regret. Brendan was no fool. The angst in James had nothing to do with his quick right hook. It had everything to do with Nora and the son he'd never acknowledge.

"I'm not looking for a fight. And I'd rather not experience your boxing prowess again, if it's all the same to you," Brendan started quietly, judging James's reaction as he spoke. Wariness. But not outright hostility. That was good. "But why didn't you go after them?"

The steely glare Brendan received for his suggestion convinced him to prepare for another blow. Apprehension morphed into confusion when James dropped onto the other end of the sofa with a shake of his head.

"I'm not like you."

That was obvious to anyone who'd met them. They'd never approached life in the same way, even before Brendan dedicated his life to honoring God.

"You don't have to be like me. You can be you and still make better choices."

James pulled his pocket watch, a twin to Brendan's, from his pocket and flipped it over and over in his palm. His eyes stared blankly at the timepiece. "You know what this is?"

To Brendan, it was a reminder that his family had expectations, and because he couldn't meet those, he would always be a failure in his father's eyes. But James was their father's pride and joy. Had he ever come close to tasting their father's disappointment? Brendan shook his head.

"It's a noose."

James dangled it from between his thumb and forefinger, letting it swing. The imagery was too close for Brendan's comfort. Too many associates had met that horrible fate. Sure, the chain tightened around his neck every time he failed to "be a man" and join in the family business. As much as he dreaded it, a day might one day come when he became as unacknowledged as James's son. But James? Never.

A sad chuckle escaped James's lips. "It's true. I know you think I can do no wrong in our father's eyes, but the pressure is always there. Do you know what he told me when I told him about Nora being knocked up?"

The crude term rankled. Still, it was his brother's story to tell. Brendan would let him tell it his way. He shook his head.

"Congratulated me on it. Told me I'd delivered a great blow to Nora's family. Then reminded me my fun was over, and I wasn't to even entertain the idea of continuing communication with Nora or acknowledge the child in any way."

Domineering. Calculating. Two terms he used frequently in describing their father. It wasn't until Nora's situation that Brendan added cold and heartless to the list. For a man who laughed freely and gave much to his family and friends, the description was incongruous but very much true. With his tendency of refusing to engage in illegal activities, Brendan had ample opportunity to experience both sides of the man. Acid churned in his gut when he considered his father's ways.

James rubbed a hand over his face. "You know what I did? Nothing. I stood there with a stupid grin on my face like I'd planned this strike at our family enemy. I ate up the praise and took my place as our father's number one, second only to him."

Guilt laced each word ripped from James in the telling. Brendan could feel the pain in his own chest. How much worse did it hurt his brother?

"That's the first time," James continued as a finger flicked the watch into motion once more, "the noose of family loyalty tightened around my neck. I determined I would never feel it again."

"You can choose a different path."

"No. I can't. Our father decided my path a long time ago. Come what may, it's the one I'm following to my grave."

Everything in Brendan screamed at him to argue, to show his brother the truth. Standing against their father wasn't easy, but it was possible.

"I'll stand with you." He silently implored James to see reason.

James pocketed the watch and stood, looking down at him. "You and what army?"

Chapter Seventeen

"Do you think we should get an extra pumpkin or two?" Dot glanced over her shoulder to Evangeline in the back seat of James's car.

She shrugged. For the last three weeks, Evangeline and Brendan stuck to their resolve about avoiding outings with Dot and James. However, with Thanksgiving less than two weeks away, Evangeline relented when Dot begged her to please reconsider. They would do whatever Evangeline decided.

"Why do we need extra pumpkins?"

"I thought maybe you and I could make a couple of pies to deliver to the Barnett family. Last I heard, he was still unable to return to the mines. I doubt they'll have much in the way of fixings for Thanksgiving dinner."

Evangeline rummaged through her handbag. The money her mother gave her for the pumpkin patch would only cover the ones needed for their family Thanksgiving dinner. But she found additional bills left over from her allowance, which should be sufficient.

"What a marvelous idea. I'm so glad you thought of it."

"It will be the perfect finish to their turkey dinner."

Evangeline laid a hand on her friend's shoulder. "Dot? How

will they have a turkey dinner if they can't afford pumpkins for a pie? I could probably ask Mother if we can package up some of ours to share, but I doubt we could do a whole turkey for them."

"Didn't you hear?" Dot's eyes brightened. "Mr. Birger donated turkeys for several out-of-work miners in town."

James nodded. "I heard tell he provided those, plus potatoes and green beans for at least ten different families."

"Mr. Birger?" Brendan frowned. "Charlie Birger?"

Evangeline sat back against the seat. "It's not all that unusual, to be honest. I've seen Mr. Birger toss a cigar box full of coins for the children in town to gather up."

"And remember the ice cream social?" Dot turned again. "Mr. Birger provided all that ice cream and even bought up the extra at the end of the evening."

The tilt of his head gave Brendan a skeptical look. Evangeline sighed.

"As strange as it seems, Dot's correct. I know his dealings at Shady Rest and the surrounding counties is deplorable, not to mention illegal, but it doesn't stop him from helping others in Harrisburg. True, he's turned angry and violent toward town folk at times. At least, according to the stories floating around bridge club and quilting circles. But for the most part, his dealings with people there are neighborly."

Dot nodded. "Billy Cranston even said Mr. Birger refused him entrance to Shady Rest because his mama asked that he be kept far away from the gambling and drinking. He told Billy if he was going to lose his money, it wasn't going to be at one of his establishments."

Brendan listened to the praise coming from the women in stunned silence. Mr. Birger's reputation was earned, though they argued the opposite. Of course, hard as he was, Brendan's own father treated his family well. It was possible Mr. Birger thought of the people of Harrisburg as the family in his charge. Or maybe he simply wanted respect from those where he lived. He could only guess what drove men like him to show a side in complete contradiction to their business demeanor. Regardless of the reasons for it, the behavior only served to garner sympathy for someone who could not be trusted. And there lay the danger.

"Evangeline," Brendan placed his hand over hers. "Please understand men like Mr. Birger are not benevolent Santa Clauses bringing hope and love to the masses. It doesn't matter how many turkeys they provide to those in need. Charlie Birger is a dangerous man, immoral in his business dealings. And gathered from stories not shared by women around a pot of tea, he's got plenty of blood on his hands."

Evangeline patted his hand on top of hers. "You don't need to worry. I was merely pointing out the idiosyncrasies, not attempting to paint the man as some sort of Robin Hood."

"The man is dangerous."

"My father mentioned this morning that trouble seems to be brewing. More than usual. I understand your concerns."

"I don't think you do." Brendan glanced toward Dot. "And I know you don't. If you did, there's no way you'd frequent his establishment as freely as you do."

Dot scoffed. "You worry too much, Brendan. I've never been in danger at Shady Rest. And even if I was, I've got James here to protect me. Isn't that right?"

"That's right, baby."

"You shouldn't be encouraging this, James." Brendan nearly shouted. Sucking in a deep breath, he tried to calm himself. "You, better than anyone, know what the man is capable of. It's one thing for you to put yourself in his path. It's unacceptable for you to knowingly place Dot in that position."

James reached across the seat to pat Dot on the knee. "Maybe he's right. You don't belong at Shady Rest. That's why you're going to stay put while I take a moment to deal with a few things."

Confused, Brendan glanced out the window. He'd been so caught up in the conversation, he hadn't realized they'd veered from the road leading to the pumpkin patch to make their way to Mr. Birger's place. Anger burned in his chest. His brother had lost his mind. What excuse could he possibly have for such irresponsibility?

"Don't even think about it." Brendan ordered through clenched teeth. "We're going to turn around, drive out of here, and head straight to the pumpkin patch."

"Calm down." James laughed. "I'll only be a minute. Then, we'll go get your precious pumpkins."

James exited the vehicle with Dot right behind.

"Wait for me." She hurried after him. "I'm coming with you."

Evangeline made a move for the door. If he didn't do something, she would follow them both straight into the lion's den. He grasped her arm, careful not to hurt her but firmly enough to make her pause.

"We can't follow them." Brendan hoped she would see reason. "We shouldn't be here."

He took quick survey of their surroundings. If he wasn't mistaken, the two men flanking the barbeque shed were openly armed. Not unusual in itself, but given it was only midday, there was cause for concern. There had been whispers of tensions mounting between rival gangs that Evangeline mentioned earlier. Only days ago, someone drove past this very spot and tossed dynamite out the window. Thankfully, no one was injured, but any attack didn't sit well with people like Charlie Birger.

"Come on." Brendan opened his door. "We're going to get out of here. James and Dot can pick us up back on the road."

Evangeline did as instructed, joining him at the rear of the car. There was a strange electricity in the air. It wasn't right. And what was that sound in the distance? It wasn't an automobile, but it sounded like a motor of some sort. Unease crawled up his spine.

Brendan willed away the discomfort with a lift of his chin and took Evangeline's hand. Alert was good. Fear could be deadly.

They'd only made it halfway down the drive when a man stepped from behind the trees lining their path. Eyes narrowed, he stared them down. The barrel of his gun, aimed at them, glinted in the sunlight.

"We don't want trouble." Brendan held out his free hand in surrender. "We'll just head back to our automobile now. No trouble at all."

They backed away slowly. The man made no move to follow or threaten further harm. He wanted them to stay on the property. But why? And was the engine sound drawing closer? He couldn't be sure. After several steps, Brendan fought the urge to turn around. If he was wrong, they'd end up shot in the back. But surely, he would have attacked when they were closer. Brendan was counting on it. He chanced a quick peek over his shoulder to find the path clear once more.

"Just a bit more, and we'll be safe in the car." He was careful to look straight ahead as he tried to reassure Evangeline. Her hand was ice inside his own. Though she did admirably at staying calm, her body shook next to his. She was petrified.

The men at the stand spotted their return. Not taking their eyes off Brendan and Evangeline, they moved to the front of the building to speak to each other. One lifted his weapon, using it to point toward the area where the man had turned them back.

Moving in tandem, they strode to the car. Brendan opened the door and ushered Evangeline inside. Before he could join her, movement in the field between the barbecue stand and the cabin caught his attention. James and Dot. At least he hoped it was them. It was hard to tell from this distance.

The engine now roared overhead directly behind Brendan. A plane? Out here? The way the men stopped their advance and ran back toward the shack, shouting and waving wildly gave Brendan his answer.

The plane flew over his head, toward the field. The field. James and Dot! Brendan took off at a sprint no longer caring about the men and their guns.

"James! Dot!"

The engine drowned out his cries. Something dropped from the plane as it made its way over the field. The first bomb exploded, shaking the ground beneath his feet. Dirt, grass, and smoke filled the field blocking his vision.

He could hear a woman's horrified scream. Why could he hear that? He shouldn't be able to hear a single noise with the explosion still ringing in his ears and the plane's engine still roaring overhead. Above him, the plane circled back. Two more bombs rushed to the earth. More explosions. The screaming stopped.

Please, God. No.

Without a thought to his own safety, Brendan rushed forward. He didn't know where the men from the barbeque shack were, but he didn't care. Covering his mouth with his sleeve did nothing to keep Brendan's mouth from filling with grit. He coughed as sucking a breath through his nose proved worse than opening his mouth. The scents of loosened earth, burning flesh, and his own fear-filled sweat were a potent combination. Doubling over, clutching his middle, Brendan added the stench of vomit to the mix. Swiping his sleeve across his mouth, he pushed on.

How much farther out had James and Dot been standing? He should have reached them by now. He stumbled. Palms met rock-pocked ground, cutting into his skin. Against his better judgment, Brendan steeled himself with a deep inhale before finding what tripped him. The air rushed from his lungs and his shoulders sagged. Tree roots unearthed by the blast. *Thank you, Lord.*

Saturated past capacity, the atmosphere freed its grip on the dust and grime, letting it settle once more. Just ahead, a form lay still on the ground. A man, his back to the sky, as if he'd been running away. Tattered clothes proved he hadn't moved quickly enough.

An unearthly wail filled the air. It took Brendan a moment to register it was ripped from his own lungs. He scrambled over to the body. The clothes were familiar enough. James. Tentatively, Brendan reached out to the burn-marred flesh. Turning his head to the side, Brendan wretched once more. He grasped James's shoulder, turning him over.

Odd. Facing away from the blast, James's features held only grime—no noticeable injury. He was almost peaceful in death. A stark contrast to the chaos and ugliness of the scene. Brendan swiped tears away, not caring about the mud trails streaking his cheeks.

As much as Brendan wanted to kneel there, beside his brother, cradling his head in his lap, he couldn't stop now. Dot had been with James. Where was she? He scanned the area, finding her body only a few feet away. Whether it was fear or pain pinching her features, Brendan couldn't say. Either way, it meant the release of death may not have come immediately. Her leg bent at an awkward angle. The dynamite weaponized a nearby tree, sending limbs and branches like shrapnel everywhere, including Dot's chest. Even those may not have taken her life, if not for the blood-stained rock her head rested on.

A whimper drew Brendan's attention from Dot. Next to James's body, Evangeline stood with her hand to her mouth, sobs shaking her from head to foot. Horror-filled eyes stared at Dot's mangled form. Anger pulsed through Brendan. Evangeline's innocence was stripped away in a single moment. No one should bear witness to this senseless, violent aftermath. Much less a woman.

He went to her, carefully putting himself between her and her friend's body. She stared straight through him. Shock, most likely.

"Evangeline" He kept his voice soft.

Nothing.

"Evangeline."

Still no change. He grasped her shoulders and gave a quick shake. "Evangeline."

Her eyes found his. Still, she said nothing. His own awareness was little better, but was now quickly returning. Men swarmed out of the cabin toward them. Each armed and angry. If he wasn't mistaken, two of them were those who'd been by the shack. His and Evangeline's presence before the bombs dropped had not gone unnoticed. Did Charlie Birger's men think they had something to do with it?

They couldn't wait around to find out. Friend became foe often enough in a gangster's world to encourage a shoot first, ask later mentality. With tensions already high, he couldn't take the chance. Not with Evangeline.

He grasped her hand, tugging her in line behind him when she didn't move of her own accord. Distance was their only hope.

"But, Dot ..."

The painful, pleading whine pierced his heart. He sealed the wound the way his family's lifestyle had impressed on him at an early age.

"We can't do anything for her now." His tone was clipped. He hated the harshness, but it was reality. "We've got to reach the car."

Evangeline tugged against him the entire way back. He couldn't blame her. She had no part in this life. At least not before him. Opening the door with his free hand, he loosened his hold so she could get in. The wild look in her eyes caused concern. She was going to bolt. God forgive him, Brendan wrapped his arm around her waist and shoved her into the seat.

"Do not move." He slammed the door and sprinted to the driver's side. He sped toward the road, praying silently she wouldn't do something foolish, like jump from the moving automobile. A shadow in the trees beside the driveway reminded him Charlie's men weren't the only ones there. He'd be willing to bet the stranger was one of Shelton's boys, making sure his boss's attempt was successful.

Shots rang out around them. Brendan yanked Evangeline down until her head was almost resting on his leg. She fought, but keeping her safe was the first priority, even if she didn't understand.

"Stay down." The order came through gritted teeth. Keeping one hand on the wheel, he used the other to hold her still.

Sporadic sounds of metal hitting metal confirmed they weren't out of danger yet. Brendan pressed the gas pedal into the floor. He doubted either side would give chase, but they had to get out of the bullets' range.

After the shots stopped, Brendan assessed the situation. Alone on the road, he allowed Evangeline to sit up. She pushed away from him, against the door on the far side. A quick glance was all the attention he could spare. It was enough.

She stared at him. A thin trickle of blood added color to her lips in stark contrast to her pale skin. Had he done that when he pushed her down? Or maybe when he shoved her into the car? Guilt ate at his insides. The danger they faced was far worse than a busted lip, but he'd never meant to hurt her even if it was superficial.

He dug a handkerchief from his pocket. Still moderately clean considering the circumstances. He offered it. Evangeline stared at his hand, unmoving.

"Your lip. You're bleeding."

She accepted the offering and gingerly touched the wound. Even the light contact provoked a wince. Brendan focused on the road while his mind raced to formulate a plan. James put them in danger from both sides. It was up to him to get them out.

Home to Chicago? Though possible, it could also take them from frying pan to fire. An unforgivable wrong had just been committed against his family, even if James was not the intended target. Father would be out for blood. Retribution was a way of life.

Evangeline would be no safer in his father's environment than she was here. If his family was involved, she would know bloodshed and loss. Besides, Father would push harder than ever to obtain Brendan's cooperation with the family business. That is, if he didn't disown him over the loss of his favored son.

Family. Evangeline held her loved ones in the highest esteem. But Judge Moore could offer little in the way of aid for this predicament. The reach of law enforcement and the judicial system was limited in light of the gangster element, especially in southern Illinois. And the attack happened in the neighboring county, tying Judge Moore's hands.

"I want to go home."

Brendan almost missed Evangeline's whispered wish. Of course, she wanted her family. She couldn't realize the jam they were in.

"I'm taking you home to your mother and father."

Evangeline's only answer was a nod. Brendan sat straighter as a new idea came to him. It could work. It had to. He glanced at the woman beside him. It was the only way. But Evangeline was going to hate it and possibly him in the process.

Chapter Eighteen

"Mabel, take her upstairs. Clean her up."

Brendan cringed at the harsh order, but he'd done no less since the bombing. Once the women were out of sight, Judge Moore turned fierce eyes on Brendan. Life with his father put him face-to-face with far more dangerous men. Yet none of them managed to make him feel like the worst of scoundrels with a single glare.

"In my office."

The judge didn't wait to see if Brendan followed. He didn't have to. No man in his right mind would ignore the authority in his tone. No. They would do exactly as Brendan now did. Trail behind the older man and dutifully take a chair across the massive wood desk from him.

"Explain what happened and why I shouldn't have you arrested on the spot."

Brendan nodded. "Yes, sir."

Starting with the estrangement from Dot and James and the way the coming holidays moved Evangeline to a spirit of hope and second chances, Brendan recounted the tale. While the judge's lips stayed silent, disappointment, fear, and rage played across his face at various points in the telling. Opportunities to sugarcoat certain details presented themselves. Brendan refrained. Judge Moore deserved the whole truth, especially in light of what he was going to ask the man to do.

"I cannot express how sorry I am that I had to treat Evangeline so roughly." Brendan sighed. "But if we didn't leave immediately, the situation would have escalated."

Judge Moore steepled his hands on the desktop. "While I don't relish the idea of my daughter being manhandled or injured, I agree it is far more desirable than the alternative. I can well imagine Evangeline's inexperience with the evils of life left her ill-prepared to react. You did what you had to do to keep her from worse harm?"

Brendan nodded. "I believe so, yes. And the bullets lodged in the automobile would seem to testify to the fact."

"And you don't believe either you or Evangeline are out of danger?"

"No, sir. It's the exact opposite. Charlie Birger's men are out for revenge after the attack. We were seen, but we weren't interacting with anyone. They don't know why we were there, and I'm afraid with tempers high, they won't ask."

"And Shelton?"

Brendan raised a shoulder. "I can't testify to whether or not it was Shelton's men. Though that is my guess. Whoever it was, he witnessed Evangeline and me when we tried to leave on foot. We were turned back. Obviously, he believes we are aligned with Birger. And we've seen his face. A dangerous combination."

"So, the rumors are true?" Judge Moore rose from the desk and wandered to the window. He lifted the edge of the heavy curtain and peered out. "A gang war is coming to Harrisburg?"

"I believe it already has."

"And you and Evangeline may be dragged into the middle of it?"

"Yes, sir."

"What do you propose we do about the situation?"

Brendan motioned to Judge Moore's chair. "I'll detail my plan. But first, you need to take a seat."

He waited for the judge to comply before lifting his chin and swallowing hard to dislodge the nerves knotting his throat. "We have to run."

Judge Moore's eyes shut. His elbows rested on the desk with fingers steepled in front of his face. Brendan accepted the man needed a moment of silent contemplation. It was better than the alternative. Brendan didn't relish the idea of being carted off to jail in handcuffs with the irate judge bellowing at him the entire time.

Evangeline's father raised his face and pinned Brendan to his seat with a scowl. "While I'd never trade my daughter's life for propriety, you're asking me to aid you in destroying my daughter's reputation without any guarantee of safety in return."

"No, sir." Brendan shook his head. "I plan to ensure both Evangeline's reputation and her physical well-being."

The judge's eyes narrowed. "Chicago is out of the question. I don't care what kind of protection they can offer. My daughter will not be ushered into a mobster's family."

Brendan couldn't blame the man for his vehemence on the matter, no matter how misplaced. "I would never think of it. I have an uncle in Tennessee, though due to his refusal to support the family's lifestyle, my father no longer considers him so. We'll go to him. He'll take us in."

"That's all well and good for once you arrive. But by then, my daughter's reputation will be in ruins, traveling without a proper chaperone. No one will stop to ask if there are extenuating circumstances."

Lord, give me strength and clarity. Brendan prayed to the only One who could pave the way for him. As non-committal as Judge Moore had been to the first portion of the plan, he definitely wasn't going to like what came next.

"First, I need to go collect some of my belongings since we're considering a long-term move out of the area. Then ..." Brendan cleared his throat. "I intend to marry your daughter."

"I won't." Evangeline's arms crossed in front of her chest.

Her mother's warm hand on her shoulder buoyed her resolve. At least one person was on her side.

"This does seem a bit excessive, dear." Mother employed the silky tone that had often won her husband to her side. "Maybe we can find another way."

Evangeline fumed. How had Brendan managed to convince her father of this cockamamie plan? Besides, she agreed with her mother. It was too much. Evangeline wasn't convinced of the danger Brendan warned lurked around the corner.

She wasn't completely convinced he'd seen a mobster's car that "crawled at a snail's pace" past his house when he went to retrieve his belongings. He claimed relief at knowing he'd parked away from the house to keep his presence from being made known.

Nonsense. The cold chill traveling up her back meant nothing. Anyone could have driven by. Someone's visiting relative that was unclear of their destination. It didn't have to be something nefarious.

Turning pleading eyes on her father, Evangeline softened her tone. "Please. I don't want to do this. Please. Don't make me."

"There is no other," Father's voice caught, "way. And we don't have time to argue about it."

Her mother fluttered a hand over her heart with all the drama of a stage actress. For once, Evangeline appreciated the gesture.

Evangeline worried her heart-shaped locket between her fingers. It seemed to whisper to her to do her father's bidding. Family. Respect. Honoring one's parents. Illegal activities aside, her family dynamics weren't far removed from Brendan's.

Father God, I need Your strength. I can't believe this is being asked of me, but I'll follow wherever You lead. Without a clear sign from you, I'll obey my father's wishes.

"At least let me help fix her hair."

Her mother's plea was frivolous in light of the day's events. But the knowledge that she wanted more for Evangeline created a small flicker of warmth inside her chest, where everything else was as cold and dark as a condemned mine.

"Fine." Her father rifled through his desk drawers. "I have to find the certificate anyway. But be quick about it."

Once in Evangeline's room, her mother handed her the brush from the vanity. "You take care of your hair. Use that beautiful set of butterfly combs we gave you for your birthday. You'll look lovely."

Evangeline held the brush motionless in her hands. "I thought you were doing my hair. Isn't that what you told Father?"

"Yes." She stepped away to rummage through the closet. "But we have limited time and a lot to do. I will not send my only child away with nothing. You brush. I'll pack."

The soft-sided valise Evangeline kept for trips was pulled from the closet and plopped on the bed. Her mother motioned for Evangeline to start brushing as she flew past her to the hall closet. Pulling the combs from her jewelry box, Evangeline began the process of pulling the sides of her hair back and up to fix them in place with the combs.

Mother was right. It was lovely. And it was likely the last time she would stand here in her room, with the mother she loved hovering in the background. She did love her parents, despite the countless times they'd frustrated her. All the irritations and habits that annoyed her so much before lost importance when she considered what she was about to do.

"Put that in your bag." Mother motioned to the brush as she entered with a larger suitcase. "Fill the bag with any personal items. Your Bible or whatever else you may want. I'll get working on your clothes."

Evangeline did as she was told. Her Bible, a photograph of her family, and the doll she'd gotten for her fifth Christmas were carefully wrapped in shawls and placed in the valise. Other than her locket and combs, there wasn't any jewelry she cared to take. Evangeline dragged her cloche hat from the corner of the vanity. From underneath it, something shiny fell to the floor.

Tears welled up as Evangeline picked up with gaudy jeweled headband. The jewels, cheap reproductions of diamond, glittered in the light.

"One day," Dot had said. "One day you and me are going to see big city Chicago. We'll find a couple of dandies, real Oliver Twists. We'll dance the night away. We'll do the Charleston with every good-looking man in the place and fall madly in love and finally be free. And when we do, you'll need this to catch their eye."

Evangeline tried to explain she didn't need freed. With faith, freedom resided wherever she laid her head at night. Dot had changed the subject, but Evangeline had kept the gift. Even covered in fake jewels, the present was extravagant coming from Dot. Beautiful, lively, confused Dot. And now she'd never again have the chance to offer her true freedom. It wasn't fair.

Evangeline's hand flew to her mouth as her sob escaped. Her mother turned. Clothes were unceremoniously discarded on the bed as she crossed the room to fold Evangeline into her arms.

"My poor baby." Her mother took the headband and wrapped it with enough care for the finest jewels before placing it in the valise. "We will ensure Dot is laid to rest in a fine spot. Her family won't have to take care of a thing. She may not always have made the wisest of choices, but she was always as loyal as they come. We won't let her be forgotten. I promise."

"We don't have time for this." Her father's bellow from the bottom of the stairs shattered the emotional current in the room.

"Let's get these zipped up. What we've missed, we can't help."

Her mother stuffed the last items haphazardly in the suitcase before buckling it shut. Evangeline did the same with the valise. Her mother hoisted the heavier case from the bed, but Evangeline reached out and took it from her, leaving the more manageable valise for Mother to carry. One last look around her room.

Moving past Evangeline and through the doorway, her mother turned at the top step. "It's time, sweetheart."

Not sure if the suitcase or her own feet were heavier, Evangeline made her way down to her father's office to marry a man she wondered if she knew at all.

Chapter Nineteen

How many miles had they driven in silence? All his early attempts at putting Evangeline at ease failed miserably. Not even the ferry they'd taken across the river had enticed a question or comment. In the hour since they left her parent's house as husband and wife, he'd barely glimpsed the side of her face, so intent was she on staring out the window at the trees and fields passing by. Her father agreed his plan was for the best. His blessing was more freely given when Brendan expressed the depth of his feelings for Evangeline. However, it wasn't Judge Moore driving away from Harrisburg with him. It was Evangeline, and she was obviously not as willing as her father.

"Are we going to see your parents?" The words were spoken softly to the window.

Brendan was sure they'd discussed the plan. Of course, there was a lot to take in, and he couldn't be sure his new bride wasn't still in shock. He smiled in her direction, though he doubted her mind registered the gesture.

"No. My parents live in Chicago." Maybe small bits of information would be best.

"Why aren't we going to Chicago then?"

"We can't."

"Why?"

Words that could be perceived in other circumstances as disappointment, were instead monotone and disinterested. She wasn't upset they weren't seeing his family. Her questions were only to gather information with no emotional weight whatsoever. How much would she take in considering her current state?

"You know my family's lifestyle."

"So? Whether you like it or not, yours is the life of a gangster."

It couldn't have stung more if she'd reached across the space between them and slapped him. Every choice he made purposefully distanced himself from the mob life. He wanted no part of it. The greed, the selfishness, the violence. They were qualities he actively fought against in his life. And he'd lost everything because of it. He had no brother by his side and no home to return to in Chicago. She was his life now.

And she wanted no part of him.

He cleared his throat. "One day, I hope you realize that isn't true."

"Gangsters take what they want." She scoffed. "Seems to me that's exactly what you're doing."

It was the aftermath of the death and the fear. There was no other explanation. She had to know he was doing this for her safety and reputation. He hadn't planned to marry in this way. He wanted to court her, earn her heart, and show her he meant to treasure it for the rest of their lives. Then, he would ask for her hand. Circumstances may not have worked in their favor, but his care for her was real. *Please, God. Let her see how much she means to me. Give me the words she needs to hear. I'm completely lost.*

Not completely. Brendan had his faith. So did Evangeline. That was more than he could say for James and Dot. Sorrow flooded him, nearly suffocating him with its weight. Following closely behind was the voice whispering into his mind how he'd failed his brother. If only he'd done more or prayed harder, maybe his brother would not only be alive right now but in a relationship with God.

Suddenly, correcting Evangeline's misconception didn't seem as important.

Though those on the outside looking in wouldn't see it, the wall Evangeline's words erected between them was as real as the papered wall of the childhood bedroom she'd never see again.

Guilt niggled at her harsh judgment. Every time it urged an apology, Evangeline stretched her lips into a humorless smile, breaking open the cut on her lip. The sting brought accompanying tears she refused to allow Brendan to see. Instead, she used the pain to steel herself against her desire to make amends.

Dot's memory was worth her discomfort. After all, she'd failed her friend in the worst possible way. No, she held no accountability for Dot's death. Guilt rested on the shoulders of the illegal elements in the area and those who refused to stand against them.

She would pay penance for her failure to lead Dot back to the truth of her childhood, back to faith. Words or example, it didn't matter. Neither made a dent in Dot's desire to live for herself. Not that she was totally selfish. Dot cared about others. But nothing would stop Dot from making something of herself like she imagined her mother did when she left. Not Evangeline and certainly not God.

I failed Dot. I failed You, God. Now, Dot's gone forever. I wanted her to believe. Why couldn't she have one more chance? Just one more and maybe she would've accepted. Maybe I could've explained it in a way that finally made sense to her. Instead, she's dead, and I'm heading...

"If not Chicago, where are we going?"

Brendan didn't look away from the road in front of them. "I have an uncle in Tennessee."

"Tennessee?"

"I know it's a long trip, probably between seven and eight hours if we drive straight through."

"Will we?"

"Drive straight through?"

She nodded.

"I'm not sure." He shrugged. "We will have to stop for gasoline. And if you need a rest from the car, please, tell me. Or if you get hungry or, um, have any other needs to attend to."

Were husbands and wives usually hesitant to mention hygiene subjects in front of one another? Evangeline didn't remember her parents discussing such things. Then again, she wasn't privy to all her parents' conversations. Maybe she would ask. No. There was no one to ask. She'd been traumatized, married, and uprooted all in the space of a single afternoon.

Brendan glanced her way. "You will tell me. Won't you?"

"Yes."

"Good." Brendan focused on the road once more. "And if you'd rather we stop for the night, I'm sure we can find an adequate hotel along the way."

Evangeline straightened her shoulders. Spend the night with Brendan in a hotel? While perfectly proper considering the ceremony that took place in her father's office, Evangeline wasn't sure she could muster the courage to sleep in the same room, let alone bed, with a man.

Would Brendan demand what was due a new husband? Could she refuse? Evangeline understood little about such things. Another subject she would have broached with her mother had she and Brendan enjoyed a normal courtship and wedding. Every time Evangeline thought the situation couldn't get any worse, reality left her tumbling through the air like the aerialist at the circus they'd visited. Only that performer had a partner in place to catch her at the last minute. Evangeline doubted her new husband was prepared to do the same.

"You don't have to worry about how we'll pay for it." Brendan glanced her way again. "While you and your mother went to brush your hair, your father gave me enough to see us make it to Tennessee comfortably."

Betrayal. That's what her father's intervention was. She didn't doubt her parents love. And their tears as she said good-bye were genuine. They only did what they determined best under the circumstances. But it didn't feel that way now. She doubted it ever would.

And her new husband. How strange those words sounded. She, Evangeline Grace Moore, no, Evangeline Grace Dunne, was now a wife with a husband. A husband. No longer a prospective old maid for elderly women to worry about at their quilting bees or bridge parties.

No. Now, well, who knew what people would say about her? Would her beloved Miss Myrtle whisper about the time the judge's daughter ran off with a gangster after a shotgun wedding? Of course, there was no baby. But with all the rush and secrecy, Evangeline didn't doubt there'd be talk.

"I'm ruined." The words slipped out of their own accord.

"What was that?"

Evangeline licked her lips. Dare she speak of such things with him? While Brendan was her husband, years of censoring oneself did not simply fall by the wayside. What a predicament.

"If you must know," Evangeline glared at him. The ramifications of everything she'd witnessed and the circumstances spun out of her control pushed her past propriety's boundaries. "I was wondering how many times I'll be labeled a chippy by those who used to believe me a woman of faith and virtue?"

Pleasure zinged through her at his wide-eyed stare. His mouth dropped open and closed again without uttering a single sound. He turned back to the road, uncomfortably clearing his throat. She'd rendered him speechless. Perfect. He deserved it for the jam he'd gotten her into.

Focused on the road, he spoke quietly. "Please, don't refer to yourself like that again. Even in jest."

His sincerity threatened to be her undoing. Evangeline lifted her chin. Forget propriety. She possessed a mind, and she was going to share it. "Why not? You don't think half the town, including the ones in the pews, are speculating about the gangster who knocked up the judge's daughter? And you call me naïve."

"Please." He swallowed. "I know this isn't easy, but please, don't talk about yourself like that. You've too much virtue to even contemplate such crass terms."

"Not that virtue serves me at all in this mess."

With one hand, Brendan let go of the steering wheel and reached toward her hand on the seat between them. Before he could make the contact that could prove her undoing, Evangeline shifted her hand to her lap. Married or not, he wouldn't be so bold as to snatch it from there. He sighed and returned his grip to the wheel.

"Your father will set the record straight. And those who really know you won't consider it for even a minute. Those who do aren't the type you'd want as friends anyway."

"That's the berries for you." Evangeline refused to look at him. "They aren't the family and neighbors you grew up with. No one's going to think less of you after all this."

"Are you serious?"

Evangeline jumped at the sharpness in his tone as he bordered on yelling. Though everything in her screamed to face him, she would not.

"Yes. I am." She hated the wobble in her answer.

Her body swayed one way and then the other, smacking against the door, as Brendan swerved to a grassy area beside the road. Had the man lost his mind?

"Look at me."

The order rankled. The chill in it was worse than wet hair in a snowstorm. All previous hints of civility were discarded. What would happen if she disobeyed? Evangeline determined not to push the boundaries to find out. She turned.

Brendan's shoulders relaxed. "Thank you."

A nod was all she could manage.

"You're wrong, you know." He waited, but she offered no response. "My brother is dead, and my father will lay his murder at my feet. I didn't protect him. As Dunnes, we have each other's backs, even if we don't agree. And really, leeway isn't given for disagreeing. What my father says is law. I'd already been ranked as the inferior son. The cowardly one who refused to take his place in the family. Now, I'm less than that."

Pain pulsed off him in waves. Still, Evangeline sat silently. His hurt weighted the air between them.

"You asked why we weren't going to Chicago."

She nodded.

"I told you the truth. I don't want that life for you. For us." His mouth worked before he swallowed. "But even if I did, I doubt I'd be received as a Dunne any longer."

Evangeline was unsure how to reply. Brendan didn't wait for her to speak. Rather, he moved them back onto the road to continue their journey. The pressure of unshed tears pulsed in her head and pushed against her ribcage. Turning away, she stared out the window once more. This time to find relief while hiding her tears.

Chapter Twenty

Though the road stretched out for miles ahead of them, darkness swallowed it up only a few feet in front of them. Brendan scanned the ditches as far as his limited vision would allow. They'd made it this far without succumbing to bullets. He'd do everything in his power to see they made it without hitting a deer or opossum, either.

The motor and the steady in and out of Evangeline's shallow breathing were the only sounds brave enough to invade the silence. She'd long since fallen asleep. He didn't dare wake her. The trauma of the day, along with the emotional upheaval, had worn her out.

Fatigue settled in his bones several miles back, though he couldn't pinpoint the exact moment. Maybe it was after revealing the depth of his own loss. Evangeline listened. The tears and silence following his revelation left little doubt she heard him. Carrying judgment and anger before the telling, the tears afterward offered catharsis. The lack of communication changed from belligerent to thoughtful.

He pulled up to a yellow stop sign. Though no other traffic was present, Brendan took a moment. A sign announced the small town that stretched out from that intersection as Park Haven. His uncle wasn't far, but he had no idea where he lived.

Once he'd turned his back on the family business, the family turned its back on him. Beloved uncle turned complete stranger with one choice. But Uncle Patrick always favored his youngest nephew and managed to sneak a post card or two in the earliest years after he moved. The return address listed Park Haven, Tennessee, and nothing more. At least it gave Brendan a starting point.

Reaching Park Haven was only one more piece of a puzzle put in its place. So much could go wrong. Patrick Dunne might live a hermit's life, unknown to the townsfolk. Or in the fifteen years since he'd left, his uncle could have moved on. Any number of possibilities might stymie their efforts, and Brendan was exhausted enough to concoct many outlandish ones.

Brendan pulled out his pocket watch. Much too late for respectable people to accept visitors. Entering a speakeasy or roadhouse to get information was out of the question. He'd just run from that life. He wouldn't return even to find his uncle.

He drove slowly down what appeared to be the main street of the town, scanning the buildings as he went. A hotel offered a possibility. If another option kept him from waking Evangeline, he would take it first.

A plain, brick building sat at the end of the street. It wasn't anything special, even by the standards he'd seen in Harrisburg. But a sign hanging on the porch railing declared it the jail. Surely a police officer should be present, unless out on patrol or making arrests.

Brendan pulled up in front of the building. It was his best shot. Keeping an eye on the automobile where Evangeline slept, Brendan knocked on the door. No answer. He rapped harder against the wood. Still nothing. With the side of his fist, Brendan pounded against it. The door jerked open.

"This better be worth waking me up." The impatient voice belonged to a disheveled middle-aged man.

Interrupting the man's sleep wasn't Brendan's best move, but it was the only one currently available. Brendan stepped back and nodded apologetically.

"I'm sorry to wake you." His polite smile was met with a hard stare. "My wife and I are trying to locate my uncle. He lives around here. At least, we think he does."

"And I was your only way to find him?" Irritation laced each word.

Brendan glanced down the darkened street before offering another smile. "Yes, sir. In my experience, the only places open at this time of night aren't the type of establishments I'd want to take a lady to, or myself for that matter."

Frustration turned to skepticism in the officer's eyes. "And you're looking for your uncle?"

"Yes, sir. Patrick Dunne."

"Preacher?"

The man's eyes narrowed. Brendan stood still while the officer scrutinized him. Not sure what he was looking for, Brendan opted for silence.

"You look enough like him." The man rubbed his beard covered chin. "Definitely a strong resemblance. But Preacher don't talk about any family."

Brendan nodded. "I don't doubt that. My uncle left our home in Chicago when I was a small boy." Again, a wary expression. "I just took a wife, and I thought it was high time to let bygones be bygones, especially since the quarrel was between my father and him. I was always fond of Uncle Patrick. I'm sorry rectifying the situation has taken me so long."

"And you don't mean Preacher any harm?"

"On my honor, sir. I love my uncle, though I've given little enough proof of it through the years."

Honesty paid off as the man gave him directions including such descriptions as "turn left at the big oak by the fence post" and "follow the road until the woods finally give way." Brendan thanked him, apologizing once more for the rude awakening.

With the end of their journey in sight, Brendan found extra stores of energy to keep him going.

Though the address on the postcards led them to Park Haven, Uncle Patrick's farm, according to the officer, was actually nestled in a clearing several miles outside town limits. He'd judge twenty to thirty based on the time it took to find it. A small log cabin sat to one side of the clearing with an outhouse nearby. What would Evangeline think of those accommodations? He doubted she'd used an outdoor privy as the daughter of a judge.

A full garden separated the cabin from a small barn on the far side of the clearing. With gray smoke curling against the navy night sky like a cloud, the peace of the place seeped into Brendan's weary soul. An oasis in a desert, though he'd never seen one in person to make that judgment.

Pulling up to the house, Brendan decided against waking Evangeline until he'd determined their welcome. Uncle Patrick didn't seem the unforgiving sort. The officer had called him Preacher. But it might have been like naming the giant Tiny or the clumsy girl Grace. Better to let her sleep peacefully until he was certain.

Brendan didn't resort to pounding on the door this time. Shuffling answered his first knock. He waited patiently for the door to swing open. The man behind it resembled Brendan's father and yet looked nothing like him at the same time. Was that possible?

Uncle Patrick stared for the space of several heartbeats before a smile spread across his face. Without preamble, he put his strong arms around Brendan, pulling him close. With one arm tight across his back, the other cradled Brendan's head against his shoulder.

"My boy. My boy. I prayed one day you'd come."

Tears were evident in Uncle Patrick's voice. How had Brendan doubted his welcome? His own tears poured out without warning. He was eight years old again, experiencing the only unconditional love he'd ever known. Feeling broken beyond repair when that love was taken from him, only to find it, even better than he'd known as a child, when he came to know Christ as a teenager. Even now, after all those years, resting in his uncle's arms was familiar, right. *Thank you, Father God, for bringing me home.*

He prayed it without doubt. Uncle Patrick was home for Brendan. One day, maybe Evangeline would feel the same. With thoughts of her, Brendan pulled away from his uncle's embrace. Brendan swiped the heel of his hand under his eyes, removing all traces of his tears.

"Uncle Patrick, I have someone I'd like you to meet." Brendan's shoulders straightened. "But first, I need you to understand why I'm here."

Uncle Patrick motioned to a pair of weather-worn rocking chairs to the side of the door. After they'd both taken a seat, Brendan began with the highlights of his time in Chicago, including finding his faith, and his move to Harrisburg. Though he recounted only the most needed details surrounding their arrival in Tennessee, more tears flowed as Uncle Patrick learned of James's death.

"I'm beyond blessed you thought to come to me." Uncle Patrick rocked slowly in his chair while allowing tears freedom to fall. "I'm afraid you wouldn't find a welcome back in Chicago."

Brendan nodded. "True."

"My brother is a hard man." He patted Brendan's arm. "While he would claim his love is unconditional, his approval is not. James's death will hit him hard. And I'm afraid you will catch the brunt of his anger."

"I've no doubts I will." Brendan agreed before recounting the hurried wedding and escape from retribution.

Uncle Patrick stared at the automobile. "And you care for her, this woman you've taken as your wife?"

"I do."

"Does she know of your feelings?"

Brendan shrugged. "I'm not sure anymore. I believe she did,

at least before chaos ensued. Now, I'm not sure what she sees or how she feels in return. It's all such a jumbled mess."

"It's a good thing you serve a God who creates beauty from ashes, my boy." Uncle Patrick's smile crinkled his eyes. "It'll take patience, but God will work. You watch and see."

Brendan wanted to argue. Yes, God did do exactly as his uncle said. But not every mess was wrapped up with a pretty bow. Sometimes God worked in the mess. Still beautiful, of that there was no doubt, but the difficulties didn't always end.

Still his uncle smiled. "Go and fetch your bride. I'd love to meet her."

Chapter Twenty-One

A lightening of the darkness behind Evangeline's closed eyelids announced morning's arrival, but she couldn't will the heavy drapes over her eyes to open. And she didn't even need the weights her mother attached to the dining room's lightweight curtains back home to prevent daylight from breaking through. Her fatigue accomplished the task on its own.

It didn't matter that she'd fallen asleep while Brendan drove. Or that as soon as she'd mumbled a greeting to his uncle, at least she thought that's how he was introduced, and been shown to a bedroom she'd fallen back asleep. Memory could be playing tricks on her, but she thought the man had said he and Brendan would be sharing the room next to hers. Had she thanked him for the information? All she could remember was flopping down on the top of the covers and letting sleep claim her once again.

The morning sunshine warming her face even as she laid there made no difference. Evangeline's emotions, her spirit, and her body were exhausted.

Somewhere drifting between awake and asleep, Evangeline's senses aroused. The sizzle and smell of frying bacon reached her, tugging her further from her dreams. The earthy scent of fresh coffee added to the allure of the day. Her mouth watered.

She pushed up out of the bed, taking time to straighten the covers before she followed her nose to the kitchen. In front of the stove, babysitting the pan of bacon, stood the man she'd met last night.

He was shorter than Brendan but only by an inch or so giving the impression maybe he'd been as tall or even taller until life stole his height. His hair was dark, like Brendan's, but liberally peppered with gray.

A floorboard creaked under her foot. The man turned. Evangeline drew in a surprised breath. It was like looking into the face of Brendan's future. James could not be denied as Brendan's brother, but their similarities were nothing to this. One could tell they were brothers. But this man. Evangeline doubted Brendan's father resembled him as closely as his uncle.

"Good morning." His smile reached his eyes. "Uncanny. Isn't it?"

Evangeline nodded.

He laughed. "It irritated my brother, Brendan's father, especially considering he gave Brendan my name as a middle name. James favored Sean almost as much as Brendan favors me. Temperaments too. Those who didn't know assumed Brendan was my son instead of my nephew. If I wanted to rile up Sean, all I had to do was play along."

"Is that why Brendan thinks his father prefers—preferred James?" Too late to take it back, Evangeline realized she'd let news of James's death slip into her question. Her fingers covered her lips in a vain attempt to cover her quiet gasp. "I …"

Patrick smiled. "It's all right. Brendan informed me of James's passing." The smile faded. "I'm afraid, though, Brendan isn't misguided about his father's preferences."

"You can't mean it."

"I do." He flipped the bacon in the pan. "Sean always pitted the boys against each other. James was the dutiful son. Brendan did the one thing his father wouldn't tolerate. He questioned. I left when Brendan was eight years old, but even then, his tendencies not to take his father's word as gospel put a wedge between them. From what Brendan's told me, it only got worse."

"I can't imagine a father not loving his son."

"You may not be able to." Brendan's resigned growl came from the doorway leading outside. "But I didn't have to imagine. It was life."

Evangeline ached for little boy Brendan and what he went through. Her parents may not always have given her a faith example to learn from, but she never had cause to doubt their love. What would it be to grow up without love? Well, not entirely without.

"At least you had your uncle." Whether she was offering him a silver lining or trying to convince herself of it, she wasn't sure.

Brendan scoffed. "Yes. I had my uncle. Soaked in his love for the first eight years of my life. Until, of course, my father drove him away, leaving me with no one. My father preferred my brother, my mother deferred to my father, and my brother often held his position as favored one over me. But the love I had for the first eight years of my life? That was enough to keep my head up and my feet moving forward through adulthood."

Saturated in sarcasm, his words accomplished their goal. With painful barbs, they put the naïve little girl in her place. If she'd meant to encourage him, she failed to lighten his load. As he stomped back out the door, letting it slam behind him, Evangeline realized how far off the mark her comment had been.

"I didn't mean it the way it sounded."

"Of course, you didn't. Would you please fill those mugs with coffee?"

Unlike Brendan's words, his uncle's brought calm with their sincerity. While he scooped bacon onto their plates, Evangeline poured the coffee.

"Should I fill one for Brendan?"

The man shook his head. "He can fill his own cup and plate

when he calms down and decides to join us again." He winked as he set her plate in front of her. "Better to leave a man to his temper than feel the brunt of it yourself. Even if you're offering him food."

The lilt in his voice reminded Evangeline of his family roots. "Is that an old Irish saying?"

"If by old Irish saying you mean, I'm both Irish and old, then yes, I suppose it is." He laughed. "No. That one is a Patrick Dunne original. Now, let's offer thanks to our Maker so we can fill our empty bellies."

Evangeline bowed her head but peeked at the man across from her. His prayer was as easy as the man himself, speaking to God as a friend. And despite what he declared, there was nothing old about him. He might be somewhere in his late forties or early fifties, but he moved and spoke with the strength of one who worked for a living and kept in good health.

"Mr. Dunne, this looks wonderful." Evangeline picked up a piece of crisp bacon. "Thank you, both for the meal and for allowing Brendan and me to stay with you."

"Enough of that." He waved his hand as if swatting a fly. "There's no Mr. Dunne here. I'm Uncle Patrick to Brendan, and I'd be pleased if I was to you as well, or at least Patrick."

A knot of emotion lodged in her throat. Evangeline swallowed. "I'd like that. Especially seeing as my own family is lost to me."

Patrick patted her hand. "I know it's a hard road you're on now. But I want you to remember something. No matter where life leads, you're always loved. Mothers and fathers hold their children's hands for just a little while … and their hearts forever."

"Another Patrick Dunne original?" Evangeline smiled at the sentiment.

"Not at all." Patrick shook his head as he let his natural Irish brogue turn his words into music. "That one came straight from Ireland, lass."

Laughter followed and continued throughout the breakfast.

The cloud of fear and crush of guilt lifted from Evangeline for the first time in twenty-four hours. Whatever she expected faded into irrelevance in the face of Patrick Dunne. Everything about Brendan's uncle encouraged a hope that not even Brendan's anger and absence could knock from its perch.

Chapter Twenty-Two

"Where's Evangeline?" Brendan pushed off the stone wall he'd lounged against as Patrick moved out of the line of trees, shedding their leaves for a long winter rest, into the small meadow.

With a wide, steady stride Patrick quickly reached him. "She's back at the cabin washing the breakfast dishes."

"You've put her to work? We've not been here twelve hours. I can't believe ..."

A raised brow and tight lips stopped Brendan mid-tirade. Patrick crossed to the narrower side of the building, lowering himself to sit on the stone steps of the porch that spanned the width of the front. A rich, cherry wood double door with a slight peak to its rounded top loomed behind him.

"What is this place?" Brendan sat next to his uncle.

"You've posed two questions now and not let me answer one."

Though the words held censure, humor was evident. Brendan nodded.

"I did not, as you say, put Evangeline to work. The lass practically begged me for the chance to be of use."

It was in her nature to help others and do her part. Brendan shouldn't have jumped to conclusions. "How did you know where to find me?"

"Who said I was looking for you?"

"Weren't you?"

Patrick shook his head with a laugh. "Not in the slightest. I know when a man needs time to himself."

"Then why are you here?"

Raising his thumb over his shoulder, Patrick pointed at the doors without turning. "This is my chapel. Well, in truth, it's God's chapel. But He's asked me to build it. I filled the wash bucket for Evangeline, gave her directions on how to find me, and I came to pray and work as I do every day."

"Evangeline is coming?" Brendan stood, brushing the dust from his trousers, before moving to the yard at the bottom of the steps. He glanced toward the path Patrick had appeared from.

His uncle frowned. "Settle down, Brendan. She's your wife, not some wild animal to give wide berth."

"I frighten her."

Brendan fidgeted under Patrick's watchful stare. When he could take it no longer, he paced from one corner of the porch to the other and back again. The silence continued. He could almost see the gears of his uncle's mind working beneath his narrowed eyes and unsmiling face.

"Why would the lass fear you? Has it always been such?"

"No." Brendan cupped the back of his head with his hands. "No. For a while I believed quite the opposite. Evangeline enjoyed my company and welcomed my suit. I messed up, Uncle. Yesterday. When James was killed. I'm the reason Evangeline is afraid of me."

"Hmm."

Maybe the words would flow easier if he allowed his feet to move. Brendan paced again. If nothing else, it kept him from the probable disappointment in Patrick's eyes as he detailed the rest of the story.

"Last night, I told you the important details of what led us here. But I wasn't the only one who wandered into that field. When I realized Evangeline followed me and saw James and Dot mangled, I was horrified. No woman should ever see that kind of evil. All she wanted to do was grieve her friend, but I couldn't let her. I'm sure you remember—the life of the mob is more about appearances than truth. Evangeline and I *appeared* guilty to both sides."

The fear gripping him was as palpable as it was the day before. Even as they assaulted his senses, Brendan prayed the smells and sights of the day would lose their potency over time. His heart beat hard to ensure his body had everything it needed to flee, not understanding the time for running was over. His eyes slid closed as he breathed in through his nose and out through his mouth. After a few moments, the taste of dirt and smell of blood faded, leaving the sunshine and a cool autumn breeze to return him to the grass filled meadow with the little chapel once more.

"She didn't understand. I dragged her through the field and forced her into James's car. When the first bullet hit, I shoved her head down out of sight and held her there until the danger passed." Brendan fought a gag at the memory. "I have never treated a woman so roughly in my life."

Patrick clasped his hands on his knees. Staring at those hands, Brendan refused to look the man in the eye.

"You did what you had to do to keep her safe."

"It gets worse."

"How could it?"

"I told you about my discussion with her father." He leaned against the stones of the stair's railing. "He agreed coming here was the best way to keep her safe."

"Seems wise enough."

Despite the day's chill, sweat moistened the hair he ran his hand through. "Trouble or not, neither of us could stomach Evangeline's reputation destroyed. It's what prompted his agreement to marry us."

"A reasonable course of action."

Brendan sighed. "Reasonable? Yes. But Evangeline joined us to find the matter, and her fate, decided. She had no choice."

"I see." Patrick stared ahead at nothing in particular. After a few silent moments, he turned his gaze to Brendan. "But you care for her?"

"You sound like Judge Moore." Brendan lowered himself to the steps beside Patrick. "He asked the same question. Yes. Before this whole mess began, she was well on her way to stealing my heart."

An easy smile stretched across Patrick's face. "That's good news. You fancy her. She fancies you somewhere beyond her need to make sense of the senseless violence she's seen. The only thing left is to win her heart."

"As if that's easy." Brendan huffed. "I've done little else but think about our predicament since we said our vows. And I've yet to devise a plan to help me earn her love."

Patrick's hand stung against his shoulder as he clasped it. If possible, his uncle's smile grew as he added a hearty laugh.

"There's your problem, boy. You'll never plow a field by turning it over in your mind."

The groan escaped before Brendan could suppress it. "I'm too tired for riddles. Poetic though they may be."

"The time for thinking is over. Your problem calls for action. Win her heart. Court her the way a woman longs to be courted." Patrick inclined his head toward the bare tree line. "The war for her heart may not be as long as you think."

Following the motion, Evangeline emerged. She paused a moment as she registered who sat on the steps. Shoulders pushed back and chin raised, she crossed the meadow. It didn't bode well in the fight for her heart, whatever Uncle Patrick might think.

Even with her current posture, Evangeline's beauty was undeniable. Brendan smiled at the thought of how her eyes lit up when she laughed. How warmth spread through him at every brush of her hand on his, even more so at the touch of her lips to his. Equal to the effect her nearness brought, if not more so, was the pull toward her as he considered her loyalty, her giving nature, her loving spirit. She was a woman of exceptional beauty to her very core. And she was worth every effort he would exert in trying to win back her affections.

As she approached, Brendan stood, offering her his seat on the stairs, no matter how primitive they might be. Though he left ample room between them, Evangeline still edged away. As discreetly as possible, Brendan raised a brow at Patrick hoping his message was clear. *See for yourself. Evangeline fears me.*

Unwilling to give in to the irritation her reaction prompted, Brendan forced a polite smile and nod to both his companions. "If you'll both excuse me. I've been too idle after such a long drive. I believe I'll take the opportunity to stretch my legs."

He left because of her arrival. There was no question. Despite her newly developed lack of trust in Brendan, her chest ached at the thought. Evangeline dropped as gracefully as she could manage onto the step next to Patrick. Unsure what to say or do, she sat silently, wringing her hands in her lap.

Patrick nudged her with his shoulder. "Seems like you have something on your mind."

"I shouldn't bother you with any of this. You barely know me. Besides, Brendan is your nephew, your family."

"Maybe I wasn't clear enough earlier." Patrick fixed her in place with a look. "You are family now too. As for who I know, my time with Brendan ended when he was still a boy. I know Evangeline Dunne as well as I know Brendan Dunne, the man."

Maybe he was right. All her life, Dot was there for Evangeline to pour her thoughts out to. Even if her advice wasn't always sound, she listened. If Evangeline was angry, Dot was too. If Evangeline was sad, Dot cried with her. Evangeline never faced a problem without the support of a friend.

"He regrets it, you know." Evangeline rearranged her skirt.

"What does Brendan regret?"

"Having to marry me." There she admitted it. "I think he suspected all along it would happen, and he's angry because my father forced his hand."

Patrick rubbed the back of his neck. "I'm not convinced that's the case."

"If it weren't for me, he could have gone back to his family in Chicago. He'd be under the protection of his father, but instead, he is saddled with a wife he doesn't want."

Instead of answering, Patrick sat up and stared at her. His head tilted to one side as he frowned. If he had a question, he wasn't asking it.

"It's true." Evangeline shrugged. "I know he wasn't always his father's favorite. But I'm sure he wouldn't have turned Brendan away. And it seems like maybe he's cut out for that life more than he originally thought."

"What makes you think so?"

The hint of impatience in Patrick's voice propelled Evangeline to her feet. While she didn't have any fear of him becoming violent, reason told her he wouldn't want to sit next to someone who thought poorly of his nephew.

Evangeline gnawed on her bottom lip. The door was open. Now, she needed to walk through it. "I witnessed it at the, I mean, when they died. It was there—in his reaction."

"What was?"

"Brendan's anger. It's there, just under the surface. I'm not even sure he recognized it. He was a stranger. When he realized I was standing there, I couldn't deny it. He was furious. It pulsed off him in waves I could feel."

"The loss was his too."

Evangeline shook her head. "It was more than loss. He dragged me to the car. Shoved me inside, and slammed the door." She touched the rough reminder of the night left on her lip with one finger. "Brendan forced my head down onto his lap and held me there. It's the first time in my life I've been injured by another."

"He struck you?"

"No." Evangeline didn't have to replay the afternoon to know he'd not hit her. But his treatment left her fearing for her safety. "He was livid, though. More than I've ever witnessed in a man."

"My experience is a bit greater than yours. As loathe as I am to admit it, his reaction is not uncommon. I doubt you've been in such dire circumstances before."

Evangeline repositioned the shawl over her arms as cool, moist air raised gooseflesh on her skin. "I can't argue that, and I hope I never have occasion to again."

"That, from my understanding, is why you're here."

"He says it's to keep me safe. To keep me from a life dictated by the gangster activities of Brendan's family."

She glanced to Patrick. Maybe she could read the truth in his eyes as she spoke. "But this was my father's doing. Brendan might have joined his father, though he denies it. He might have delivered me somewhere safe, here even, and returned to his previous life. While Brendan may have broached the subject, it wasn't without reason. My father would insist on propriety. After all we'd been through, he was more concerned with my reputation. Now, Brendan has a wife he never wanted. I'm afraid it only tightens the hold his anger has on him."

"Unless I'm wrong, and that rarely happens," Patrick grinned as he spoke, "the situation is not as dire as you suggest. My nephew mentioned you were courting before this mess."

"Yes. And I believed him kind and strong in faith."

"Did this one event change him so completely?"

Evangeline slid her locket back and forth over its chain. That kind of transformation, so drastic and immediate, wasn't plausible. Was it possible? Even considering the horrors of the day. There was only one answer she could see.

"It was there all the time." At Patrick's frown, she realized the need to clarify. "He wasn't lying, per se. At least, not to me. I believe he was lying to himself. Telling himself he was not a violent person. Maybe he was protecting himself from the hurt of not being his father's favorite son. A rebellion of sorts."

Patrick's smile was gentle. "His refusal to be a violent person created the rivalry with James in the first place."

"But all that anger."

"May not be what it seems." Patrick stood, going to the chapel door. "Sometimes an angry word disguises a caring heart."

A wry smile twisted Evangeline's lips despite the serious conversation. "Another Irish proverb to light my way?"

"No." He opened the door, pausing long enough to turn back to her. "That wisdom comes straight from Patrick Dunne."

Evangeline chuckled. It would take years to sift through the sayings Patrick favored in conversation and determine their origin. Of course, given their circumstances, time was theirs in abundance. Her smile faded. Was there truth hidden in Patrick Dunne's wisdom, as he called it?

Could her own heightened emotions be playing a cruel trick on her? While Brendan's anger couldn't be denied, was it possible it wasn't directed at her? Could his rough actions be born of something other than his inner self? How would she know?

Father God, I feel so inadequate. I'm a helpless victim of circumstances, and it's brought me to a foreign place both in reality and figuratively. I don't know what's right anymore. I don't want my fear stealing my judgment. But I don't want to fear at all if there's no reason. Lord, guide me to the truth. Help me know what to do with this man who is now my husband for better or worse. And, please, please, let it not be for worse.

Chapter Twenty-Three

An hour spent in silent prayer changed a man. Patrick was right. Action was needed if Brendan was ever going to succeed in winning Evangeline's trust and love. What man didn't want his wife to feel those things for him? Despite the tension between them, Brendan hungered for his wife's affection. She'd captured his attention from the day they met, and his heart followed shortly after.

Before proper courtship began, another matter demanded focus. Brendan returned to the chapel steps. From inside the unfinished building, his uncle's clear baritone mixed with the sound of a saw. Brendan rounded the corner. His breath caught at the sight of Evangeline sitting on the steps, leaning against the rock banister. Peace filled her expression as she lounged there with her head inclined to the side and her eyes shut, listening to the hymn his uncle sang.

She appeared so restful. Brendan hated to intrude, but they'd wasted enough time avoiding one another. The clearing of his throat brought her head up. His heart plummeted as wariness entered her eyes and all signs of peace fell away. It tempted him to surrender before the first skirmish in this battle for her heart began. But he wasn't given to quitting at the first sign of trouble

HEATHER GREER

or even the fifth. He would see this through. Evangeline was worth it.

She was also preparing to leave if her sudden rising proved any indication. If he didn't hurry, he would miss his chance. His long, quick strides put him at her side before she could flee. Though he reached out to take her hand, he thought better of it, reaching in his pocket to take out his watch instead. He clicked it open, glanced at the hands, and placed it back where it belonged. A believable cover to decrease her chance for discomfort.

"You were so relaxed sitting there in the afternoon sunshine." He let his gaze roam everywhere but her face. "Disturbing you is the last thing I wanted. But I hoped you would take a stroll with me. I need to tell you something."

Standing there in silence while she debated wasn't easy. Slightly narrowed eyes assessed him. She weighed her options. Words to plead his case pressed against his resolve to allow her time to choose, building up like the steam in a heating kettle. Only there was no spout to relieve the pressure. At least, not one he would employ.

"I'm still feeling the effects of the night." Evangeline placed a hand over the locket against her chest. "Do you think we could keep it a short walk?"

Hope rose and fell and rose again, as quickly as a toy yo-yo he'd once seen as a child. He'd agree to anything as long as it meant Evangeline was speaking with him instead of running away. Of course, to say that would probably increase her reticence.

"I understand. I promise we won't go far."

Manners ingrained from childhood prompted him to offer his arm. At her hesitation, Brendan considered dropping it to his side. Before he chose, Evangeline hooked her arm around his with a tentative smile. She was trying too. No matter what transpired, he had to remember that.

Together, they strolled through the meadow grasses toward the tree line. In his time praying, Brendan stumbled on a place Evangeline would love, one that might possibly help her find peace as they talked. While they ambled down the worn dirt path, neither spoke. While the wind had few leaves to rustle on their way, the fallen ones crunched beneath their steps, and a few birds engaged in song to fill the silence.

Tranquil. Brendan imagined the entire area gave definition to the word. At least, it would be if he and Evangeline didn't have this oppressiveness hanging over them. The sooner they laid their differences to rest, the better.

The path they walked opened to a river. The clear, still water pooled under a small fall where the stream tumbled over a rocky edge only a few inches high. Was it even called a fall when the height was so minuscule? He didn't know. It didn't matter. The effect was charming.

Flat rock made up a large portion of the river edge around the pool, providing the perfect place to sit and talk. Brendan led Evangeline to a spot far enough from the water to stay dry and held her hand for balance as she lowered herself onto the cool, hard surface. He hadn't considered how the autumn temperatures might be most noticeable while sitting on the rock.

"Would you like my coat to sit on?" The air might prove a little cool for him, but it was better that Evangeline was properly cared for.

Her shy smile was reminiscent of the Evangeline he'd first met. Angling her legs to the side, she smoothed her skirts.

"I'm fine. Thank you."

Brendan joined her on the rock. Lifting his head to the sunshine, he closed his eyes, soaking in the calming atmosphere of the place. When he opened them once more, it was to Evangeline's scrutiny. It was time to say what needed said.

"I want to apologize." He forced himself to look into her eyes, let her see his sincerity. "This isn't how I wanted our relationship to go. From the moment you stood behind me at Shady Rest, and I realized you were in danger but too in shock to comprehend it, everything I did was for your safety."

He raked a hand through his hair. How did one apologize for

something they weren't truly sorry for? "It makes me sick to think in your time of distress, I caused you more. And while given the chance to do it again, I would repeat every action to keep you safe. I regret you had to witness any of it. I'm sorry my actions were so rough and impatient."

Pained eyes stared back at him. "You were so angry. Furious with me."

"No." Brendan scooped her hand into his, praying she wouldn't yank it away. "No. I was never angry at you. I was furious *for* you. The reprehensible choices of evil men cost you your friend and your innocence. That was inexcusable."

"I know evil exists, Brendan. I'm the daughter of a judge. I know what men are capable of in the pursuit of power or riches."

He rubbed the back of her hand with his thumb. "I understand. But knowing with your mind and experiencing with your entire being are two very different things. One may make you sad, even prompt you to action. But coming face to face with it can terrify. I've known it to break men, steal their hope."

Whether she was taking it all in or biding time to walk away, Brendan couldn't tell. But he was saying his piece. Doing what he could to salvage the situation and take responsibility. It was up to Evangeline to decide what she would do with his words.

"I didn't want that for you." He pushed a strand of hair back from her face. "And then, when I realized both sides assumed we were allied with the other, all I could think was it wouldn't matter what you'd seen. If I couldn't get you out of there immediately, you'd end up ... we'd end up just like James and Dot."

He hated the catch in his voice. Even now the vision of her lying in Dot's place was potent enough to bring tears. The way she froze stuck in his mind, making his heart race despite the danger being long past.

"You were in shock. There but not responding." His voice strained against the emotion. "I couldn't lose you."

While his tears remained behind their dam, Evangeline's streamed quietly down her face. He lifted his hand to wipe away the moisture. Before he reached her cheek, she clasped her hand around his, drawing it to her lips. Her skin was soft as it pressed against his knuckles. After she'd kissed each one, she lowered his hand to her lap where she kept it cradled in her own.

"I didn't realize." Her voice was as light as the breeze but full of warmth. "I am so sorry."

"There is nothing to apologize for. Shock is a natural response to traumatic events. Once it sets in, it becomes your master. You couldn't take in the danger or act in any way to escape it."

Evangeline stared at their hands twined together. "While I'd never before experienced or even seen it, I understand the concept of shock. That's not why I apologized."

"I'm not sure I understand."

"I think I've judged you too harshly. I didn't see my struggle. Only your reaction. Your anger, your forcefulness." Evangeline met his gaze. "I interpreted it through a flawed lens. I determined the same violent tendency, desire to control, and hunger for vengeance housed in those terrorizing our area and others of their ilk ran through your veins as well. I decided your family's way of life fit you better than you imagined."

While glad she realized her assessment was faulty, knowing Evangeline, however briefly, thought he was suited to the lifestyle he'd worked so hard to escape made bile rise in his throat. Even knowing it came from a place of terror didn't squelch his disappointment.

"That is never going to happen. I can assure you. I want no part of my family's dealings."

"I know that now. Do you think you can ever forgive me?"

Brendan chuckled. "I have a feeling our appeals for forgiveness could circle indefinitely."

"Then how about this? We wipe the slate clean of all our grievances up to this point. We're both forgiven. And now, we're free to forget the nightmare and move on."

"Agreed."

Brendan was rewarded with a smile promising Evangeline was

HEATHER GREER

ready to do exactly as she suggested. While the promise of renewing the relationship they'd started before loomed before him, a nagging thought tempered his hope. He and Evangeline might be ready to let go of the past, but would the past be so easily dismissed?

Chapter Twenty-Four

E vangeline hummed along with the hymn of praise Patrick sang on the cabin's front porch. Catching onto the tune was easy for her, but the words were unfamiliar. Intent on learning them, she paused setting the table to listen as he began the second verse.

"Before His presence let us come with praise and thankful voice. Let us sing psalms to Him with grace, with grateful hearts rejoice."

Beautiful. How often since they'd come to stay with Patrick over a week ago had she taken time to nurture a grateful heart? Too often, the enemy whispered to her mind about the things she lost. Her home. Her family. Dot. That one tormented her constantly.

But on Thanksgiving Day, it was time to hush the enemy inside and remember how much she'd been given. Patrick opened his home to them without question. They'd escaped the gang in southern Illinois without getting caught in the crossfire. And while they didn't enjoy a traditional marriage, she and Brendan had put aside their misunderstandings and extended the forgiveness they both desperately needed. Since then, his attention resembled the courting they'd done before tragedy struck.

Yes, she had a lot to be thankful for despite her life's circumstances feeling as jumbled as a pile of jacks waiting to be scooped up by a careless child's hand. She laid the last fork on the table and went to retrieve the pumpkin pie from the oven.

Hearing the door open, Evangeline glanced over her shoulder as she balanced the hot dessert on her towel padded hand. Patrick's smile as he breathed in the spicy aroma brought one of her own. Whether or not her efforts deserved the appreciation was another matter altogether.

"Our cook always made the Thanksgiving meal. Your instruction has been most helpful, but I do hope I haven't ruined our dinner."

"What is made in love can never ruin." He moved closer and inhaled the scent once more. "Besides, it smells like it's going to be delicious."

Evangeline set the pie on the counter to cool. "Is that another Irish proverb for me?"

"Wrong again." Patrick's laugh filled the room. "That is another straight from the mind of Patrick Dunne."

"And the song? Is the tune from Patrick Dunne as well?"

He shook his head. "Not at all. The melody is from Ireland, herself. I was a boy when my mother taught it to me."

"It's beautiful. And a fitting reminder I've been given more blessings than anyone deserves, even if my mind sometimes whispers to my heart it isn't true."

"You've had plenty of reason to feel that way." Patrick took her hands in his, turning her to face him. "But now those times are behind you."

"What if they're not? What if someone from home figures out where we are? What if we must run again? What if Brendan and I aren't a good match after all? A lot could go wrong. I don't even know how to prepare for it."

"Don't be breaking your shin on a stool that's not in your way."

"Wisdom from Ireland?'

His smile spread across his face. "Well, I'll be. You finally got it right. Of course, the wise words aren't only from the Irish. God's word tells us the same. We're not to carry around worries for tomorrow or what might be. We're only to use what's given to us today."

"Thank you for the reminder, both in what you said and what you sang."

"Would you like me to teach you the song? It might help you refocus when those doubts and fears keep nagging."

"I'd love that. Thank you."

Brendan grasped the rope dangling in the well, lifting the full bucket from its depths. Dipping his arms into the cold water up to his rolled-up shirtsleeves, he rinsed away the film of dirt clinging to his skin after mucking out the horse's stall and filling its trough with hay. The fenced in pasture would provide the needed sustenance for the horse, the goats, and the cow come spring. But Patrick assured him this late in the season, the animals needed a bit more than nature could provide.

Never having been on a farm before, Brendan was just beginning to acclimate to a manual labor-filled life. Nothing he'd done in Chicago prepared him for the work, and his muscles still ached with the reminder. But it was good, honest work.

Clean enough to pass inspection and join the others at the table for dinner, Brendan strode across the lawn. He paused on the bottom porch step. His uncle's rich voice blended with Evangeline's in singing an old Irish song of praise. While her speaking voice was decidedly feminine, it didn't prepare Brendan for the haunting soprano joining Patrick's baritone. Soft, yet strong, like the woman herself.

"Amazing." Brendan whispered, unwilling to draw attention to his presence.

Another item to add to the list of things he was learning

about his wife. She owned the pure voice of an angel. One that would transport him to the throne room of heaven as they worshiped in song each Sunday. Maybe, one day, if he was gifted the blessing of knowing Evangeline as his wife in every way, he'd get to enjoy that voice lulling their baby to sleep.

Heat crept up his neck at the thought. Better not to entertain such ideas. One day it would happen, God willing. And he truly believed God was willing. But he and Evangeline were only now renewing the relationship they'd known before their loss. Trust and friendship were difficult stones to set. But once they were firmly in place, love would rest, unshakeable on their foundation.

He and Evangeline had been closing in on love before his family's thirst for power and money rained death and fear down on them. Images of Dot and James, bodies mangled by the blast, played in his mind. His hands clenched, seeing Evangeline turn into a shell of her vibrant self as she stumbled along behind him. The sights were devastating as he lived them. Reliving them at times like this, or worse, when they played unhindered in his dreams, stoked a burning anger in his chest he prayed time would douse.

If not for his father's sinful greed, his brother would still be here. Evangeline would have her friend. James and Dot would still have the opportunity to turn to God. Instead. No. He couldn't think about that now.

"Everything is set." Evangeline's declaration broke into his fuming. "As soon as Brendan returns from his chores, we'll be ready to feast."

That was his cue. Time for daydreams and nightmares passed. Two deep breaths to hide the flame of anger, though nothing ever extinguished it. For today, Brendan would fix his thoughts on Evangeline and Uncle Patrick. For them, he could be thankful.

He reached for the door and forced a smile.

"It smells like heaven in here. A feast fit for Thanksgiving Day."

"Well, then," Evangeline laughed, "get in here and we'll feast and give thanks for all the blessings God's given us."

Brendan took his place at the table with a silent prayer to keep his demons at bay. This was a day of thanksgiving. His anger would keep for another time. The spark heating in his chest wasn't dying any time soon.

Chapter Twenty-Five

The thud of hammer to nail provided an odd rhythmic accompaniment to the melody Evangeline hummed. Giving one final tap, Brendan let his hands drop from the threadbare quilt he secured to the chapel's window opening. That was the last one. Seven gaping holes, framed for the windows Patrick was waiting to arrive, were now covered with an odd mixture of old, borrowed quilts.

"I hope Patrick reminds everyone to bring lanterns tomorrow." Brendan frowned at the dimly lit room. With rock walls and all the points of natural light covered, the little sanctuary was more like a catacomb than a place of worship.

Evangeline swiped an oil doused rag over the simple wooden pews Patrick had somehow procured. "The people will appreciate dim over cold. The wood stove in the back corner wouldn't do a lot of good at keeping out the November chill if those window holes were left open."

"I suppose you're right." Brendan gathered the various tools Patrick had left scattered around the room before traipsing off to invite everyone to services on Sunday. "I'm not sure why we couldn't wait for worship until the windows got put in though."

"It's only fitting, really." Evangeline straightened, put a hand to her lower back and arched it. "This is the Sunday after Thanksgiving. Might be nice to have electricity, though."

"I can't see that as a possibility any time soon. Even back in Harrisburg, there are several without it. And that isn't nearly as remote an area as this."

"Oh, well." Evangeline shrugged.

As she went back to work, Brendan studied Evangeline for signs she was in pain. Other than her stretch, she showed no indication of discomfort. Pride welled up. His wife was content to hum and clean, despite the roughness of the circumstances.

With the judge for her father, Evangeline never had to experience the roughness of life. Electricity, automobiles, even indoor plumbing were her normal. A housekeeper made meals and cleaned up afterward. If she wanted them, she could have milkshakes and bagged potato chips every day with the allowance her parents gave her.

Now, she was oiling the pews in a little chapel in the middle of nowhere without even enough light to allow for dust swirls to dance in the rays. And come tomorrow, he'd have to remind her to see to personal matters before they left the cabin. While it was equally rustic in its lack of electricity and indoor plumbing, at least his uncle had the foresight to build an outhouse. Patrick said they would build a couple on the chapel grounds, but if they didn't accomplish the task soon, it would have to wait until spring thawed the ground.

"I'm sorry." Evangeline straightened. "I didn't realize you were done. I'll hurry and finish dusting the pews so we can leave."

Brendan grabbed a broom. "No. Take your time."

She eyed him with a tilt of her head and eyes slightly squinted.

"I'm not finished. I've got other things to do. There's no hurry at all." To prove his point, Brendan strode out the door and began sweeping the crisp leaves that had blown free from their branches and been deposited on the porch and steps.

Evangeline took up her humming again, and he could only assume the cleaning that went with it. While she didn't seem to mind it, and possibly even found a way to enjoy the work, Brendan regretted the need. His own mother never worked a day in her life.

While his father may have been a lot of things Brendan wanted no part of, he couldn't fault the care given to his mother. Many of the lavish gifts were status symbols to be sure. But Brendan could call to mind many loving looks and teasing between the two of them. Even as the matriarch of their family made it clear she disapproved of their illegal activities, the love she had for her husband was undeniable. And his father's answer to her love was to spoil her, telling her she deserved all she had and more.

"Evangeline deserves it too." Brendan wasn't sure if he was telling himself or informing God. "Too bad she's hitched to me. I can't change it."

"Change what?"

The broom clattered to the ground as Brendan swung in the direction of the voice.

"Patrick!" Brendan caught his breath. "Don't you know better than to sneak up on someone? You scared me half to death."

Patrick chuckled. "I apologize." He held up his hands. "Truly. I'm sorry. I didn't mean to startle you."

"If you promise not to do it again, I'll forgive you."

"Forgiveness shouldn't come with caveats."

"Fine. I'll forgive you without stipulations."

Patrick leaned against the railing at the bottom of the stairs. Uncomfortable with his inspection, Brendan continued sweeping, though no leaves remained.

"What is it you can't change?"

Brendan searched the tree line around the chapel. "You wouldn't think the trees could keep dropping leaves like this. You can sweep them off, and an hour later they're back worse than before."

"Walk with me."

Patrick pushed off the stair railing. With little choice but to follow his uncle's lead, Brendan joined him. At the bottom of the stairs, he spun and marched back to the top. Opening the door, he searched the interior.

"Patrick and I are going for a little walk. I didn't want you worrying."

"Thank you." Evangeline waved her rag at him. "You go on. I'll finish up here and wait for you to walk me back to the cabin, if you don't mind."

Brendan nodded. "It would be my pleasure. We won't be gone long."

Looking back over his shoulder several minutes later, Brendan barely spied the chapel through the trees. If his uncle wanted to speak with him so badly, why wasn't he saying anything? They could as easily walk in silence back to the cabin with Evangeline.

"Maybe we ought to head back." Brendan picked a stubborn, low-hanging leaf off a tree as he passed.

"Or you could tell me what it is you're powerless to change?"

There were no more leaves to provide distraction. Evangeline wasn't around to overhear. With barriers to their discussion effectively removed, Uncle Patrick wouldn't take no for an answer. Tenacity ran through Dunne veins as surely as blood.

Brendan tossed the leaf he plucked into the creek. A large rock at its edge provided a place for Patrick to sit while Brendan leaned against a tree. He gazed at the flowing stream. Its peace could lull him to sleep if it weren't for the topic of conversation.

"It's Evangeline."

A deep *V* appeared between Patrick's brows. "Evangeline? Why on earth would you want to change the lass? She's as sweet as they come. A quick learner and a hard worker to boot."

"That came out wrong." Brendan picked at the bark with his fingernail. "I don't want to change Evangeline. I want to change things for her."

"Nothing is going to bring back her friend or wash away her memories of what happened."

"It isn't about changing what happened." Brendan flicked a piece of bark into the water. "I mean, I would if I could. But there's no use even thinking about what can't be. Did Evangeline tell you her father is a judge in Saline County?"

If the sudden change in the direction of the conversation was a surprise to Patrick, he didn't show it. He sat stretched out on the rock, with his legs out in front of him, leaning back to rest his weight on his forearms.

"I believe she might have mentioned it. Or maybe you did when you first arrived."

"Harrisburg is no Chicago."

"Is it supposed to be?"

Brendan shook his head. "No. But it is fairly metropolitan and growing in number each year. It might not take long for it to catch up."

"And you think Evangeline will miss city life? I didn't take her for the sort to enjoy the somewhat less than savory opportunities living in a metropolis might offer."

"No. Never Evangeline. Dot, her friend, fancied herself a flapper. Lived for the day she could go to the big city and experience the excitement of life. That was the draw for her with James. He only wanted a fling, but she believed he would introduce her to the life she craved."

"But not Evangeline."

"No." Though it was framed as a statement, Brendan was compelled to answer. "But there are amenities that come with being the daughter of a judge. It goes beyond indoor plumbing and electricity. Judge Moore's position provided physically for his daughter, but it also brought her a measure of respect."

"You think people around here won't respect her?"

Brendan smiled. "People can't help loving her. She's caring and real. But it's different, you know?"

"I'm afraid I don't."

"My mother never lacks anything. And when she goes out, people treat her like she's the most important person in their world. My father, with his many faults, has given that to her. It's the lifestyle Evangeline has known. It's what I can't provide. The only way I'm going to be able to is doing the one thing I said I would never do. I'll have to play by my father's rules."

Patrick removed his shoes and waded into the edge of the water. He stared intently into the ripples before bending to pluck a small, flat rock from the creek bed. Cocking his arm to the side, he let the rock soar over the water until it skimmed the surface and skipped across a few times before gravity pulled it under.

"I can't speak for Judge Moore." Patrick searched for another rock. "But I've seen what you're speaking of where your father and mother are concerned. And you've got it wrong."

"What do you mean?"

He let the new rock follow the same bouncing path over the water. "It's not respect your mother's presence garners. It's fear of your father. There's a difference. And I'd be willing to wager, Evangeline wants nothing to do with that."

"At least she'd have the life she's accustomed to. I've got nothing to offer. No job. No training. I'm worthless outside of my father's empire."

"There's a saying."

"Isn't there always?"

A few unamused slow blinks were betrayed by Patrick's attempt to fight a grin. "Nothing wrong with a good saying, boy. Years of repeatin' only proves its worth."

"On with it then. What's this nugget of Irish wisdom?"

"'Better a man of character than a man of means.' Your father has the means, but you have the character. I can't help wonderin' which one Evangeline would want most."

"Speaking of Evangeline," Brendan pushed off from the tree trunk, "we'd better get back to her. She's going to think we've abandoned her. Besides, it won't be long till your stomach's rumbling makes it impossible to hear any wisdom coming from your mouth."

For all his words, Patrick understood when to let silence have its time. Though he matched Brendan's stride as they returned to the chapel to collect Evangeline, he allowed Brendan time to mull over his words. Brendan was glad for it.

Was the desire to provide the niceties of life wrong? He didn't think so. And while Patrick may have been correct where Brendan's mother was concerned, he didn't think Judge Moore inspired the same feelings of fear in the people of Harrisburg.

Could Brendan inspire the same respect for him and Evangeline without the fear? Staying with his uncle would make it impossible. Could he return to his father without embracing the life he loathed? Was there a middle ground where he could appease his father and provide for Evangeline without spotting his soul with sin?

Of all the questions haunting each step, there was one that nearly drove Brendan to his knees. How could he even consider returning to his father when that life had just taken his brother from him?

Chapter Twenty-Six

"Seventy times seven." Patrick scanned the faces of all those gathered for worship. "And sometimes, the command to forgive must begin at your own doorstep."

It was unreasonable to consider. Patrick Dunne was not singling her out from the pulpit. Evangeline had seen his gaze skim over each one. It hadn't landed on her any longer than it did anyone else. And yet it pinned her to her seat.

Applesauce. Patrick Dunne was a man like any other. He couldn't know what was in her heart as she hadn't shared it with him. This feeling of being singled out was all in her head.

"This week, we celebrated Thanksgiving. One of the biggest blessings we have in life is a forgiving God. But what happens when we don't allow God's healing forgiveness to take place? When we refuse to forgive ourselves of the shortcomings God has already pardoned us for?"

How Evangeline begged God's forgiveness for her failure with Dot. She straightened her shoulders against the back of the pew as *what ifs* tumbled through her mind. Maybe one more prayer or one more conversation would have changed Dot's fate. If Evangeline had convinced Dot that James wasn't good for her, maybe her friend would still be alive.

But she'd failed. And Dot had paid the price. While it wasn't sin as such, Evangeline's burden rested heavy on her. It might as well have been sin with the eternal results her failure brought.

"Peter had a choice."

When had the topic shifted to Peter? Evangeline forced her attention back to Patrick.

"He denied Jesus. Three times he'd failed the man he'd given three years of his life to. The man he'd walked beside, learned from, and ultimately watched sacrifice himself. In this passage, we see Jesus restoring him. The debt was paid on the cross, the sin was acknowledged and forgiven. But Peter had to choose. Would he put away the guilt or wallow in it?"

Patrick shut the Bible resting on the simple pulpit in front of him. "The sin was forgiven. But how much good would forgiveness provide if Peter couldn't move on? He'd experienced the conviction of sin that brings repentance and life."

Patrick patted the cover of the Bible. "Second Corinthians tells us godly sorrow brings repentance without regret. It leads to life and salvation. But at this point, Peter faced a different kind of sorrow. We call it guilt. It's the world's cheap counterfeit of conviction, and it has no place in our lives. It tells us the forgiveness God offers isn't good enough for our situation. Peter put away any urge to wallow in his guilt, and God was able to use him to build the Church. What is your guilt keeping you from?"

While Patrick stood at the back of the chapel, shaking hands and offering a word to each attendee, Evangeline and Brendan wove their way through the pews picking up any bit of litter remaining behind. They didn't speak as they straightened. It was just as well they didn't. The morning's thoughts were still playing a rowdy game of tag in Evangeline's mind.

"Thank you both." Patrick retrieved his Bible from the pulpit after the last family left the building. "I think we're ready to head back to the cabin."

With her arm looped through Brendan's as they strolled down the worn path, Evangeline couldn't lag behind, though she might enjoy a walk later. The rhythm of her steps might help her work out the knotted threads of her thoughts. For now, she tried to attend to what was being said.

Patrick glanced around Brendan to include her in the conversation. "What did you think of today's service?"

"I was surprised." Evangeline decided to focus on the physical aspects of the service. She still needed to work through the ramifications of the message. "I expected a more, um, structured experience."

Patrick frowned.

"I don't mean to offend." Evangeline offered an apologetic smile. "It's only that the church Brendan attended in Harrisburg is known for being more, um, formal. And I got the distinct impression his family attends the same type of church."

"That they do, my dear." Patrick laughed. "But I'm not a priest."

"I thought Brendan's whole family ..." Evangeline stopped. Had she misunderstood Brendan? She bit her lip.

Brendan patted the hand nestled against his arm. "My family chooses to worship in the same tradition as many other families from Ireland do. But Patrick has always been the black sheep. Isn't that right, Uncle?"

"Yes." Patrick chuckled. "I determined two things long ago. The first is that I wouldn't be party to the family business. The second was that I didn't need the traditions so heavily practiced in our family's church to exercise my own faith. Oh, don't misunderstand me. I believe a man can come to saving faith in services where traditions are favored. My own faith began there, but tradition isn't a prerequisite to personal faith and salvation."

"Then, if I'm not being a busybody by asking, why did you leave? Wouldn't it have been easier for your family if you'd stayed?"

"Considering it was the proverbial straw that broke the camel's back with both my brother and my father, yes, it would have been easier to stay." Patrick nodded. "But I felt God calling me to something different from what I grew up with and what would ease family tensions. I'm to preach the gospel, plain and simple. To do anything else, even when that thing is not wrong on its own, would be a sin for me."

"I don't understand how something that's not wrong could be a sin, especially if it could heal the rift in your family."

Patrick smiled. "Let's put it in an everyday context. Is it a sin to visit a sick person?"

"No." Evangeline scoffed. "Taking care of those in need is scriptural."

"What if your father, who you still lived with, forbade it?"

"He wouldn't."

"But if he did. Would that make it wrong for you to do it?"

"I suppose, since there are other ways I can accomplish God's instruction to care for the sick, then, yes. Disobedience to my father would be sin."

"See?" Patrick's grin grew. "It's the same for me. There wasn't anything wrong with the path that would please my family, except that God instructed me not to take that path."

Evangeline looked up at Brendan. "Then maybe instead of my opinion of the service, we should be asking you for yours."

He shrugged. "I have no issue with Patrick's services. Like my uncle, my relationship with God is personal. While I've grown through the teachings in my family's church, I've also grown through my own private times of study and prayer. Though I've stayed in the church out of respect to my parents, I don't feel a particular need to worship in the way they're accustomed to worship. I'm as comfortable in Uncle Patrick's chapel as I am in my family's church."

"And if you'd left your family's church?"

Brendan swallowed. "Like Patrick, the affront would have been too much for my father. Any standing in the family, even an acknowledgement of being family, would have been taken from me."

The trio entered the cabin's clearing in silence. Turkey

vegetable soup waited to heat on the stove inside, but Evangeline followed the men to the well.

"Don't kid yourself." Patrick pulled the bucket from the inky depths. "When trouble came, you found me. Your family ties are severed."

Evangeline accepted the dipper of water Patrick offered and took a slow drink of the cool liquid. Passing it to Brendan, she couldn't ignore the dullness in his eyes. His pain was obvious. If Patrick was correct, Brendan had lost his entire family with one choice. His reality brought an ache to her chest.

Evangeline touched the necklace at her throat as she made her way to the cabin without waiting for the men. Leaving her own family left her feeling a bit adrift. But hope was still hers to own. One day, God willing, the gang wars and violence would end. She could reunite with her family.

Chapter Twenty-Seven

Evangeline settled onto the bench seat of the buckboard next to Patrick. The suggestion to take Brendan's automobile into town was vetoed though it would be quicker. The windows Patrick ordered for the chapel arrived, and Patrick doubted there would be room to carry them safely if they didn't use the wagon.

"You settled back there?" Patrick turned to Brendan behind them.

"Yes, sir. Just try not to hit too many ruts on the road, or I may bounce out."

Evangeline tucked her skirt under her legs and eyed the bench. "We might be able to squeeze you in up here. You'd be less apt to bruise if we bump along at all."

"No." Brendan shook his head. "It's better for you and Patrick to be comfortable. We'd be squished like sardines if I tried to sit there too. I was just having some fun with you. I don't mind being back here. Really."

With arrangements settled, Patrick clicked to the horses and snapped the reins, setting them off. Evangeline grabbed the plank beneath her to steady herself with the motion. She'd never had occasion to ride in a wagon, other than the few times she'd been on a hayride with friends from church. Or the last one she'd attended with Brendan.

The conversation between Patrick and Brendan flowed, though Evangeline paid it no mind. The tightness in her belly had nothing to do with the sway of the wagon. Instead, memories of their last hayride assaulted her. What should have been a sweet memory was tainted by the atrocious behavior of those around them.

Dot would tell her not to be a bluenose. Everyone was just having fun. A pang settled in her chest. As much as she didn't appreciate her friend's laughter and judgment at her expense, Evangeline would give anything to hear it again.

"Are you feeling well, Evangeline?" Patrick's query broke through her morose thoughts.

A weak smile was all she could muster. "Yes. I'm fine. Just woolgathering, I suppose."

"If you need a break, we can stop for a moment."

"Oh, no." Evangeline placed a hand on his arm. "I'm fine. No need for a fuss."

Brendan squeezed his face and shoulders between them.

"What am I missing forced back here all by myself?"

All he needed was to ask if they were almost to their destination and his transformation to small child would be complete. As his gaze shifted between them with a back-and-forth tilt of his head, the cloud over Evangeline's soul evaporated leaving sunny laughter to bubble up.

With a hand to the top of his head, she gave him a playful shove back into his place. Her smile froze as she realized what she'd done. How could she let herself act so forwardly with a man? She frowned. Brendan wasn't just any man. He was her husband.

But what did that even mean? They didn't enjoy the loving touches and teasing remarks she'd often witnessed between her mother and father when they thought they were alone. A kiss to her cheek. Her kiss to his hand. She sighed. One beautiful kiss brushed across her lips. Those represented the extent of their intimacy.

Theirs wasn't the typical union. It couldn't be. But there was attraction. And before the nightmare that plunged them into life as husband and wife, there was love. Immature and untested. But it was there.

Evangeline couldn't deny love on her side of the relationship, though still in its infancy and battered by recent events. The feelings Brendan had for her were less sure, but she believed if love wasn't present, it was nearing. Did that make her actions forward or simply flirty? If only she had undeniable proof of his love.

What Brendan wouldn't give to know what was happening inside that beautiful blonde head of hers. She'd sequestered herself inside her own mind. Watching her profile from his seat, the serious expression without a hint of smile was proof enough of the depth of her thoughts.

Even the tiny smile she'd given Patrick showed no warmth. Brendan's attempt to lighten the mood, inserting himself between them, earned him the joy of hearing her laugh. However, immediately after her flirtatious push, her cheeks turned rosy.

Completely adorable. If not inappropriate due to Patrick's presence, he might question the reason for her blush, if only to make it deepen. He would never tire of seeing color bloom on her cheeks.

Brendan smiled. He wouldn't have to. Unless familiarity stole her modest reactions, Brendan would have a lifetime to tempt the reaction. Even if she developed immunity to the things that caused it now, Brendan was sure he could muster up enough creativity to find new ways to tease the pink into existence. Surely, there had to be a few ways to keep the spark of playfulness through the years.

Feeling the heat in his own cheeks, Brendan ran a hand

through his hair as if doing so would dislodge his wayward thoughts. Common sense told him it wasn't wrong for a husband to think in this way toward his wife. Reality chided that theirs was not the typical spousal relationship, and such ideas should be avoided.

"You're sure the windows are ready to be picked up?" The question was inane, even to Brendan. They'd already discussed it before setting off for town. But he needed a distraction, and that was the best he could muster.

Patrick nodded. "Mr. Whitcomb told me so at service yesterday."

At least Patrick was gracious enough not to remind him of their previous talk. "Are we installing them this week?"

"That's the plan. I want to get them in before temperatures drop any lower." Patrick navigated the wagon toward the town's only general store. "Those quilts worked out fine for our Thanksgiving service, but they'll do precious little when icy breezes bring snow."

"Do you believe snow is coming soon? Maybe for Christmas?" Evangeline's eyes lit with the possibility.

Chicago always received too much snow for Brendan's liking. But if a white Christmas elicited joy in Evangeline, he'd pray for it every day until then. There'd been too much cause for tears and not nearly enough call for laughter during the previous weeks. Besides, Evangeline was as beautiful when her eyes sparkled as when she blushed.

"I don't know." Patrick scanned the sky as if the answer was written in the clouds. "It could. Happens often enough around these parts. But even if there's no snow, the dropping temperatures are enough to require a more permanent solution than the flimsy material currently draped over the holes."

Evangeline rubbed her hands together. "Oh, I hope it snows. It's a rare Christmas back home that doesn't at least have a dusting, if not enough to build a snowman. And my father always made snow ice cream with the first good snow of winter. I know it sounds silly, but I think it tasted best when it was from a Christmas snow."

The wagon pulled alongside the general store, and Brendan hopped down as Patrick pulled the horses to a stop. He hesitated only a moment before framing Evangeline's tiny waist with his hands to swing her down to the ground. A wobble as her feet touched the earth was all the convincing Brendan needed to keep his hold on her. When she turned those innocent, brown eyes toward him, Brendan realized how close to him she'd landed. A mere inch or two more and she'd be snug in his embrace. His heart flipped in his chest at the way she tucked her bottom lip between her teeth and how it couldn't completely hide her smile.

It did, however, shift his focus. A tilt of his head, and their lips would meet. Their single kiss played through his memory, sweet and soft, like a love song. Or a siren's song, beckoning him to indulge once again.

The clearing of a throat broke the spell. Patrick smirked, his brows raised. Brendan loosened his hold on Evangeline and took a step back. Crimson stained her cheeks.

It wasn't a feminine blush. Brendan was sure Evangeline was shamed at the encounter, and it nearly stopped his misbehaving heart. If they were alone, he could reassure her Patrick's warning was only given due to the public display. They were husband and wife. They shouldn't feel guilt over enjoying flirtatious glances or the sparks created by little touches.

Doubt crept in, stealing some of his certainty. The logic remained true, but did the oddity of their union nullify traditional schools of thought? No. He would not have his wife believe looking at her husband with desire or seeing the same in him was something shameful, even if they didn't yet take the liberties afforded them by marriage.

Brendan teased her palm with his fingers. When she didn't pull away, he clasped her hand in his. "As much as I'd rather gaze at your beautiful face all morning, we have windows to pick up."

The little gasp from Evangeline before she averted her eyes

convicted Brendan. If he and his wife were going to move beyond necessity and reclaim the feelings they'd shared before they wed, changes were needed. Wooing the woman he loved required intentionality. And though he couldn't pinpoint the exact moment it happened, Brendan couldn't deny his heart had shifted from merely falling to being completely head over heels in love with his wife.

Shoulders back and a grin on his face, Brendan joined Patrick with Evangeline at his side. "If you don't mind, I think Evangeline and I will browse the aisles."

Patrick opened the door and waved them through. "Not at all. Park Haven isn't far from the cabin, but it's not as convenient as opening the front door and strolling down the block either. Take your time. We're in no hurry."

While his automobile would make visiting the town easier, every mile would require fuel. Without funds coming in to refill the tank, Brendan needed to exercise care in its use. Patrick was right. It might be a bit before they returned to the limited conveniences of the town. Would Evangeline let him know of her needs?

"Here." Brendan opened his billfold and pulled two dollars from inside. He offered the bills to Evangeline. "I told you your father provided what we needed to arrive here comfortably. I want you to have this in case there are items you need to purchase."

She tried to push his hand away. "Thank you, but I have a little left from my allowance if I need anything."

"Please. I insist."

His hand hung in the air for an eternity before Evangeline accepted the bills and slid them into her handbag. The additional funds might not be necessary, but this way, without a doubt, she'd be able to get anything she needed. Though, she might not want to with him standing next to her.

"I'm going to look around a bit. If you need more, just find me."

He didn't wait for a response before moving down a random

aisle. Before he moved too far, he turned and pretended to peruse the contents. Evangeline stared after him momentarily before making her way down a nearby aisle.

Content that she would find him if she needed him, Brendan took stock of where he stood. Hand blown and painted baubles filled the shelves in front of him. Christmas decorations? The last thing he needed was glass ornaments and electric lights they couldn't use at the cabin even if they did end up getting a tree.

On his way to find a more useful aisle, a twinkle of silver caught his eye. Not a necessity, but Evangeline would love it. He could save it for her Christmas present. No. This one would be a special surprise for no reason other than allowing him to see her beautiful smile.

The ornaments glittered under the lights. Inspiration struck. He'd devised the perfect Christmas gift for Evangeline. Now, to find it.

Relief flooded Evangeline. She absentmindedly patted the outside of her purse. There were a few items she needed, but embarrassment would have kept her silent. She inspected the aisles, hoping Lister's Towels had made it to more rural areas like this one. The last thing she wanted was to explain her womanly needs to her new husband.

She sighed as she spied the needed item on the shelf. Adding them to her wicker shopping basket, Evangeline roamed the rest of the store taking in all it offered. A set of handkerchiefs displayed next to a small Christmas tree caught her eye. They would make a perfect gift for Brendan. She tucked them under her other items in case the man in question joined her. Then, she headed to the sewing and notions section of the store.

Within minutes, she found everything she needed and made her way to the register. Evangeline couldn't erase the smile from her lips as she joined Patrick at the wagon. She'd gotten everything she needed, plus gifts for Patrick and Brendan, and hadn't even used a penny of the money Brendan gave her. The rest, she would save for the future.

"Did you find everything you needed?" Brendan inquired as he joined them.

"Yes, thank you." She clutched her bag close to her side. "And you?"

A mischievous twinkle lit his eyes. "Yes. I believe I did."

"And the windows are loaded and ready to go." Patrick climbed onto the wagon seat. "There's a restaurant in the hotel. Why don't we pick up a few sandwiches to enjoy on our trip back to the cabin?"

"You two wait here." Brendan assisted Evangeline into the wagon. "I'll go fetch them for us."

Evangeline twisted on the seat. Her gaze followed Brendan as he hurried down the sidewalk toward the hotel. Something was changing between them. The looks. Holding hands as they walked into the store. Even making sure she could purchase the things she needed without awkwardness.

While their relationship couldn't recapture the innocence from before the bombing, the day proved the attraction and care were still present. Maybe even more so as they were married, and certain freedoms came with that designation.

"Might want to turn around." Patrick's suggestion drew her from her thoughts. "I'm going to pull this wagon around and meet Brendan outside the restaurant since that's the direction we need to go anyway."

Evangeline did as instructed. Stowing her purchase under the seat for safe keeping, she grasped onto the board she sat on to steady herself as the horses lurched forward. Patrick maneuvered the wagon in the opposite direction with ease and stopped in front of the hotel as Brendan exited the building with a large brown paper bag.

Accepting the parcel from him, Evangeline waited for him to climb into the wagon and situate himself in an area where the windows were in no danger from him. Once settled, she extended the bag toward him.

"Can you hold these until we get moving?" She waited until he accepted it. "Thank you."

She braced herself for the inevitable jerk as Patrick started them on their way home. When they were moving at a steady clip, Brendan once again poked his head between driver and rider.

"Everyone ready to eat?" He didn't wait for an answer before retrieving a sandwich from the bag and offering it to Evangeline. "I got ham and cheese sandwiches. I hope everyone is fine with that."

"It sounds perfect." Evangeline unwrapped the sandwich before handing it to Patrick. "Here you go. I can't imagine trying to drive and wrestle a sandwich wrapping at the same time."

She accepted a second sandwich from Brendan, waiting to take the first bite until Patrick offered a blessing on their meal. When Brendan held out another open bag between them, Evangeline squealed. Potato chips. It was nice to know one of her favorite treats had made it to the little town of Park Haven.

Taking one from the top of the bag, Evangeline let it crunch between her teeth. her eyes slid shut at the crisp, salty goodness. "Mmm."

"Have another." Brendan rattled the bag. "I know you love them."

A sheepish smile turned her lips as she stole another. "I can't deny that. Whoever invented these knew exactly what they were doing."

"I don't know." Patrick took one of his own. "But I'd say the man had to be Irish. No one but an Irishman would think to turn a potato into something this delicious."

Brendan's laughter was as comforting as the chips. "Of course, Uncle Patrick. No one who isn't Irish has ever grown a potato."

"I didn't say that. But if it's a potato you're using, I guarantee the Irish did it first and will always do it best."

Evangeline made herself take another bite of sandwich before plucking another chip from the bag. "If it means I enjoy more chips, I'm in full agreement with you Patrick."

"Of course, you are." Brendan rolled his eyes. "Origins of the chip aside, there is one important question left to answer."

"What's that?" Evangeline brushed stray sandwich crumbs from her skirt.

Brandon held up a golden chip. "Who gets the last one?"

Chapter Twenty-Eight

Brendan followed the soft melody floating through the yard to find Evangeline in the chicken pen spreading feed across the soil. Unfazed by the fury of wings flapping around her as hens gobbled up the grain almost before it hit the ground, she continued her song.

As he waited for her to notice him, an idea formed. When she finished her task without giving any indication she saw him, Brendan entered the enclosure, careful to keep the door from making a sound. He crept close.

"No-o-el, No-o-el, Born is the Ki-ing of I-is-rael."

He leaned close to her ear from behind her. "You sound like an angel."

Feed filled the air along with Evangeline's scream. Panicked clucking and the flurry of wings as the chickens startled added to the chaos. Brendan wasn't sure whether to duck away from the irritated hens or Evangeline as she turned toward him, swatting without mercy.

"Whoa." Brendan laughed, moving out of range. "It's just me."

She glared. "Don't ever do that to me again!" She covered her heaving chest with her hand. "You could have given me a heart attack. I had no idea you were there. And you got the chickens all in a tizzy."

Brendan made a point to look around her at the poultry who'd immediately gone back to their scratching and pecking on the ground. He raised a brow.

"Well, they were riled up."

"I don't know. They settled a lot quicker than you."

Her shoulders straightened as her chin lifted. "Are you comparing me to hens, Brendan Dunne?"

"Not at all." Brendan stepped close. Plucking a stray feather from her hair, he offered it to her. "Although if you continue sprouting feathers it might give some people reason to question."

She snatched the feather from his hand. "You know good and well that feather is your doing, getting them all antsy like that. Everything was the berries before you showed up, scaring us senseless."

Brendan smiled at her use of the slang she only used when excited. "Scaring you? Yes. I'll admit that. Senseless? No."

He inched closer. Cheeks pinked by the cold air and eyes bright, she drew him to her without trying. "You, Evangeline Grace Dunne, have a sharp mind. It pairs nicely with your kind spirit and beautiful smile. You are a picture of loveliness, both inside and out."

Rose bloomed in her cheeks having nothing to do with the temperature as a shy smile formed on her lips. The way she avoided eye contact endeared her to him even more. Love came easily with a woman like Evangeline.

Brendan paused. When did attraction grow into love? It didn't matter. The truth was there in his heart. He loved his wife. And he would do all in his power to show her for the rest of their lives.

As she raised her gaze to his, the revelation and attraction blended like the colors of a sunset, warm and inviting. The tin bucket she held prevented him from reaching out to her, from enjoying the softness of her as he cradled her hands in his.

He should deliver the message he'd sought her out to give and be on his way. Contentment stole over him. The idea of staying next to Evangeline, freely drinking in her presence, despite the cold, tempted him from the task.

She let go of the feed pail with one hand allowing her to rub one arm before the bucket moved again and she repeated the action on the other side. Brendan might not pay the temperature any mind, but Evangeline was chilled.

"I'm sorry I startled you." Honestly, he would probably enjoy repeating the offense for the rest of his life to see her reactions, but it wasn't the time to get into that. "I only wanted to let you know Patrick and I are heading to the chapel to begin window installation."

Evangeline nodded. "I figured you would. I know he's anxious to have Christmas services. And don't worry about coming back to the cabin for lunch. I'll prepare something and walk it over to you. That should save a bit of time for the work."

"Always thinking of how to help others is one of the things I love about you, Evangeline."

Wide eyes met his announcement. Those perfect lips opened in an *O*, teasing him with thoughts of a kiss. Brendan leaned in slowly, happy to oblige. She didn't shy away as the space between them reduced to a breath.

"Yes, Evangeline." His whisper warmed the air between them. "I love you."

He waited only until she raised her lips to meet his before claiming the kiss. As her lips warmed under his touch, Brendan lifted a hand to brush from the softness of her cheek back into the waves of her hair. Encircling her waist with his other arm, he pulled her close.

Neither paid mind as the bucket she held fell to the ground beside them and hens raced to retrieve the fallen seed. A shiver having more to do with heat than cold raced through him as

Evangeline's delicate hand slid up his back and nestled in his hair. He groaned against her lips and deepened the kiss a moment before forcing himself to put space between them.

The chicken yard with hens flapping at their feet was not the ideal place for romance. Besides, Patrick could come looking for him at any minute.

"I should be going." Brendan shattered the spell between them. "Patrick is waiting."

He stepped around chickens to the gate before turning back to Evangeline, rooted in the same spot. A wink brought another blush of color to her cheeks. "I look forward to seeing you at dinner time."

The magnitude of his actions and words surged through him with energy that demanded release. Running around the yard like a schoolboy was out of the question, but Brendan could not contain his goofy grin.

He loved his wife. Just thinking about her silky lips against his tempted him to return for another kiss. But beyond the need to help Patrick with the windows, another thought convinced Brendan to stay the course.

He had made his love known. Evangeline had not returned the sentiment.

Love. Evangeline bent to scoop the pail off the ground as she considered what had transpired. Brendan professed his love for her and punctuated it with a kiss that left her knees as weak as a newborn foal in spring. Even with cold in the air, she could still feel the heat of his touch coursing through her.

Attraction was one thing. In Harrisburg, he'd shown appreciation for not only her looks but also her spirit. The circumstances around their flight to Tennessee may have put them on shaky ground, but even then, it was present behind all the hoopla they dealt with. But love?

"What am I supposed to do with love?"

A fat, brown hen flapped in response. Evangeline shook her head and strode from the chicken enclosure. Her husband told her of his love, and she sat there talking to the chickens like a ninny. There were clothes to wash and dinner to make. And hopefully, enough time to accomplish those tasks and sort out her mixed-up feelings before delivering the meal.

Brendan didn't appear flustered when she didn't return his sentiment. Knowing he wasn't anxious or angry, Evangeline didn't have to have all the answers right away. But it was necessary to examine her feelings about him. In the end, the answers might not be the ones he wanted to hear, but at least they'd both know where they stood in the relationship.

An hour later, Evangeline was closer to untangling the mass of clothes in the washing tub than the thoughts running through her mind. A hand to her lower back as she straightened in attempt to find a moment's relief from the ache residing there did little. If she'd known the back-straining work involved in cleaning garments without the aid of an electric washer, Evangeline would have appreciated that blessing a little bit more.

Not that she did the washing at home, with or without electricity. Her mother hired that chore out to the housekeeper. Their home ran with precision and very little help from either her or her mother.

"If you could see me now, Mother." Evangeline touched her locket. "Doing laundry by hand, feeding chickens, and learning to cook. Other than maybe learning to cook more, I'd never have given these chores a thought back home."

Home. Evangeline paused at the word. Was Harrisburg home? There was no chance to return in the foreseeable future. She and Brendan hadn't lived long in the little cabin, but they were settling in well.

"Shouldn't home be where my husband is?"

Evangeline ran the first shirt through the wringer before placing it in the wicker basket. Once full, she'd tote the damp garments to the clothesline. She stopped and blew on her hands. Washing clothes would never be her favorite chore, but at least in spring and summer it wouldn't leave her chilled to the bone and sporting cold chapped hands. She retrieved another shirt from the rinsing tub.

"Lord, I'm content here with Brendan and Patrick." At least she thought she was. "But it's only been a few weeks. How would Mother and Father feel if they thought I sloughed them and all they've done for me into the slop bucket like last night's supper scraps?"

Confusion whipped her thoughts about as mercilessly as the tornado that tore through the area near Harrisburg the year prior. Even with the tornado's path pushing it northeast away from Harrisburg, the lesser storms it brought with it were horrible enough. The devastation left was still present in many areas and would be discussed for years to come.

She hoped her personal twister didn't create the same lasting destruction. Her parents sent her with Brendan, but it was for her safety. They did what they thought they must. Marriage was a formality to keep her reputation intact. Thoughts of love hadn't entered the equation. What would they think if they found out she was falling for Brendan?

Even if she could secure her parents' blessing for love to grow, it was wrong to consider such frivolous nonsense in the face of her failure and loss. It had to be.

"Especially after so much tragedy." Evangeline's frustration poured out into the clothes as she worked the crank on the wringer with more force than she realized she possessed. "How can I even think of falling in love when someone I loved just died?"

Her grief alone should prevent love from forming. Dot was her best friend, and she'd failed to reach her. Failed to help her see the deadly path she'd been on. Evangeline couldn't get her to see the truth in time, and now it was too late. Her friend was gone, forever.

"But, Lord," she prayed as she hefted the basket on her hip and trudged toward the clothesline. "if it's so wrong, why does my stomach do a flip every time I think about Brendan's declaration of love? And why do I feel like my heart is going to burst out of my chest if I can't share how I feel about him?"

Chapter Twenty-Nine

"I hope it's acceptable that I used the leftover corned beef for sandwiches." Evangeline retrieved one of the kitchen towel-wrapped sandwiches from the pail she carried and handed it to Patrick before giving Brendan his. "Oh, and there are some dried apple slices I pilfered from the root cellar in there as well. I couldn't find a fresh one anywhere."

"Thank you."

Brendan brushed his thumb across her hand as he accepted his dinner. The touch sent Evangeline's nerves skittering about inside her. Unsettled by the morning's thoughts, running away was her best option.

"I'm going to leave you men out here with your dinners." She opened the chapel door. "I want to see how you're coming along."

Evangeline scurried inside the chapel. With quilts still hanging from four of the six windows, the interior was dim except for where she stood at the back of the room. Two windows, opposite each other, let sunshine filter through. Whether the windows were completely finished or not, Evangeline couldn't ascertain, but the difference they made was remarkable. The chapel would be lovely.

A quilt draped shape stood propped against the front of the

chapel behind the pulpit. She'd inquired about the narrower opening in the rock wall when she first saw the chapel. Patrick mentioned a stained-glass window. But he'd not described it, and she'd not seen it. Curiosity nudged her in its direction.

Upon closer inspection, Evangeline realized the window was encased not in a single quilt but in layer after layer. Each one was carefully folded around the window with their ends tucked securely behind it. She didn't dare try to remove them herself. With her luck, she'd pull the window over with the quilts and shatter the artistry underneath.

"It's going to be beautiful."

Evangeline startled at Patrick's voice in the empty room. Taking a step away from the mound of fabric, Evangeline said a silent prayer of thanks that she hadn't been touching it when Patrick surprised her. Better to put space between herself and the window before an accident happened.

"I'm anxious to see it."

Patrick traipsed up the aisle toward her. "Well, then, lass, what do you say we take a gander at it."

"What are we looking at?" Brendan spoke from the back of the chapel as he entered.

"The stained-glass window." Evangeline sounded like a child with a present dangled in front of her, but she couldn't help it. The church Brendan attended in Harrisburg sported the colorful glass, but hers did not. And the opportunity never arose for her to see it either from inside or up close.

Brendan joined them. "You were going to look at it without me? After I grew up on tales of this window and how magnificent it is?"

"I'm sorry?" Evangeline's brows puckered. "Didn't you hire this window made or purchase it like the others?'

Patrick ran a hand lovingly down the cloth draped mass. "No, lass. I doubt any window made here and today would be as bonnie as this one. Crafted in Ireland, this one traveled with the Dunne family when we first arrived in America."

"And the family entrusted its care to you?"

Patrick shook his head. "Not entirely. The window was displayed in a small family chapel on the land our family worked. After the landowner's passing, his nephew inherited the place. He was not a fair man. My da, Brendan's grandfather, was in too poor health to make the voyage. But he sent my brother and me to the United States. Thought we'd know a better life here."

Evangeline dropped onto the front pew, drawn into Patrick's story. By knowing the Dunne family, might she better know her husband?

"But the window?"

"Patience, child. I'm getting there." Patrick's laugh took any sting from his words. "Our landlord in Ireland was friendly and charitable, and I often spent time with him in the chapel. He was the first to impress on me the ability to enjoy a personal relationship with God without adhering to the traditions I'd been raised in. I'd believed the truth of scripture, that Jesus died for my sins. I was God's child, of that I had no doubts. But there was something powerful to me in knowing I could come to God on my own, simply, in praise or in repentance."

"So, he gave you the window?"

Patrick held his hands up with a shrug. "Yes, in a fashion. He's the reason I wanted it. The new owner had no use for the chapel, wanted it torn down. When Sean and I left for America, I summoned enough courage to ask for the window. It's a tie to the family and land I left behind and to the man who taught me so much."

"And your brother, Sean? Was this when your break with him occurred?"

"Yes." Regret filled his eyes. "But not in the way you might be thinking. It wasn't so much about our differences in worship styles, though that's how you'd hear him tell it. I believe in any church where Jesus's death is preached as the payment for our sin, you'll find those who are faithful and true believers and those whose faith is only show. That was the real dividing line between

215

my brother and me. But then, it's been years. I cannot account for where Sean is at the present."

Brendan took a seat next to Evangeline. "I'm more than able to. My father is a powerful man in Chicago, and, as such, appearances are everything. That includes being a faithful churchgoer, though faithful is a gross exaggeration applying only to his attendance. By his own words, the only person he truly has faith in is himself."

"I figured as much, especially seeing how you two fled here and not to Chicago." Patrick lowered himself to the stoop of the stage with the weight of disappointment pushing his shoulders down. "Sean and I rarely saw eye to eye, but my belief that true faith is accompanied by living God's way instead of our own was more than my brother could handle. His unscrupulous ways clashed with my convictions. It came to a head, and Sean refused to acknowledge me as a brother any longer. That's when someone mentioned Park Haven in passing, and the Spirit stirred in me to relocate."

Brendan enclosed a fisted hand in the other. "Father often called you a coward. Said you didn't have the stomach for what had to be done to protect the family's interests."

"It is better to be a coward for a minute than dead the rest of your life."

"Let me guess." Evangeline tapped her chin with one finger. "That one is straight from Ireland?"

A smile spread across Patrick's features. "You're getting good at this. We'll have you an honorary Irishwoman before you know it." He glanced at Brendan. "But your father was correct. I wanted nothing to do with what he did in the name of protecting the family."

"I wasn't judging." Brendan pulled his watch from his pocket. "Father gave James and me these with the admonition to take our places in the family." He dropped it back into its hiding place. "I never measured up, and I held to what I remembered of you every time he berated me for my cowardice. I never thought you were weak. Quite the contrary. In your strength of conviction, I found enough of my own, though I never fully left the family until now."

Patrick smacked his hands against his knees and rose from the stoop. "Enough weaving tales of years long since spent. This lass wants to see the stained glass window, and see it, she shall. Come. Give me a hand, Brendan."

Within minutes, the quilts rested in a neatly folded stack on the floor next to a window rivaling any museum painting. While it leaned against the wall with no light filtering through it, the colors were dulled and darkened. Still its beauty inspired. Though not as complex in pattern as those housed in the church in Harrisburg, its simplicity drew her.

"It's beautiful." Evangeline carefully traced her fingers over the odd shaped cross in the middle of the pane.

She'd never seen such a cross before, with a circle intersecting its four arms like a halo. The interior of the cross was a million shattered pieces with shades of red, blue, yellow, and a smidgen of green. The background boasted a single color. The rich blue lent a sense of peace to the chaos of the fractured cross. An intricately knotted border wove around the outside edge of the window. Evangeline leaned in close to inspect the pattern. It probably had an official name, but she had no idea what it would be. Two golden-yellow ropes entwined together, like plaited hair, in a repeated pattern to the top of the window. At the very top, the pattern broke, leaving space for a different design resembling a strange three-petaled flower. A circular band near the center drew one's attention to the place where the trio of eye-shaped petals intertwined. The effect, even without sunlight streaming through it, was impressive. A work of art with a beautiful history of faith.

"When will you install it?" The other windows were needed. There was no doubt about that. But Evangeline was anxious to see this window in all its glory.

Patrick lifted one of the quilts from the stack and arranged it over the glass. "Soon enough. It'll be the last one we hang. Not that I'm superstitious, mind you. It's not a good luck charm for the chapel." He draped another quilt over the first. "God's blessing is all we need and all we seek. But something feels right about letting it be the final piece."

"Then let me get out of your way." Evangeline stepped from the stage and made her way down the aisle. "You have work to do."

Chapter Thirty

The stomp of heavy feet on stairs alerted her to someone's approach, but Brendan and Patrick weren't due back to the cabin for hours. Evangeline's breath caught as a knock shook the door. She gripped the broom like a shield, though it would make a pitiful one.

Had Birger's minions found her? Or maybe it was Shelton's gang? Brendan assured her they'd traveled far enough to ensure their safety. And no one was aware of their destination to let it slip in conversation with the wrong people.

"Hello?" A feminine voice called out.

Evangeline's breath escaped in a rush as she opened the cabin door to a shrunken old woman. Behind her, a mule, still attached to its small cart, munched what remained of the grass under its hooves where it was tethered to the porch railing.

"Hello. Can I help you?"

"When my boy came home talking about a new woman in these parts, I must admit, I thought maybe he'd gotten into a bad batch of moonshine. But here you are in the flesh. And my, aren't you a fetching one."

Her voice cracked and whined like a door in need of a good

greasing, but underneath, the remnants of a family matriarch laced each word with confidence. There was no doubt about it.

The woman tilted her head to the side, sharp features and a sharper nose giving her the appearance of a disgruntled bird, beak and all. Evangeline's smile was true, but she must admit not brought out due to the dictates of manners and hospitality engrained in her since childhood.

"Well, aren't you going to invite me in out of this cold?"

No. It was definitely not brought out by the manners she'd swiftly forgotten in the face of this strange little woman. Evangeline moved out of the doorway and waved her surprise guest inside.

"Forgive me, please." She closed the door and accepted the woman's coat and wool scarf to hang on the pegs by the door. "I wasn't expecting anyone, and I believe surprise got the better of me. Come have a seat and let me get you a nice cup of hot tea to warm you."

The woman shuffled across the small room and plopped down on a kitchen chair. "I don't want no tea. Thank you. But I will take a cup of coffee. You've got that, right?"

Evangeline retrieved a mug from the cabinet. The blue coffee pot rested on the burner where Patrick and Brendan left it after breakfast. As it was hours until the dinner hour, it shouldn't be too strong yet. She filled the cup and set it before the stranger.

"Sugar?"

The woman swatted a hand through the air. "Black is fine. Now, why don't you sit down and join me? Let's have us a little chat."

"That sounds wonderful." How Evangeline managed to respond appropriately, she would never know. This woman's strange appearance left her off-kilter. With absolutely no idea how to proceed, Evangeline sat across from her guest.

The woman's shrewd gaze took in everything from Evangeline's flour-dusted apron to the mess on the counter with one sweeping glance. Assessment complete, she turned back to Evangeline.

"I 'spose you're makin' a pie?"

"Yes, ma'am."

"You be sure to stew those apples until they're a nice pink color."

"Yes, ma'am."

"Got yourself enough lard for the crust?"

"Yes, ma'am."

"Be careful not to over mix it. You don't want a tough crust."

"No, ma'am. I won't."

"You're not from around here?"

"No, ma'am. I'm from Harrisburg, Illinois. My husband and I just relocated to the area to be near his family."

"Preacher don't have no family."

"Yes, ma'am. He does. He has his nephew, my husband. And he has me."

Evangeline was surprised how easily the answer sprung to her lips. Though she hadn't considered it before this woman's questioning, the truth of it settled in her heart. Patrick and Brendan were her family.

"Very good. Very good." The woman clucked before taking a final swallow of her coffee. "Me and my Arthur've worried about him. Out here all by his lonesome. We're his closest neighbors. Took him under our wing when he arrived and showed the lay of the land. Good to hear he's got his people now."

"I'm glad he had someone to look after him back then." Evangeline smiled.

The woman pushed up from the table and shuffled back to her coat and scarf. "I gotta be goin'. Dinner won't make itself, and Arthur's all but helpless in the kitchen. Don't make yourself a stranger. You need anything at all, you just tell Patrick to send for me."

Before Evangeline could make it to the door, the woman exited and made her way down the steps. By the time Evangeline reached the porch, her guest had unhitched the mule and was mounting the small cart. Once she had the contraption pointing in the direction Evangeline assumed would lead her home, she turned and waved.

"Be safe." Evangeline called as she returned the gesture.

Returning to the forgotten pie, Evangeline mulled over her neighbor's visit. Back in her heyday, Evangeline guessed the woman would've been what Dot would term a bearcat. She showed spirit and spunk even in her old age. And whatever oddities the woman might possess, she did seem partial to family.

What a strange word. Family. The concept was one she'd not given much thought.

"Any thought, truth be told." Evangeline kneaded the dough against the floured counter.

Dot owned the title of best friend. But that hadn't made her family to Evangeline's mother and father. To call her friend sometimes pushed past her parents' sensibilities, especially as she and Dot aged, and Dot became wilder in her ways.

Church ladies cared, but her parents didn't consider them family either. If Evangeline listened to her father, nearly every one of them was nothing but a busybody with too little sense and too much time on their hands. Evangeline loved them all, even the nosy ones. But she'd never thought of them as family.

No. Family, in the Moore household, only meant her parents and her—the three of them. For a time in her childhood, her grandparents were included. But they'd died before Evangeline reached her teens. And since family meant blood alone, Evangeline's family was their little trio.

"Oh, bother." Evangeline had been kneading the dough while her thoughts wandered about. She'd failed to heed her visitor's words. She grabbed the rolling pin and flattened the mound. If the crust was tough, they would simply have to deal with it. Next time, she would pay more attention.

She concentrated on the task long enough to finish the pie and slide it in the oven before allowing her thoughts to return to family once more. Legally, Brendan became her family the night they said their vows. Something had shifted since then, though she couldn't pinpoint when. Over the last few weeks, he'd worked his way into her heart.

When he'd said those three words, she'd not answered in return. She wasn't sure she should. The idea her parents might object still gave her pause, but she couldn't deny the simple fact that she loved her husband and wanted to consider him her family.

Even Patrick, though in a different way, had a place in her heart. Without an uncle growing up, she had nothing to compare to. However, his love and concern for her well-being physically, emotionally, and spiritually was like that of her father. This had to be the attitude of an uncle, or at the very least some sort of family.

"Thank you, Heavenly Father." She paused in her dinner preparations. "The loss of my family and friends is a deep wound. I'll continue to miss them and ask You to reunite us in the future. But you've not left me alone. You've blessed me with new family, and that is a gift I'll always treasure. Help me embrace it wholeheartedly."

"Mmm. Mmm." Brendan sniffed the air as he entered the cabin with Patrick. "Something smells like sugar and spice and ... apples."

"I made a pie, silly." Evangeline giggled without turning from the dish basin. She flung a soapy hand in the air, waving it toward the table. "If you've both washed up, sit yourselves down."

She grabbed a towel and dried her hands before scooping a bowl from the small stack beside the stove. She ladled something from a pot and set it in front of Patrick with a hunk of bread. Beef stew. He inhaled the steam as she set another bowl in front of him. How had he missed its rich aroma? Only the draw of apple pie could do that.

With meals on the table, Patrick said grace. Brendan groaned as the first bite hit his tongue. Evangeline may not have experienced extensive training in the kitchen, but she was quickly catching on.

"This stew rivals anything our cook made growing up."

Brendan's compliment brought color to Evangeline's cheeks. If he didn't have to eat and get back to work, he'd be content to stare at her lovely face all afternoon. Chores waited, though. He savored another spoonful.

"Thank you." Evangeline dipped her bread in the broth. "I had a visitor today."

Patrick's head popped up as he set his spoon back into his bowl. "Who was it?"

Though he worked to keep his tone casual, Brendan sensed an underlying tension. There'd been nothing amiss since they'd arrived in Park Haven. Maybe Patrick was being a bit too cautious.

"I don't know, but she came inside to chat for quite a while."

Brendan's heart tripped ahead with unease. "Do you think allowing her in was the best course of action?"

Evangeline's hand over his was warm and steady. Not a single sign of nerves. She'd deemed her visitor a non-threat and acted in accordance with that assessment. Though everything worked out fine this time, a serious talk about her safety was in order. He'd seen too much in his brief years to discount the possibility of those who might want to do them harm.

"Believe me, when she first knocked, I thought my heart would pound out of my chest. I found the entire visit exceedingly odd, but I didn't get a sense the woman was a menace." She turned to Patrick. "And she knows you. She said she and some man named Arthur 'took you under their wing' when you first arrived."

A rush of breath escaped Patrick's lips. "Arthur and Beatrice Smithfield. Of course, I know them. Perfectly harmless, though as you said, exceedingly odd when it comes to societal norms. It doesn't surprise me at all that she spent the entire visit and never gave you her name. Wouldn't even have crossed her mind."

Brendan's gaze bounced between them. A frown formed and he did nothing to curb its appearance. "It's wonderful that Beatrice is harmless, and I'm glad you had the opportunity to meet one of the neighbors. But what about Arthur? What if he dropped by when you were by yourself?"

"Arthur wouldn't be an issue." Patrick stood with his cup and went to the stove to refill his coffee. "You met him at church on Sunday. Elderly man who could barely look you in the eye because he's so bent with age. Took him a good five minutes to make it from the back pew to the bottom steps outside, and not because he stopped for chit-chat."

Brendan nodded. "Yes. I remember him. I would still feel better if the door remained locked while we're out. You can't account for everyone in the area. What if an unfriendly transient passed through?"

A wistful smile played with the corners of Evangeline's lips.

"I am relieved you see reason in this case."

The smile faded. "Oh, no. I don't agree in the slightest. I will concede to trying to look out the window before I open the door, but I will not be unneighborly without threat or reason."

"But you were smiling?"

"I thought you rather gallant in your attempts to protect me." Her cheeks pinked. "My own private hero determined to see me safe."

"This isn't a laughing matter, Evangeline."

She patted his hand. Unwilling to give, he pulled away from her touch. He couldn't allow her to soften him, not about her well-being. A huff escaped her as she stared at him.

"No. It isn't funny." She crossed her arms in front of her chest. "But I'm safe enough to be left here alone while you work at the chapel. Safe enough to do the laundry or whatever other chores need doing. And I'm safe enough to walk your dinner to you whenever you decide against taking a real break and coming back to the cabin."

She pushed back from the table and practically stomped to the counter. Pulling a knife from the drawer, Evangeline proceeded to cut the cooled pie with more force than necessary. Once she plated three slices, she dropped the knife in the wash bin, picked up all three plates with more balance than a person should possess, marched back to the table, and placed dessert before each of them. Resuming her seat, she took a bite.

"If I'm safe enough for all of these activities, I'm safe enough to know when to open the door and when to bar it shut."

Brendan glanced at Patrick. He needed support in this battle. The older man kept focused on his plate.

"Please, Uncle Patrick. Tell Evangeline I'm right."

"Clarity of motives often cuts the path to the perfect compromise."

Brendan rolled his eyes along with his head. "Isn't that just the bee's knees? We're having a serious conversation, and your only addition is an old Irish phrase."

"I believe," Evangeline interjected with a saucy tilt of her head, "that one is a Patrick Dunne original."

Perfect. Now they were working together against him. His shoulders drooped. Maybe he deserved a little bit of it though, after he'd allowed the conversation to frustrate him into using the slang he believed unnecessary nonsense. Fine. He would let it go for the moment.

"Good ear, Evangeline." Patrick toasted her with a forkful of pie.

"Old or new. What exactly does it mean?" He trained his attention on his uncle. "In plain English, please."

Patrick swallowed his pie and took a slow sip of coffee. "Well, lad, it means you both need to listen to the other." He pointed the fork at Brendan. "You can claim your leadership as the husband and demand the door stay locked. And Evangeline will do your bidding, but she will resent it."

The fork swung Evangeline's direction. "You can passionately fight and argue with the idea. But Brendan's bull-headed side will come to the fore. You'll eventually agree to follow, but you'll have lost a measure of respect as a level-headed and capable woman in letting your untethered emotions take the stage."

Evangeline frowned. "What do we do instead?'

"I'm glad you asked." Patrick leaned back in his seat, threading his fingers together behind his head. "The answer is to lay down your desire to be you and learn to work together as one."

Brendan laid his fork on his now empty plate. "I'm not entirely sure what you mean."

"I'm not married. Never have been." Patrick's smile included both Evangeline and Brendan. "But I've known many friendships and opportunities to work together with others. It's taught me a thing or two."

"Before you go on. Let me get these out of the way." Evangeline collected the empty plates and deposited them in the wash bin.

Brendan took the pause in conversation to refill his cup and Patrick's. Once everyone was reseated, Patrick continued.

"We've a perfect example right under our roof. Brendan and I are working together to hang the windows at the chapel. I couldn't do it on my own. Lifting, holding, and setting require more than two arms can handle. For the window to be properly secured, we have to work together as one."

"But you've told me what to do all week." Brendan splayed his hands in front of him on the table. "I simply follow your instructions."

Patrick nodded. "That is true. But why?"

"I guess because I've never hung a window and don't know how."

"Exactly!" Patrick's palm smacked the table. "In this instance, I have the knowledge and we both have the ability. But what if we were to work on your car. How would that change?"

Brendan smiled. "I'd have the knowledge, and we'd both have the ability. I'd lead the way."

"And I'd follow your lead. In marriage, God's word tells us the man is to be the head of the family. However, a wise man understands God's given him his wife as a complement and will value her knowledge and abilities as much as his own. There will be times when what she knows makes her advice the wiser option. Other times, his ideas on a matter would carry more weight."

"And in times like these?" Evangeline shifted her locket back and forth across its chain. "Am I to simply follow along when I'm not in agreement?"

"That's a bit more difficult." Patrick pursed his lips. "But you can still work together as one, even in these issues. By openly discussing your sides, the motives of both of you become clear. Brendan isn't trying to control you. It's his desire to keep you safe. And Evangeline isn't trying to be difficult or headstrong. She wants to be neighborly and helpful both to our household and others."

Brendan sighed. "We still don't have an answer for this situation."

"No. But it does give you a starting point. You're on the same side. Together, you can come up with a solution that best answers the needs of keeping Evangeline safe for Brendan's peace of mind and still allows Evangeline to be a productive member of the family and a caring neighbor as she wants to do."

"It does make sense." Evangeline glanced his way with a tentative smile.

Brendan nodded. "I think we can work with that."

"Good." Patrick stood. "I'm going to go check on the livestock and give you time to find your compromise."

As the door shut, Brendan gave his full attention to Evangeline. "Please, tell me what you want out of this situation. I'm ready to listen."

Chapter Thirty-One

"Brendan says you're joining us today." Patrick buttoned his heavy coat.

Evangeline swept the broom across the floor one last time before returning it to its spot in the corner. "Did you think I would miss the hanging of the stained-glass window? I want to be the first to see it with light streaming through."

"Of course, you do." Brendan laughed. "It's all you've talked about since Patrick let you take a peek under that pile of blankets."

Evangeline raised her chin. "It seems only fitting. It's the last piece of the chapel. Now, we'll all enjoy a fresh start, and it's just in time to hold a Christmas service."

Patrick moved out of the way so she and Brendan could put on their coats. In minutes, they were out the door and marching down the well-worn path through the barren woods toward the chapel. Their laughter-studded conversation echoed through the trees.

Evangeline rubbed her mittened hands together. Cold enough for her to catch her death, but still no snow. Disappointment dampened her spirits. Christmas and snow were like watermelon and summer. It didn't seem like one without the other.

She scanned the sky looking for hope, and there was no Christmas star shining overhead offering that. With Christmas Eve on Sunday, the good Lord had four more days to order the proper weather. She would even settle for Christmas Day, so long as she had a white one.

"Come on slow poke." Brendan glanced back at her from where he and Patrick walked ahead and waved her forward. "We'll never get that window hung with you lagging behind."

Evangeline skipped ahead. Snow or not, the day was beautiful, and the stained-glass window waited. Threading her arms through Patrick's on one side and Brendan's on the other, Evangeline's spirit was lighter than it had been in ages.

A song of praise filled her heart and overflowed from her lips as they walked. Patrick soon joined in. While Brendan refrained from singing, she did catch him quietly humming along with the tune. It was a good day, indeed. Maybe she didn't need snow on Christmas after all. Of course, it would still be a nice surprise.

Evangeline ran her hand over the gold knot pattern edging the window. "This is lovely. I can't believe little shards of glass can come together to make something as beautiful as this. It's a work of art."

"That it is." Patrick wiped grime from his hands and joined her beside the window. "And it's not just a fancy decoration. It means something too. Take that cross. Many think it predates Christianity in Ireland and was used in worship of nature and the pagan sun god."

Evangeline's hand flew to cover her mouth. "Oh, that's horrible. Why would a Christian use the image if it meant something ungodly?"

"The story says early Irish monks used the image of the circle to represent Christ's halo or his status as God in explaining the Trinity to those who'd been involved in pagan worship. One legend says Saint Patrick brought the Celtic cross to Ireland. Regardless of where it originated, believers, mostly the monks, began using it to reach the lost in Ireland. Often, carved crosses included scenes from the life of Christ in the design."

"It's a great picture of redemption." Brendan gazed up at the cross from where he gathered the tools needed to install the window. "God takes the lost, person or Celtic cross, and gives it new purpose for Him."

Patrick pointed to the knotted design. "And that edging you're so drawn to is called the sailor's knot.'

"Hmm." Evangeline studied the shape. "It's a fitting name. The rise and fall of the knots evoke thoughts of ripples along the water."

"The one at the top is the Trinity knot."

"I can see why." Evangeline nodded. The odd flower's design made more sense when paired with its name. "And do these patterns carry special meaning as well?"

Patrick clapped a hand across Brendan's shoulder. "You've found yourself a wife as intelligent and inquisitive as she is lovely, my lad."

"That I have."

Brendan's appreciative smile filled Evangeline's cheeks with heat. Unsure how to respond to the pleasure welling up inside, she turned her attention back to the window. "I suppose that means the sailor's knot and Trinity knot are associated with specific themes?"

"Yes. They are." Patrick ran a finger along the sailor's knot. "This one is two ropes twined together and though it's one of the simplest knots, it has great strength. It's said to represent love and harmony."

He pointed to the Trinity knot. "Like the Celtic cross design, the Trinity knot is said to have pagan roots related to the worship of their false gods. But, again, Christians recognized the benefit of using the design to explain the Father, Son, and Holy Ghost. An image the pagans already understood helped ease the transition to faith in the one true God."

"Why would the designer of the window choose these two types of knots? Why not simply choose one?"

Patrick shrugged. "I can't say for sure since I never met the man. But I like to think it was purposeful." He retrieved a large Bible from a nearby table and flipped through its pages. "When I look at this design, I can't help thinking about Ecclesiastes. In chapter four, several verses list the benefits of unity. Starting in verse nine, the passage reads, 'Two are better than one; because they have a good reward for their labour. For if they fall, the one will lift up his fellow: but woe to him that is alone when he falleth; for he hath not another to help him up. Again, if two lie together, then they have heat: but how can one be warm alone? And if one prevail against him, two shall withstand him; and a threefold cord is not quickly broken.'"

"We need each other." Evangeline reasoned. "And together we need the Trinity."

Brendan nodded. "It's a picture of how God's people are supposed to work together."

"My thought exactly." Patrick rejoined them. "But it's deeper too."

"How so?" Brendan frowned.

"I think it speaks to more than friend and church relationships. It's a lesson for those, yes, but also for marriages. Genesis tells us when a man and woman marry, they leave their families to become one, like the sailor's knot. Two ropes, beautifully twined together for strength. However, the man and woman aren't the only ones in the marriage. God desires a position at the head of every marriage. Faith, God's leadership, is essential to create a strong union to weather life's stormy seas."

"That's a lovely thought."

Brendan nodded. "I don't know that I would've ever considered it, but it makes too much sense to ignore."

"Yes." Patrick chuckled. "And now that you've endured my

spontaneous sermonizing, it's high time we got this window installed."

Evangeline stepped from the stage. "I'll sit over here, out of the way."

The men went through their tools and supplies to confirm everything they needed was close at hand. While Patrick explained the process step-by-step to Brendan and double checked their measurements, Evangeline mulled over Patrick's words.

She rubbed the pendant around her neck between her fingers. What did Patrick say? They leave their parents and become one. Physically staying with her parents had not been an option. The moment their vows were said, Evangeline was packed into the automobile and driven hours away. But had she become one with her husband?

They'd only shared a kiss. That was hardly becoming one. To truly join with her husband would mean, well ... Heat surged up her neck into her face. It was forward to think such things, but Brendan was her husband.

Glancing up at him, she smiled. He brushed a hand through his hair as he listened to Patrick's instructions. She remembered how soft those locks were. She'd run her fingers though them once. But his hair was coarse in comparison to the softness of his lips against hers. Desire sparked inside. It wouldn't be a chore to become one with him in that way, no matter how her cheeks warmed at the thought.

Even sharing such intimacies wouldn't complete their oneness though. What Patrick spoke of went beyond the physical to a sharing of ideas, giving each other the first place after God in their lives, and being united in all areas of life.

How many times had she already failed? In considering what her parents might think above working to strengthen her bond with Brendan, she'd given them the honored place they always held. She had refused to leave them and join to her husband.

Brendan and Patrick hoisted the window. Moving with great care, they inched their way to the opening.

Pride rushed through Evangeline at the selfless way Brendan protected her from the dangers at home. No—in Harrisburg. Here with Brendan in Park Haven was home.

And now, he worked beside Patrick each day learning a new way of life to provide for them. It couldn't be easy walking away from everything he'd known, even if he didn't agree with his father's way of life. Yet he did it. For her.

"Wait." Evangeline jumped up from the pew and rushed up to the stage. "Don't set the window just yet."

"Is something wrong?" Brendan grunted as he gingerly set his side of the window down in time with Patrick.

"We need to do something first." She turned and held up her hair with one hand. "Would you please undo the clasp of my necklace?"

"I guess so." Confusion laced his words, but Brendan did as she asked and then handed her the locket.

Evangeline dangled it in front of her. "This was a gift from my parents the day I turned thirteen. It holds a picture of my parents on one side and my photo on the other."

"It's very pretty." Brendan ran a hand through his hair. "But why are we discussing this now?"

She clasped his hands in her own and dropped the necklace into them. "Because I want to give it to you."

"I think it would look better on you."

"No." Evangeline laughed at his face, scrunched in confusion. "Not literally. Figuratively. Through the years, this pendant has come to represent everything my family, my mother and my father, mean to me. They've been my providers. The ones I go to for advice, and the ones who've warned me when I've gone astray. They introduced me to faith, and other than God, I've considered no one's thoughts higher than theirs."

"I suppose that's as it should be."

Keeping one hand on his, Evangeline used the other to motion toward the window. "I want what the window depicts. A marriage, not in name only and for protection alone. Coming together as one in all aspects of life, our bond strengthened by our shared faith and looking to God to lead our home."

"And I can't do that," Evangeline held up the locket once more, "while holding on to this. While looking to my parents instead of looking to you, my husband. I want to give you the place you deserve in my heart."

Brendan stared through her, his expression lacking both smile and frown. Evangeline tucked her bottom lip between her teeth. Had she erred in being so bold, so forward? When he turned and plodded to one of the windows closest to the stage without a word, fear gripped her lungs, holding her breath captive.

Tears filled her eyes, though she refused to let them fall. Evangeline turned to Patrick whose expression warned of his own emotional battle. Shame pushed her tears from their hiding place. Shaking his head, Patrick stepped toward her with arms open. Evangeline stepped into them accepting the support they offered.

"Shh," Patrick whispered close to her ear. "It's going to work out. Just wait."

Evangeline moved away from his embrace and wiped her eyes. Movement by the window drew her attention. Brendan strode to join them. Unsure what to expect, Evangeline straightened her shoulders, bracing herself for the worst.

"Please." Brendan stood in front of her but didn't touch her. "Forgive me."

Evangeline swallowed. "For what?"

"When you shared just now, it cut me to the quick. You want a real, God-honoring marriage with me, and I failed to provide you with the opportunity."

"You didn't know."

He shook his head. "No. But ignorance doesn't excuse me letting my pride get in the way of fully committing to you and our marriage."

"I'm afraid I don't understand."

His hand clasped hers. Leading her to the nearest pew, he sat and patted the seat beside him. She joined him. Without a word, Patrick hustled past them and out the door, giving them privacy.

"When James and Dot were killed, I didn't hesitate to marry you. I was already falling in love with you, though I didn't stop long enough to consider that then. My feelings have only intensified over the last few weeks, but still I wrestled with the idea you were stuck with me due to circumstances."

"Please, I never felt stuck."

"I know you don't. But in my mind, I determined you would someday. You and I grew up with so many modern conveniences. Automobiles, shops within walking distance, cooks and maids, indoor plumbing. Now, we have none of those conveniences."

She covered his hand with her own. "I don't need any of those things."

"I know, but I wanted you to have them. I wanted to provide them for you. I'm ashamed to say, I found myself contemplating if there was any way I could go back to my father, provide all the things you deserve, and still stay morally clean."

"You would go back to that life? After it took Dot and James? Knowing how wrong and dangerous it is?"

His hand slipped out from under hers. Rubbing his face, Brendan groaned. "No. That's just it. I couldn't do that no matter what my father could provide us. But I felt like I was cheating you with my refusal."

"Oh, Brendan."

He stood and peered down at her. "Evangeline, I don't have anything to offer you beyond my name. I don't know a trade to provide for us. All I can promise you is I'll strive to be the man of God you deserve as a husband and trust Him to provide everything else. Is that enough?"

A weight lifted from Evangeline with his words. They both came with nothing to offer but themselves, and with God it would be more than enough.

"Yes, Brendan. I would love nothing more than to truly be your wife from today until death parts us."

A giggle escaped as Brendan pulled her to her feet and straight into his embrace. He lifted her from the ground and swung her around. If his action hadn't already left her breathless, the kiss he gave her would have. Passion, hope, and love collided together in a kiss more beautiful than the ones they'd shared before.

As Brendan stepped away from her, he dug in his pocket. He dangled his watch before her. "You gave me your locket and in doing so, your promise to let me be your family. Let me do the same for you. All my father and his lifestyle can give us is contained in this timepiece. It's a reminder that the family way, his way, always comes first. But no more. You are my first and only, other than God."

Evangeline extended her hand. The metal was cool and smooth against her palm. She glanced toward the stained-glass window. Its beauty magnified by the vows it had evoked in them. And it would serve as a reminder every day they spent in this building.

"Brendan, I've a wonderful idea." Evangeline grabbed his arms in her excitement. "Let's leave them here."

"What?"

She held up his watch. "Let's leave our parents, their expectations, and their dreams for us where they belong."

"Where is that?"

"Right there." She pointed to the hole in the wall. "We leave them at the cross. They will always be family, but now is our time to become one. To be a three-fold cord that can't be broken. Your watch and my necklace can rest here forever along with our desires to please our families instead of each other."

Brendan stared at the wall. Slowly, a smile curved his lips. He hurried to the worktable and sifted through the items on it. Evangeline could only watch the strange behavior. In seconds, he emptied nails into a bucket and returned to her. In one hand he held her locket and a pencil. In the other, a small cardboard nail box.

"This will be perfect." His announcement made little sense. "Give me a moment."

He opened the box and scribbled something inside the lid. Turning it toward her, Evangeline read the message. *A three-fold cord, forever strong*. His initials followed. Snatching the box and pencil from him, Evangeline added her own monogram, pausing only a moment before she added the *D* in flowing script. *EGD*. Before, she'd imagined changing names would seem odd. It didn't. Nothing could be more right.

She deposited his watch into the box. Brendan added the necklace before closing the lid and handing it to Evangeline.

Together, they stood before the hole where the stained-glass window would soon reside. Evangeline sent up a silent prayer. The pressure of Brendan's hand as he squeezed hers told her he did the same.

"This is it." Evangeline glanced at him. "This is our opportunity to make something special of this marriage. Are you ready to leave these distractions behind?"

Another squeeze of her hand. "I'm ready to devote myself to you and our marriage for the rest of our lives."

"Together, then?"

"Together."

Chapter Thirty-Two

L ight streamed through the window casting colors across the sanctuary. Never mind that Christmas Eve arrived on a Friday and without the herald of snow. The day was perfect for a celebratory service, and the array of colors streaming through the glass brought enough beauty to satisfy as Patrick led the congregation in song.

"A thrill of hope, the weary world rejoices." Evangeline sang out with abandon feeling the message. "For yonder breaks a new and glorious morn."

It was indeed a glorious morn. Then and now. The savior's birth. The hope of the cross. The best reason to rejoice made even sweeter knowing she was celebrating it with her husband. Brendan caught her eye, and she smiled at him as she continued singing. Glancing around the room, she recognized several faces from the chapel's first service.

Her smile grew when she spied Arthur with Beatrice leaning on his arm across the aisle. The woman glanced her direction and gave a little wave. Evangeline returned it. Their closest neighbors were such an interesting pair but caring to a fault. They'd ventured out in the cold the day before to deliver a fresh baked loaf of bread to the cabin for Christmas. Evangeline could just see the handle of the basket of cookies she'd baked and given them this morning.

The carol ended, and everyone took their seats. Evangeline did her best to attend to the message Patrick delivered though she found her thoughts wandering a few times. At each occurrence, she turned her musings into a prayer of praise before returning to the sermon.

"What is taking him so long?"

Evangeline's question reached Brendan on the other side of the cabin door. He smiled at his wife's impatience. She'd been a bundle of energy since arriving home after church. While he and Patrick appreciated their noon meal to the fullest, Evangeline had scarcely eaten a thing so excited was she to tromp through the woods and chop down the perfect Christmas tree. She'd hovered behind them as they secured it in the metal stand and made sure it was level.

He shook his head. The pungent smell of burned popcorn still lingered. Even on the porch, he caught the hint of it. The treat they were to string for garland wasn't popping quickly enough, and she'd added more wood to the stove. After windows and doors were propped open and the offensive contents of the pan dumped out by the outhouse, Patrick jokingly forbade her from touching the stove again in her excited condition. Instead, he popped the new batch of corn.

With much laughter and even a few kernels of popcorn sneaked into their mouths, the tree stood draped in a garland of white. Sprigs of holly tucked into the branches added a pop of color along with the simple red bows Evangeline tied at the end of a few branches. It wasn't the tree, decorated with store-bought decorations Evangeline's parents put up each year, but she was delighted with it. And his surprise would only make it better. He hoped.

"I'm right here." Brendan swung the door open. "You are so impatient today."

She rolled her eyes at him. "Well, you left us waiting for an impossibly long time while you ran to the barn. Isn't that right, Patrick?"

Patrick raised his hands in surrender. "I'm not getting in the middle of this."

Lips flat, her eyes narrowed. She wouldn't say it, but *traitor* ran through her mind. Nothing would convince Brendan otherwise. Holding the retrieved package behind his back while he removed his winter coat proved awkward. Unbuttoning it was difficult enough. Trying to shimmy out of one sleeve with the other pressed against his back was next to impossible.

"I can hold whatever you're hiding behind your back," Evangeline stepped closer, "while you slip out of your coat."

Brendan wasn't fooled by her beautiful smile or rendered powerless by her innocent eyes with their batting lashes. "Not a chance. You'll not touch your present until it's time to open it."

"It's a present? For me?" Evangeline clasped her hands in front of her and practically hopped up and down with excitement.

Lord, thank you for blessing me with this delightful woman as my wife. One minute mature and proper, the next filled with childlike wonder and excitement. Her enthusiasm drew out his own.

Finally, his arm slipped from the sleeve holding it captive. Freeing the other one was much easier. As soon as his coat fell to the floor, Evangeline snatched it up.

"Here." She hung it on the nearest coat peg. "Let me get that for you."

Brendan laughed. "You don't fool me, you know. You're only being helpful because you want to see what I'm hiding."

Patrick leaned against the doorway between the kitchen and living room. "You should put the lass out of her misery, Brendan.

She's been buzzing worse than a bee in summer since you left to go to the barn."

"Humph." Evangeline crossed her arms, lips jutted out in a pout. "You men just don't understand. Christmas and gifts and such are supposed to create excitement."

"I think you've got enough excitement for all of us." Brendan kissed her cheek.

That chaste kiss brought rose to her cheeks as she stole a glance in Patrick's direction. The older man ignored the gesture, bless him, and the extra color faded. Someday soon, maybe they could have a space of their own where he could freely kiss his wife as passionately as he wanted without fear of someone walking in. Of course, at the present such action would surprise his wife as much as an onlooker, but that was changing since they placed their family reminders under the stained-glass cross.

"Fine." He took pity on her. "Go sit down in the rocking chair by the tree, and you can have your surprise."

Her eyes widened. "Tonight? On Christmas Eve? I don't have to wait?"

"No. This gift is one better suited to opening early."

Patrick barely managed to clear the doorway before she rushed past. It was a wonder she didn't knock into him on her way through. Brendan followed at a more acceptable pace, though her excitement was rubbing off on him. Imagining her reaction to the present stoked his anticipation of seeing her open it.

Upon entering the room, she'd taken a seat on the sofa. Brendan smiled. She perched at the edge of the cushion, back straight, feet crossed at the ankle, her hands resting on each other in her lap. The idea to tease her flitted through his mind, but he dismissed it. It would be cruel to dangle the gift in front of her only to whisk it away in jest.

Brendan took the box from behind his back. If possible, Evangeline's eyes brightened on seeing the gift wrapped in brown paper. At least he'd taken the time to purchase a length of festive red ribbon to tie around it and found a sprig of holly in the woods to tuck under the simple bow. Her hands shot out to retrieve the present from him as soon as he offered it.

Even in her excitement, Evangeline carefully removed the greenery and bow. Making sure the paper remained as tear and wrinkle free as possible, she unwrapped the gift. Her mouth opened into an adorable *O* at the snowflakes pictured on the outside of the cardboard packaging. She slowly lifted the lid.

"These are beautiful." She pulled out a single ornament. The snowflake crafted from silver tinsel and accented with a single pearl-like bauble in the middle evoked a sigh from Evangeline.

"The box contains two dozen snowflakes." Brendan pointed to the description on the lid. "I wanted to guarantee you enjoyed a white Christmas every year."

"Oh, Brendan. It's perfect." Evangeline bit her bottom lip as she ran her hand over the ornaments with near reverence.

Tears were close to the surface. Brendan would bet his life on it. They'd be happy ones, though. This was a celebration.

"Now you have a choice to make." He shifted the focus of the room just enough to ease the emotion.

"And what's that?"

Brendan nodded to Patrick. "Do we get to help place them on the tree, or are you going to hoard all the fun for yourself?"

"As much as I'd enjoy prolonging the fun, it will be greater fun if we do it together." Evangeline offered a snowflake each to Brendan and Patrick before placing the box on the sofa cushion. "But I get to hang the first one."

With three of them decorating together, finishing the tree took only a few minutes. Brendan would have been content taking all night if it meant seeing the joy on Evangeline's face. Settling at one end of the couch, Brendan draped his arm across the back. Evangeline dropped onto the seat next to him and leaned back against him.

He stilled, except for his heart beating a wild rhythm at the pleasant surprise of her nearness. Since their decision to commit to each other alone, they'd enjoyed more handholding and stolen kisses. Still, everyday closeness and comfort in each other's touch eluded them.

While Evangeline's gaze was focused on the tree, Patrick's was trained on them with a satisfied smile. Apparently, he didn't find Evangeline's seating choice improper. That was good, because asking her to move was the last thing Brendan wanted.

Patrick stood. "As much as I'd like to sit here enjoying the tree and company, I believe a fox has been stalking the chickens. I need to check the coop one last time. Make sure everything is locked up tight. Might need to check on the livestock in the barn while I'm at it. Can't be too careful."

"Don't stay out there too long." Evangeline spoke from her place next to Brendan. "We wouldn't want you to catch cold right here at Christmas."

God bless his uncle. It was an excuse. They completed all those chores before supper. Since she'd been occupied with preparations for the meal, Evangeline was none the wiser.

"It's a beautiful tree. Don't you agree?" Evangeline snuggled deeper against his chest.

Brendan's only thoughts were for the warmth his wife created as she lounged against his side and the pleasure her closeness brought. But the tree was important to her so he glanced at it again. "It's absolutely perfect."

The silver tinsel sparkled in the light from the oil lamps positioned throughout the room. Candles fixed to the ends of the branches would increase the glistening effect, but the small tree took up a large portion of the already small room. Adding candles brought a fire hazard they all agreed was unwise.

"Maybe a trifle large for the room."

"True." Evangeline sat up, angling to face him. "In case I forgot to tell you, thank you for my present. I don't know if I've ever received one so thoughtful."

The tenderness in her eyes captivated him. Weaving his fingers through her hair, he cupped the back of her head with his hand

and gently pulled her toward him. As she wound her arms around his neck, their lips and bodies met in unison.

More intimate than their previous kisses, Brendan's desire for his wife pulsed through him. After tasting her lips, he kissed the spot at the very corner of her mouth before creating a trail across her cheek and ending at the soft curve where her jaw and neck met. Her soft moan of pleasure transformed the steady waves of desire into the crashing waves of a storm-tossed lake.

They were alone. They were husband and wife. There was no wrong in enjoying each other. Still, Brendan leaned away as far as the couch cushions allowed and loosed his hold on her, setting her right again. Though allowable, the time wasn't right.

"I'm glad you like your gift." The words came out in a hoarse whisper.

Evangeline's coy smile tempted him to abandon his conviction. When he might have given in, she turned back to the tree and settled under his arm once more. The silence surrounding them offered no angst, only contentedness.

"You might be right." Evangeline held the hand draped around her shoulders. "Even this little tree is too big for the space we have. The three of us can barely find enough room without the tree, though I hope I don't sound ungrateful. I didn't mean it that way in the slightest. I'm terribly appreciative of Patrick's willingness to take us in."

"I didn't take it that way at all." He squeezed her hand. "It's true. We're very blessed the cabin had two bedrooms, or Patrick and I would've spent the last several weeks on the floor. But the cabin wasn't built with three people in mind."

"If we're going to stay indefinitely, maybe we could speak with Patrick about adding an addition to the cabin."

Brendan lifted his free hand from the arm of the couch and rested his chin in it. "Hmm. Another idea might be asking permission to build a house on the land. There's enough space north of the barn before you reach the woods, and it would still leave the grazing area to the south for the animals."

"Would this house be a real, traditional farmhouse? Painted white? With two stories?"

"If you want two stories, it will have two stories painted whatever color you like. What about a porch with a pretty little hanging swing?"

Evangeline sat up, clasping her hands together at her chest. "Oh, a swing would be perfect. Can we have a porch that wraps around at least two sides of the house?"

"I'll wrap it around all four, if it makes you happy." Brendan chuckled at her excitement. "And we'll even add a bathroom off the kitchen and add indoor plumbing as soon as it's available out this far."

"Do you think plumbing will be available soon?"

He shook his head. "Probably not for a while. But we'll be ready for it. Now, how many bedrooms do you want?"

"I think we should have three, anyway. Our children can share, and if visitors come, there would still be room. The extra room would allow our guests or children to avoid sleeping on a couch or pallet on the floor."

Children. Evangeline wanted children with him. They'd not spoken of such intimate issues before, and since they'd yet to spend a night together as husband and wife, he'd not been comfortable broaching the subject.

With this further confirmation of her wish to enjoy a real marriage relationship came the assurance he needed his Christmas plans were well laid. Not much longer, and they'd be free to show their desire for each other without hesitation. The closeness of a couple sharing everything would be theirs, and they could turn their dreams of a house into a very real home.

Those days couldn't arrive swiftly enough for Brendan.

Chapter Thirty-Three

T he aroma of freshly brewed coffee and maple syrup warming on the stove pulled Evangeline from sleep. She burrowed deeper into her pillow and blankets, enjoying the scents. What a way to start Christmas morning.

Her eyes popped open. Throwing back the covers, she sprang from the warmth of the bed. Christmas arrived, and she was lazing in bed. Shame on her. There were gifts to give and praise to offer up, all in honor of the Christ-child's birth.

Rushing through her morning routine, Evangeline dressed in record time and retrieved the gifts she'd hidden in the dresser drawer. She hurried straight from the bedroom to the living room and deposited the gifts under the tree. A few others rested below the branches that had not been there the previous night. Fighting the temptation to steal a glance, she instead focused on the silver ornaments dangling from the limbs.

Warmth filled her. Thanks to Brendan's gesture, she would always have a white Christmas. Technically, it might be more silver than white, but it didn't matter. It meant the world to her.

"I thought someone raced through a moment ago." Patrick stood in the doorway. "Admiring the tree? Well, breakfast is ready. Let's eat and then we can exchange gifts."

"You don't have to tell me twice. I love giving gifts."

Patrick winked. "And unless I misread your excitement last night, you're not opposed to receiving them either."

"No." Evangeline laughed. "I might enjoy that a bit too."

Conversation flowed freely as the trio sat around the table filling up on pancakes, bacon, and coffee. Evangeline licked a spot of sticky, warm syrup from her lips. Paired with the salty bacon, nothing could have improved the meal. When everyone had eaten their fill, they cleaned up and moved to the living room.

"I hope you don't mind." Patrick reached for his Bible on the end table. "But I like to begin my Christmas celebrations with the Christmas story."

"Please do." Brendan pulled Evangeline closer to him on the couch. "I can't think of a more fitting start to the celebration of His birth."

Patrick read from Luke chapter two. While it didn't include the wise men's visit as Matthew did, Evangeline found herself drawn to the story of the shepherds. Everyday people called to worship by the Savior.

Not judges, like her father. Not powerful people, like Brendan's father or those in Harrisburg who made their own laws. Instead, God used a sky full of angels to announce His Son's birth to those whose station in life was more in tune with Patrick or Beatrice and Arthur. Humble lives no one else noticed.

Or Dot, who wanted love so badly she remade herself into whatever she thought would make that happen.

If God took notice of the shepherds and reached out to them in love, couldn't He have done the same in Dot's final moments?

Assurance of Dot's eternal fate would never belong to Evangeline. However, the shepherds proved a love that reaches out to the Dots of the world. God was present in Dot's field of death. Believing this, Evangeline held hope that God might have reached out personally, like he did to the shepherds, to offer one last opportunity to know the Christ child, her Savior.

As Patrick finished the reading and led them in prayer,

Evangeline wiped tears from her cheeks. Never had the story of Jesus's birth resonated so personally. *Thank you, Father, for using the story I've known and believed all my life to confirm your love for those I love. I am seen and loved by You. Thank you for Your Son.*

"Are you all right?" Brendan's whispered words tickled her ear.

She nodded. "I'm fine. Simply realizing how much we're loved and seen by God."

"Joy to the world, the Lord is come." Patrick's rich voice filled the small room.

Evangeline joined the praise without hesitation. Humming at first, Brendan soon added his voice to the song. They might not rival the voices of the angels on the hillside in perfect harmony, but their praise was true. Evangeline didn't doubt God considered it beautiful.

"This is Christmas." Patrick set his Bible on the side table. "And I'm blessed for you to share it with me this year. It's been ages since I've celebrated with family."

"It's a blessing for us as well." Brendan voiced the sentiment residing in her heart.

Patrick rose from the chair and knelt before the Christmas tree. "And now, it's time for gifts."

He chose a large box from the small assortment, glanced at the tag, and held it out to Evangeline. Lighter than she expected.

"I get to open the first one?"

"Patrick and I discussed it while you slept away the morning." Brendan pointed between the two of them. "After last night, we figured if we made you wait, you were likely to burst from excitement. We couldn't chance that on Christmas Day, now, could we?"

Evangeline swatted his arm and glared between the two. She lifted her chin. "Fine. Whatever the reason, I get to open a present. So, that's perfectly fine with me." She read the tag. "Thank you, Patrick."

"You haven't opened it yet."

Evangeline grinned and untied the ribbon. Once she removed the paper, she lifted the lid on the plain box. A pair of leather boots nestled inside. Unlike her other shoes and boots, these didn't have the heel women's shoes generally sported. And their form lacked the decorative touches she was used to.

"They're men's boots, boy's actually." Patrick shrugged. "I know you have several pairs of shoes and boots, but I thought these might be of more use to you in the garden and the barnyard. Sturdy, warm, and not easily ruined by mud or snow."

"They're perfect." Evangeline ran her hand over the brown leather. "Thank you. I can't tell you how awkward it is working in shoes with heels all the time. These are wonderful." She pointed to a flat package. "Please, open mine next."

Patrick plucked the present from among the rest and made short work of the bow and paper. "This is beautiful." Patrick lifted the green scarf from the box. "Did you knit this?"

"Yes." Evangeline beamed with the praise. "But keep looking. There's another small surprise in the box."

Patrick set the scarf across his lap and reached back in the box to withdraw a small rectangle of material. Evangeline bit her lip.

"It's a bookmark for your Bible." She couldn't wait for his response before explaining.

Patrick cleared his throat. "Bless each door that opens wide to stranger, kith and kin." His voice was hoarse with emotion as he read the line embroidered on the material. "It's perfect, lass. Part of an Irish house blessing."

"I'm sorry I couldn't fit the blessing in its entirety."

"No need for apology." He ran his fingers over her work. "As I said, it's perfect." Another clearing of his throat. "And now, it's Brendan's turn for a gift."

Instead of a package, Patrick picked an envelope from the branches of the tree and passed it to Brendan.

"From Uncle Patrick." Brendan announced as he opened the seal.

Brendan stared at the missive in silence. Though she angled

her neck closer, Evangeline still couldn't make out what the note said. Brendan licked his lips and rubbed them together. Finally, he glanced toward Patrick.

"I don't know what to say." He slid the note back inside the envelope. "Thank you doesn't seem enough."

"A thank you is more than enough." Patrick smiled. "I'm blessed to be able to do it, as much as I'm blessed to have you and Evangeline near."

Brendan passed the envelope to her. "It's for you too. The field to the north of the barn is unused. He gave it to us to build our own home."

Evangeline's hand flew to her mouth. Such an extravagant gift. "Are you certain, Patrick?"

"Yes." He nodded. "No need to feel pressure. If you're not set on staying in the area permanently, I understand. If you are, the land is yours. I built this cabin for one, and it serves me well. But it's not ideal for growing a family."

Permanent? Chicago was out of the question due to Brendan's family, but once the gangs in southern Illinois were dealt with, couldn't they return to Harrisburg? They'd discussed building a house. And though they'd discussed the possibility of building on Patrick's land, they'd never committed to staying.

"I appreciate your offer, Uncle. Evangeline and I should discuss our options before deciding for sure. Her hometown may be safe tomorrow, or it could be years from now. I feel we should still consider our choices together before undertaking such a big change."

That was all Evangeline needed. Assurance her wishes mattered to her husband. She handed the envelope back to him.

"I think taking Patrick up on his offer is the right thing to do." She offered a smile of reassurance. "We're settling in nicely here. And we don't know that Harrisburg will ever be safe. If it is, we'll enjoy visits with my family. If you're favorable to it, I say we make Park Haven our home."

Brendan turned to Patrick. "Seems I was wrong. There's no need for discussion. We're settling here in Park Haven."

"Good." Patrick smacked his hands down on his knees. "With that settled, I have another matter for you to consider before we continue our gift giving."

What more could Patrick give them? He'd already supplied the land they needed for the home they'd started dreaming of the prior evening. Patrick's excitement played across his features.

"Thomas Morgan is the local carpenter. He's getting up in years, and his only son moved away to become a lawyer down in Nashville. He's got no one to teach the trade, and he's open to taking on an apprentice. He's holding the position for you, if you want it."

Brendan ran a hand through his hair. "I've never thought about carpentry before."

"This farm is a personal one. It doesn't provide enough produce to sell for income. Because of my preaching, the town's always been careful to supply anything else I need. But you and I discussed your desire to find work, and you've shown yourself a quick study as we've worked at the chapel."

"I have enjoyed the work." Brendan turned to Evangeline. "What do you think?"

Evangeline shrugged. "Carpenters are always in demand. Houses, shelves, porch swings. You name it, and a carpenter's probably had a hand in building it. If you enjoy it, I say it's honest work that will provide."

"All right, then. I'll plan on speaking with him later this week. Between now and then, I'll pray about it." Brendan pointed to another gift. "How about we get back to gift opening, and Patrick you can start with that one."

Opening the package revealed a flat black book. Patrick turned it over in his hands and ran his thumb along the embossing on the front.

"Church Record?"

Brendan nodded. "It's for the chapel. There's bound to be

weddings and births and baptisms and such through the years. This gives you a way to remember each of them. There are sections for all the special events the chapel might host."

"I never considered keeping a record. What a wonderful idea." Patrick thumbed through the pages, blank except for a few headings and lines designated for names and dates. "Thank you."

"And if you would be so kind as to pass Brendan the smaller of the two packages left, I'd appreciate it."

Evangeline couldn't wait for him to see the present she made for him. Nerves and excitement together sent her tummy topsy-turvy as he removed the paper. He lifted the scarf from the box. It was identical to Patrick's except for the color. The deep red she chose for his would highlight his blue eyes perfectly.

Brendan flung the scarf around his neck. "How do I look?"

"Handsome as usual. And a little too pleased with yourself." Playful teasing came with greater ease each day.

Brendan's attention returned to the box. He lifted one of the handkerchiefs from inside. The blue decorative monogram was the first she'd completed. He passed it to Patrick before pulling out another.

"These are all different." He examined the green one with its fancy swirls on either side of his initials. "You did an excellent job on each one."

Patrick handed back the one he'd been given. "They are beautiful. When did you find time to knit two scarves and embroider handkerchiefs?"

"I have a confession." Evangeline laughed. "I've never been an early to bed type person."

Brendan's brows dipped low. "But you've retired early every evening?"

"Exactly."

Once their laughter died down, Patrick handed the final package to Evangeline. Another gift from Brendan. She opened it, finding an ivory garment inside. Evangeline stood and lifted the material from the box. Sheer chiffon sleeves matched the ivory material draped over the dress shell. The edges of the overlay were pulled up in the middle of the front and fastened under a rose made of the same, creating a pleasing ruffle down each side and completing the slight handkerchief hem of the dress.

"This is beautiful." Evangeline examined each facet of the dress. "I'll have to save it for something special, it's such a fine gown."

She lowered the dress and found Brendan down on one knee in front of her. A gold band held between his raised thumb and forefinger shone in the room's light. Evangeline sucked in a breath.

"It pains me you weren't able to enjoy a wedding as brides often do. You didn't even receive a ring." Brendan gazed up at her. "Will you accept it now and marry me this evening beneath the stained-glass cross that means so much to both of us?"

"Oh, Brendan." Evangeline sank to the sofa, the dress still in her hands.

"Is that a yes?"

She set the dress to the side and held out her hand, fingers extended. The ring slipped perfectly onto her finger. "Yes. I would love nothing more than to marry you, again."

Chapter Thirty-Four

How and when did Brendan manage to arrange everything so perfectly? Evangeline peeked through one of the chapel windows before making her way to the porch where she would enter. All the families who attended services filled the pews. A far cry from nuptials witnessed only by her mother and the family housekeeper.

As she climbed the steps, Patrick opened the chapel door a sliver and slipped outside. He held a bouquet of holly and evergreen boughs with ivory ribbons woven throughout.

"This is for you." He offered it to her. "Keep your wrap on until you hear a knock on the door. I promise you won't wait long. Then, I've instructed one of the guests to open the door for your entrance. I'll be waiting up front with Brendan."

Evangeline nodded, hoping nothing else was expected. Emotion stole her ability to speak. Patrick's understanding smile brought the sting of tears. He wrapped her in a careful hug.

"You look beautiful, and I couldn't be prouder to have you as a niece." Patrick released her and slipped back into the building.

Evangeline closed her eyes and concentrated on breathing. Butterflies fluttered inside her stomach without mercy. The knock sounded. Evangeline removed her wrap, laying it over the porch railing to retrieve later. The door opened.

Candlelight flickered from around the edge of the chapel. Guests had supplied lanterns to line the aisle leading to Brendan and Patrick waiting at the front of the sanctuary. Evergreen boughs tied with the same ivory ribbon hung in every window, except the stained-glass one at the front. It was a work of art on its own. Like something from a child's fairy tale.

Guests stood in unison. Evangeline made her way up the aisle, not taking her eyes from Brendan, handsome in his black suit and with love shining in his eyes. Love for her. Blessed. There was no other way to describe the feeling. Truly, overflowing with God's blessing.

The exact words and prayers Patrick offered up were lost on Evangeline. So wrapped up in her husband's adoring expression. She must have answered what was required though, because in what simultaneously lasted only seconds and also an eternity, Brendan slipped the gold band back on her finger.

"You may kiss the bride."

Brendan pulled her close and kissed her with the proper kiss expected in a public display, even in a wedding. He leaned close to her ear.

"I love you, Evangeline Grace Dunne."

"And I you, Brendan Patrick Dunne."

They stood to one side of the door as their guests filed out into the night after offering their congratulations. When the last one exited, Brendan shut the door and pulled her into his arms in one move.

"And this is how I'll kiss you for the rest of our lives."

His lips against hers tasted of love and desire. If he kept his word, a day wouldn't go by that Evangeline didn't feel cherished.

A cough sounded from the front. Evangeline's cheeks heated as she stumbled away from Brendan. They'd forgotten Patrick straightening up at the front of the chapel.

"I apologize Uncle." Brendan smiled despite his serious tone. "I was overcome with love for my wife."

Patrick reached them and pulled them each into a tight hug. "It's quite understandable. No apology necessary."

Brendan scanned the sanctuary. "With everything in order, I guess it's time to head back to the cabin."

"Not so fast, my boy." Patrick's eyes twinkled with merriment. "No couple should have to spend their wedding night in a cabin with an old man like me. Evergreen Falls is a little town not over thirty minutes from here in your fancy automobile. I've arranged a hotel room for you both tonight and tomorrow."

"That's why you wanted me to drive here." Brendan pulled his uncle in for another hug.

Patrick winked at Evangeline. "He thought he was the only one with surprises tonight. Turns out he learned it from me. I even have bags packed for both of you in the back seat."

Together, they filed out of the church. Downy flakes swirled in the air. Blessings upon blessings. God gave her a white Christmas after all, and just in time for her wedding.

Epilogue

Four Years Later

Evangeline stared out the window of the empty bedroom, frustrated and irritated with herself for feeling that way. How many times had God showered her and Brendan with blessings in the four years since their wedding?

He'd given Brendan a good apprenticeship with Mr. Morgan. In doing so, Brendan found he loved carpentry and even decorative woodwork. Together, the men built their dream house, complete with blue shutters and a wraparound porch extending to the west side of the house where she could sit in the swing and watch the sun set.

Evangeline worked the garden and cared for the chickens since Patrick's duties for the chapel had expanded, along with the congregation. Even she became involved in ministry, inviting the women of the church into her home twice a month for prayer and sewing. Occasionally, they even spent a bit of time in the Word.

Charlie Birger had been hanged nearly two years after they fled Harrisburg. With the Shelton gang also out of the area, Brendan determined they were safe enough to plan a reunion trip to see her parents for Christmas and their third anniversary the previous year. Patrick went with them, and her parents accepted both Brendan and him into the family. In fact, they'd visited Park Haven for Christmas only three months ago.

Life was good. God was good. Why did this one disappointment cast such a gray cloud over her otherwise sunny sky? Why did each monthly time she faced hit her harder emotionally than the last?

Brendan told her to stop worrying. Children would come when they came. In her distress, she'd whispered in the dark one night, "What if they don't?"

As much as Brendan wanted a family, he'd whispered back, full of conviction, "Then I'll keep loving you until my dying breath." Despite her tears, he'd taken her in his arms and kissed her doubts away.

Still. This room was meant for a child. A child that might never come.

There was a knock on the door but she didn't move from the window. Brendan was downstairs and could answer it. Voices filtered upstairs, both male and female, but they were too muffled to determine their owners.

"Evangeline, could you come here a minute?" Brendan called up the stairs. "Your parents are here."

Fear snaked through Evangeline. Her parents wouldn't come down unannounced without reason, and that reason would have to be of monumental importance. Her father's job required too much time to allow for frivolous trips. Her heels clicked against the floor as she rushed from the room and down the stairs.

"What's wrong?" She barely made it to the bottom step before blurting out the question.

Her mother swept her into a quick hug. "Nothing's wrong, exactly. But we do need to speak with you and Brendan."

"That doesn't sound like nothing is wrong."

Her father lifted his chin. "No need for sass. Your mother's right. Let's go into the parlor, and we'll explain everything."

Evangeline straightened her shoulders and forced a breath.

Her father's no-nonsense personality still had the ability to bring focus. "Where are my manners? Would you like something to drink? Water? Coffee?"

"Nothing, thanks." Her father shook his head. "We'd rather just tell you what brings us here today."

Brendan led the way, with her mother and father following behind. Evangeline took up the rear, every step laced with lead. If her father had no time for pleasantries, it must be serious indeed.

Her mother and father sat on the chairs flanking the sofa where Brendan sat. Evangeline joined him. He took her hand, offering his strength and calm in the gesture.

"A little boy showed up on our front porch yesterday." Her father commanded the attention of everyone in the room. "He's ten years old, and he says his name is Connor Dunne. Though he freely admits that last name is not on his birth certificate."

Brendan frowned. "I don't understand."

"Mabel, give him the letter, please."

Her mother sifted through her handbag and pulled an envelope from inside. Without a word, she rose and handed it to Brendan before returning to her chair.

Brendan opened the paper inside and scanned its contents. "It's from Mrs. Higgins, my family's cook for as long as I remember."

"What does she say?"

"Dear Mr. Brendan." He smiled. "Always Mr. Brendan and James was Mr. James. Father insisted on it. Anyway, she goes on. I regret being the one to inform you, but your brother found himself in a deal of trouble with Nora when he was only months past sixteen. Left her to fend for herself with the baby."

He glanced up from the letter to the others in the room. "I found out about Nora not too long before James's death. He'd actually cared about her. Wanted to do right by her when she told him he'd be a father soon after he turned seventeen, but our father's influence on him was too much. James allowed their child to become an attack against the family our father hated. After telling Nora she'd have to deal with it on her own, James never mentioned her again. I think the guilt was too great."

"Oh, Brendan. That's horrible." Evangeline placed her hand on his arm.

He nodded and returned to the letter. "The boy and his mother never came around, until just recently. Connor showed up on the doorstep with one little suitcase in tow. Nora died. The boy wasn't sure from what. Her family disowned her after finding out about her relationship with James and refused to acknowledge her son. Your father was no better. I snuck out of the house, gave him the money he needed to get to Harrisburg, and this letter of introduction. I pray he finds you and that you are the man of faith I remember from your teenage years. Please, right the wrong done this child and his mother. You're his only hope of family."

The letter's meaning sunk in. Evangeline glanced at her father. "You mean the boy is here? Where? Where did you leave him?"

Her father pinned her to the sofa with a look. "Enough dramatics, daughter. It's not as if we've stuck him in the trunk. We know how to care for a child."

"He's with Patrick." Her mother's soft voice drew her attention. "We didn't think it wise to have him present for the reading of the letter."

"My uncle knows who the child is?"

Her mother nodded. "Herb told him the basics while I waited in the automobile with Connor."

"We assumed you'd need time to decide how to handle the situation."

"The situation?" Brendan's brows rose. "My nephew is not a situation. He's family."

"Mr. Dunne doesn't see him that way."

Brendan harrumphed. "With all due respect, my father doesn't see me as family either. Not since Connor's father was killed and my father's favorite was wrenched away from him."

"I'm sorry, son." Father's chin dipped in respect. "I meant no harm. You and Evangeline need to decide what place, if any, Connor has with you."

"He's a boy in need of family." Evangeline pointed out what she would have thought obvious to everyone else in the room. "We are his family. And if he is willing, he will stay with us."

Brendan took both hands in his, shifting her to look directly at him and no one else. "Are you sure about this? It's a big step, committing to raise a boy who's half-raised already. Especially since we don't know anything about how that raising went."

The question was posed sincerely, but Evangeline could see the hope in Brendan's eyes. He wanted his nephew. While Connor wasn't the baby she'd expected God to bless her with, Evangeline's heart longed to love this child as much as the ones she'd not been given yet. Connor needed them. Maybe they needed him too.

"James left behind a child who needs family and a chance to see how much God loves him." She freed a hand from Brendan's grasp and cupped his cheek. "We can give him both. We've already got the room. And while we may have expected it to hold a crib before a bed, God sent Connor to us and, in His wisdom, prepared the way. Yes. I'm sure."

Brendan turned to her father. "It's decided then. God's given this opportunity. We won't neglect it. Let's go see my nephew."

"There's no need." Her father shook his head and checked his pocket watch. "Patrick should be here with Connor in just a few minutes."

"Then I believe now would be the perfect time to pray." Brendan bowed his head and asked God to bless them with wisdom as they stepped into the role of parents to a boy who'd just lost his mother. He thanked God for restoring another piece of his family to him. And he asked God to help them show Connor how much he was loved each day, by them and by God.

A knock on the door brought the prayer to a close. Brendan rose from the couch and strode to the front door. Evangeline hurried to follow. She sucked in a breath at the sight of the little boy on the other side. The Dunne genes were strong. Connor was the spitting image of his father.

"Hello, Connor." Brendan stooped down to his level. "I'm your Uncle Brendan. Welcome home."

The End

Note to the Reader

Dear Reader,

I never imagined I would write a historical novel, but God had other plans. I'm so glad He did, because writing Evangeline and Brendan's story was a great experience. I learned so much about the 1920s and what the area I grew up in was like at that time in history.

Being a work of fiction, most of the events and people in the book are not real. However, I wanted the story to feel like the 1920s in Harrisburg, Illinois. To do so, I researched phrases, clothes, food, local groups and events, movies, and so much more. I've included a few of those things.

Charlie Birger, the Shelton gang, Shady Rest, Holloway's Café, and Mr. O'Gara are all taken from history. And while details like the movies I allude to, the circus coming to town, and foods available at the time were all correct for the period, I may have adjusted some by a couple years to be able to include them in my story.

In writing about Mr. Birger, Shady Rest, and the trouble with the Shelton gang, I tried to capture the complex sentiment of the time. Mr. Birger was known to be neighborly to those in

Harrisburg. Even the story of him refusing to allow a local boy to partake in the offerings at Shady Rest has been reported, thought I changed the name. But Mr. Birger was also known to be deadly. The illegal activities that took place at Shady Rest and elsewhere on his orders resulted in his arrest and conviction. He was the last man publicly hanged in Illinois in 1928, two years after the events of my story.

From what I researched, the first aerial bombing in the United States did take place in 1926 at Shady Rest. While it was related to the trouble between the Shelton and Birger gangs, no one was reported hurt and no damage was done to Shady Rest. Those are details I embellished as a fiction writer for the sake of the story.

I hope you enjoy Evangeline and Brendan's story as much as I do!

Happy Reading,
Heather Greer

Acknowledgments

I thank God every day for allowing me to follow the passion He's given me and use it for Him. He's blessed me with a job I love and wonderful people to support me on this path. My family, my writing friends, Scrivenings Press and the three who are creating this series with me, and the readers who have allowed me to be a part of their lives. I thank God for each of you, and I thank you for being beside me in this journey.

About the Author

Though more at home with a mixer than a history book, Heather enjoyed digging into the southern Illinois mining town of Harrisburg 1920s. Though not as metropolitan as Chicago, the now sleepy little town was once on track to be the next big hub in Illinois complete with gangsters, bootlegging, gambling, and murder.

With a desire to understand the events and ideologies that shaped Harrisburg at the time, Heather's research uncovered an uncomfortable truth that still applies today. When times are tough, it's easier for people to be duped by evil masquerading as truth. From the KKK being widely accepted as an answer to corruption to murderous men, like Charlie Birger, being seen as a Robin Hood of sorts in the towns where they resided, one evil marched in to take the place of another evil without resistance from a large portion of the population.

Heather weaves these ideas into the fictional story of Evangeline and Brendan as a reminder to stay grounded in the Word and diligent to use it in determining good and evil. While including truth is important to Heather as she writes, her hope is that readers connect with the characters and enjoy their time in the stories.

Whether in books, on stage, or in movies, Heather loves a story that can tug at your heart and still leave a smile on your face. The ones that leave you with a lighthearted sigh of satisfaction are great too. These are the kinds of stories Heather strives to tell, and she hopes you enjoy each one.

Also by Heather Greer

Love in Any Season

A novella collection that includes

Sugar and Spice by Heather Greer

Emeline Becker, owner of Sugar and Spice Bakery, loves New Kuchenbrünn, except for the gingerbread. As the only bakery, she supplies the annual Gingerbread Festival with the one treat she can't stand. It's gingerbread everywhere.

Things get worse when Ryker Lehmann is hired as the festival photographer. He was her secret teen crush, her sister's boyfriend, and witness to her worst humiliation. Plus, he broke her sister's heart and bruised hers when he left town after graduation. Now, he's back in town, determined to fix their friendship before the festival ends.

With gingerbread and Ryker together, can Emmie make it through the festival with her mind and heart intact?

Get your copy here:

https://scrivenings.link/loveinanyseason

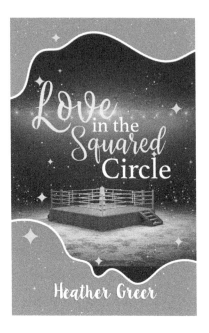

Love in the Squared Circle
by Heather Greer

Trinity Knight is not a fan of professional wrestling. But with her husband gone, it falls to her to give their son the father-son trip they daydreamed about when he was alive. After Trinity causes them to miss a meet and greet with Jay's favorite wrestler, a random act of kindness saves the trip and starts Trinity on an unexpected path.

Universal Wrestling Organization Champion Blane Sterling hears whiny children at photo ops all the time. However, overhearing a young boy comfort his mother piques his interest. Touched by their story, Blane works with the UWO Public Relations team to give Jay the experience of a lifetime.

As they learn each other's stories, Trinity and Blane are drawn to each other. But they don't just come from different states. They live in different worlds. Trinity might learn to fit into his life, but can those in her world look beyond Blane's profession to see his heart? Or will a lack of acceptance cause Trinity and Blane to lose their shot at love?

Cake That!
Third-place Winner - Contemporary Romance
2022 Selah Awards
Ten bakers. Nine days. One winner.

Competing on the *Cake That* baking show is a dream come true for Livvy Miller, but debt on her cupcake truck and an expensive repair make her question if it's one she should chase. Her best friend, Tabitha, encourages Livvy to trust God to care for The Sugar Cube, win or lose.

Family is everything to Evan Jones. His parents always gave up their dreams so their children could achieve theirs. Winning *Cake That* would let him give back some of what they've sacrificed by allowing him to give them the trip they've always talked about but could never afford.

As the contestants live and bake together, more than the competition heats up. Livvy and Evan have a spark from the start, but they're in it to win. Neither needs the distraction of romance. Unwanted attention from Will, another competitor, complicates matters. Stir in strange occurrences to the daily baking assignments, and everyone wonders if a saboteur is in the mix.

With the distractions inside and outside the *Cake That* kitchen, will Livvy or Evan rise above the rest and claim the prize? Or does God have more in store for them than they first imagined?

scrivenings.link/cakethat

Faith, Hope, and Love Series:

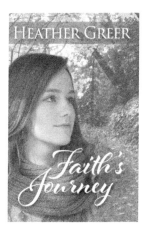

Faith's Journey

Faith, Hope, and Love Series - Book One

https://scrivenings.link/faithsjourney

Grasping Hope

Faith, Hope, and Love Series - Book Two

https://scrivenings.link/graspinghope

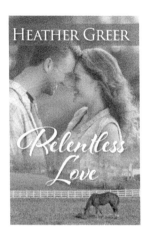

Relentless Love

Faith, Hope, and Love Series - Book Three

https://scrivenings.link/relentlesslove

Coming Soon from Heather Greer

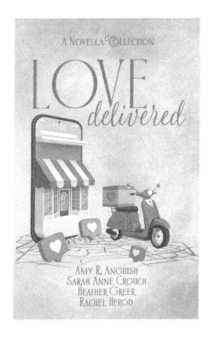

Love Delivered

A novella collection that includes

Sweet Delivery – by Heather Greer

Available February 14, 2023

After winning Cake That, Will Forrester thinks his Pastry Perfect baking dreams have come true. The sweetness fades when a chain bakery moves to town, and Will must adjust his plans to keep his customers. Hiring Erica Gerard is one of those changes.

As they work together, Erica challenges Will and offers new ideas to improve the bakery. Soon, Erica and Will start bringing out the best in each other.

But Erica harbors a secret, and if it's discovered, Will might never be the same.

Get your copy here:

https://scrivenings.link/lovedelivered

Stay up-to-date on your favorite books and authors with our free e-newsletters.

ScriveningsPress.com

Made in United States
Orlando, FL
11 December 2023

40290051R00157